Walter Besant

The Master Craftsman

Volume 2

Walter Besant

The Master Craftsman
Volume 2

ISBN/EAN: 9783337369491

Printed in Europe, USA, Canada, Australia, Japan

Cover: Foto ©Andreas Hilbeck / pixelio.de

More available books at **www.hansebooks.com**

THE

MASTER CRAFTSMAN

BY

WALTER BESANT

AUTHOR OF
'BEYOND THE DREAMS OF AVARICE,' 'ARMOREL OF LYONESSE,'
'ALL SORTS AND CONDITIONS OF MEN,' ETC.

IN TWO VOLUMES
VOL. II.

LONDON
CHATTO & WINDUS, PICCADILLY
1896

CONTENTS OF VOL. II.

CHAPTER XIV.

MORE LESSONS.

In that way began the companionship that has changed the whole of my life and Isabel's life as well—you shall hear how.

I set myself to work, as I had done with Robert, systematically. I had to drag a girl out of a miserably narrow groove in which she had lived and moved for five years without any change, almost without fresh air; without society; without books; without friends or companions; a burying alive. It is wonderful to me, when I come to think of it, that her finer nature was not wholly destroyed; most girls after such an experience would have become a mere household drudge, or a mere clerk, with, as another natural result of such a life, a snappish temper and a bitter tongue. Per-

haps the presence of her father kept Isabel from these
evils ; the old sailor was always cheerful, though fate had
given him small cause for cheerfulness. However, Isabel
passed through the time of prison with no lowering of
her moral nature. The social side, of course, suffered.
I had to show her how other girls dressed, and how
they comported themselves. I had to lift her out of
the submission and meekness so ill assorted with her
beauty. I had also to give her the world of books and
of art—an easy task, made easy by the adaptability of
the girl and her quick perceptions ; a pleasant task, as
the charge of a pretty woman always must be ; and a
dangerous task, because the girl was surely the most
lovable creature under the canopy of heaven. Of this
danger I had no thought or suspicion. I declare that
I was entirely loyal to Robert, until I discovered a fact
which changed the whole situation. The fact once discovered, the rest was natural.

My lessons in the study of Nature and Humanity
were continued during the months of June and July.
On Saturdays we went afield—to Hampton, to Rich-
mond, to Dulwich, to Sydenham, to Loughton, to
Chigwell, to Theydon Bois, to Chingford, to St. Alban's
—wherever there are trees and gardens to be seen. Or
we went up the river to Maidenhead, Bray, Windsor,
Weybridge ; or down the river to Greenwich. On

Sunday morning I took her generally to Westminster, where she heard the silver voices of the choir ringing in the roof while we sat in a corner of the transept beside the tombs. At such a time I would watch her and mark how her spirit was rapt and carried away. When the music ceased we would get up and go out and seek the peaceful cloister, cool and shady, on the south side of the church, and there sit together, mostly in silence.

'Yours are new thoughts, Isabel,' I said one Sunday morning, while we sat in this quiet place.

'They are all new thoughts now,' she replied. 'Thanks to you. What did I think about formerly? I don't remember. Terrors, mostly.'

'And now they are pleasant thoughts?'

'Oh! what can they be but pleasant? You have taken me into another world. How could I live so long, and be so contented?'

'It is a finer and a better world?'

'It is far, far broader, to begin with; and far, far finer. Whether it is better, George, I do not know. I only see it from the outside. It is happier; of that I am quite sure.'

'It may well be happier. As for its being better— I meant better in the sense of more comfortable; you mean more virtuous. Well, nobody knows, not even a

Father Confessor, whether one part of the world is more virtuous than another part. You see, we never get to the real inside of any part—not even our own corner. And most of us can never get outside our own corner at all. Nobody else ever lived in such a corner as you ; but you haven't got outside that corner yet, and you never will. We only see little bits of the world. My own belief—but I may be wrong—is that we are all pretty much alike ; all, as the children say, up and down, and round about—good, and bad, and middling. We are anxious, first of all, and above all, to get as much solid comfort for ourselves as we can.'

She sighed. 'I confess,' she said, 'that I desire happiness more and more. But it is not altogether solid comfort that I look for.'

'Your views of happiness have broadened, Isabel. What made your happiness two months ago ?'

'There was no happiness, nor much unhappiness. It seemed now as if I lived always in a sort of twilight. No trees even, except those in the burial-ground ; no flowers, no fresh country, no books, no poetry, no Cathedral music.'

'There is a pretty story, an old story, about a prisoner, and about a flower which sprang up, and grew, and blossomed between the chinks of the stones. You are that prisoner, Isabel, and the flower is your soul, which has grown up and blossomed in the dark and narrow prison. But we must not call Robert the gaoler.'

'Oh no, I must not blame Robert; pray do not think that I do. He has been so full of work and thought that, of course, he could not tell; and why should he be dragged out of his way to think of me? And my father is growing old. No, no; there is no one to blame. Not Robert—oh no, never Robert.'

Let me make a clean breast of it; not that I am penitent, but quite the contrary. I ought, I suppose, to have discontinued these little expeditions as soon as I learned what was coming out of them. That would be the line adopted by the sage of seventy springs. I had only five-and-twenty. Moreover, it is very difficult to say when friendship is transformed into love; the young man goes on; the companionship, always delightful, becomes too delightful to give up; the companion creeps into his heart and remains there until one day he awakes to the consciousness that life without that companion will henceforth be intolerable.

But we entered upon the thing loyally; we had no thought of any danger; then, no one interfered with us; we went where we pleased. I began with thinking about Isabel when I ought to have been considering the lines of a boat; I began to think how she looked, what she said; her face haunted me—her sweet, soft face, full of purity, grace, and every womanly virtue; her eyes—her deep and limpid eyes, wells of holy thoughts, charged with goodness; her voice—the tones of her voice, which had become to me the sweetest music in the world. I dreamed of these things at night, I thought of them all day, long before I understood what had happened to me, long before Isabel suspected anything. The last thing, indeed, which the maiden feared or suspected was the thing that happened. She was engaged to Robert; and I was Robert's cousin, and by Robert's permission I was showing her the world. Even a girl who knows the ways of the world, and especially the treacherous, villainous, deceptive ways of young men, and would be therefore suspicious in such a case, might have thought that there was some security in common loyalty and friendship. But Isabel had no knowledge of the world, and no experience of young men, and consequently no suspicion.

This very ignorance of danger made things more dangerous. Her ignorance encouraged her to be perfectly frank and confiding. She showed openly all the pleasure she felt in these little expeditions, and she manifested her innocent affection—I call it affection, not friendship—towards me so unreservedly that it was impossible even to tell her when the thing began, or even when the thing had grown until it became a very furnace of passion.

There you see—it happened so. It was quite natural—it was severely logical—I now understand that nothing else was possible—it was inevitable. No man going about day after day, with so sweet a companion, could fail to fall in love with her. I did fall head over heels, up to my neck, in love. That mattered nothing so long as neither Robert nor Isabel suspected it. As for myself, why, at that time, I did not ask myself what was going to happen, or what would in the end come of it. Enough for me just to enjoy the presence and the sight of her, the touch of her hand, the rustle of her dress. Why, since by marriage we are taught that the man must worship the woman, then was I married to Isabel long before she knew or suspected that I so much as held that form of faith or believed that teaching.

The end—I mean the end of unsuspecting confidence —arrived unexpectedly. It came one evening, about the middle of July, and at sunset. We were sitting in the place where I had taken Isabel first—the park near Rickmansworth. She sang hymns no more, nor did she faint at beholding the splendour and the glory of the world; but she sat in silence, gazing upon the western glow in the sky, and on the flowing river at her feet, where the glow was reflected.

Could this glorious creature be the pale and drooping maiden whom I brought here six weeks before? Now she sat upright, cheeks glowing, eyes uplifted, limpid and lovely eyes, with rounded figure and head erect—a girl full of life and of the joy of youth.

'Of all the places that we have seen together, George,' she said, 'this is the one that I love best.'

'It is where you first felt the beauty of the world, Isabel, and it was too much for you.'

'How came you to think about taking me out? It has been so wonderfully good of you, George. I can never think enough about it.'

'In my capacity of great Physician, I discovered that you were suffering from monotony, so I spoke to Robert, and we arranged it.'

A cloud passed over her face, but only for a moment.

'If our little expeditions have put colour into your cheeks and light into your eyes—your very lovely eyes, Isabel——'

'Please, George, no compliments.'

'Well, then, if they have done you good—there is a nice homely way to put it—I ought to be quite contented and happy. You see, Isabel'—this was rather a risky thing to say; one could not meet her eyes—'it

has been so great a happiness to have you for a companion, that you must just think how good it has been
of you to come with me.'

Still she did not suspect what was in my mind.
When she began to talk about wonderful goodness it
was impossible, of course, not to point out that on the
other hand I was the one who should be really grateful
and deeply obliged for days and evenings of pure and
unmixed happiness, reading the soul—so high above
my own—the sweet and lovely soul of this most sweet
and lovely maiden. I believe I have said these words
about her already. Never mind. I say, then, that I was
constrained to put the case before her in its true light.

'You say this,' she replied, 'out of your kindness. Of
course, I can never believe that you really wanted the
company of a girl so shamefully ignorant as myself.
Why, I could talk about nothing. Besides, you have
that other friend of whom you have told me—Lady
Frances. Have you not neglected her?'

'Lady Frances does not mind,' I said. 'And I have
not neglected her, and I do assure you, Isabel, that I
am perfectly in earnest when I speak about the happiness of your companionship. I wanted, at first, I confess, only to clear away the clouds from your face and
from your mind by a change of place and some kind of
amusement. I cannot bear to see any girl unhappy.

That was all I thought about at first, when we began to go about together. Afterwards——' And here I stopped.

'The clouds are gone,' she replied, 'so there is no more need for any more evenings abroad. Now, I suppose, I must make up my mind to go back to Wapping, and to stay there. Well, I have a very happy time to remember.'

'Indeed, you shall not, Isabel, if I can help it. Go back to the old life? Not if I have any voice in the matter. Besides, the clouds are not all gone. There is one that falls on you quite suddenly, and sometimes lies upon you for an hour or more. Why, it has fallen now. You cloud over suddenly, Isabel. It is some thought that comes to you uninvited. Your face must be all sunshine or all cloud. Never was such a tell-tale face.'

She blushed; but the cloud lay there still.

'What is it, Isabel? What is this cloud? Is it anything that I can remove?'

'No one can remove it,' she said.

'Is it anything—but I have no right to ask. Only, Isabel, if you like to tell me, I might advise.'

She remained silent, but the tears gathered in her eyes.

''Tell me, Isabel,' I pressed her. 'I asked you once before, in the old burial-ground.'

'I do not dare. I am ashamed. You will think me the most ungrateful of women if I tell you.'

'Then tell me, and let me scold you.'

'It is—it is'—she hung her head—'it is Robert.'

'What has Robert done?'

'It is because he has promised to marry me.'

Then the scales fell from my eyes, and I understood the cloud. I ought to have known. She told me as much before.

'Oh, he has been so good! I have told you—we owe everything to him—I am bound to him by chains—and yet—yet—— Oh, George, I am telling you everything. I am ashamed—yet I must tell someone, because sometimes I think I shall go mad; it weighs me down night and day. He has promised to marry me; his promises are sacred, and it is the thought of marrying him, never to be away from him; to be with him always; always to be his servant and to do what he orders; and never a single kind word, or one look of interest even, not to speak of—of affection. I am as disregarded as his office-boy; I am nothing more than a machine. How can I do anything but tremble at the thought of marrying such a man?'

'Then you must yourself break off your engagement.'

'No, no. I cannot. You forget, George, that we

are his dependents, my father and I, both of us. I must do what Robert wishes—all that Robert wishes.'

I groaned.

'And now you know the meaning of the cloud. I am only happy when I can forget my own future. And all your kindness is thrown away, because the thought of my own future never leaves me altogether—even with you.'

And then it was that I quite lost my self-control.

'Oh, Isabel!' I cried. 'You shall not marry him. Oh, my love! my love! you shall not marry him.'

I took her hands. She cried out and sprang to her feet. I threw my arms round her and kissed her, being carried quite beyond my own control. And I told her, in words that I cannot, dare not, set down here for all the world to see, all that was lying in my heart.

She pushed me from her, and sank back upon the fallen tree on which she had been sitting, and buried her face in her hands.

'Isabel!' I whispered. 'Isabel! if you can love me!'

She gave me her hand. 'Let me hear it once—and say it once, for the first time and the last. Oh, George —and I did not know it!'

I kissed her again and again. It makes my heart leap up still only to think of that moment.

Then she stood up. 'It is the first time and the

last, George,' she said. 'I am engaged to your cousin
Robert.'

'Yes, Isabel.'

'Now we will go home. We will not forget this
evening, George. I thank God—yes, I thank God we
have told each other. Now I shall feel, whatever
happens, that I have been loved—even I, whose promised
husband scorns me.' Her voice broke into a sob. 'But
we must never, never again speak of it. Never, never.
You have loved me for a little, and that is enough for
me—to gladden all my life. Even I have been loved—
even I——'

I made no reply, because I was fully resolved, you see,
somehow to speak of it again. In fact, I felt that it
was impossible to consider any other future than one in
which the subject would always form the chief topic of
conversation.

'Give me your promise, George,' she went on.
'Promise that you will never speak to me of love again.'

'I promise, Isabel, that I will never again speak to
you of love until Robert himself has set you free.
Will that do?'

How I proposed at that moment to persuade Robert
I do not know. How I did actually and afterwards
persuade him you shall presently learn.

CHAPTER XV.

MUTINY.

THEN and there was the emancipation of Isabel begun. It was effected, you have seen, by making her physically strong and well, by giving her courage, by providing her with something to think about, and by relieving the monotony of her life.

'You've done wonders for the girl,' said the Captain one day. 'Wonders, you have. I don't hardly know her, she's so changed. Why, she sings now, and she plays her music half the day and every day. She that used to be such a shy and timid thing, afraid of her own voice. Perhaps, Sir George'—he would never abandon the title; it gave him a sense of self-importance to be talking with a Baronet—'perhaps you don't notice these trifles, but you must have seen the change that's come over the puddings.'

'No—really? Over the puddings?'

'There's a lightness about them, more jam, since the

girl got brighter. Ah! It's quite natural. When the soul is heavy, the pudding comes out heavy too. There can't be the real feeling about the jam. And the teas are quite remarkable compared with what they were. There's a spiciness about the cake now.'

'Well, Captain, do you think that Robert has noticed any change?'

'No. He never notices anything. There's a change in him—and that's all he thinks about. What in thunder is the matter with the man to be engaged to a beautiful girl, and a nice girl too—isn't she, now?'

'A nice girl indeed!'

'And never to take the least notice, no more than if she wasn't there. I say, Sir George, it isn't natural. If he doesn't want her, why doesn't he tell her so? If he does, why not put it to her in the usual way?'

'Don't you think, Captain, that a word from you——'

'No, sir. He won't listen to one word, nor a thousand words, from anybody.'

'Consider, your daughter's happiness is at stake. Can any girl like to go on year after year engaged to a man who treats her with absolute neglect and icy coldness? Is it fair to keep a girl going on in this way year after year? Could he not, at least, take back his promise and set her free? You are her father; it is for you to interfere.'

The Captain froze instantly. 'Perhaps, Sir George, under ordinary circumstances that might be so. But you forget that we have eaten Robert's bread and slept under his roof for five years, and you forget, besides, that he is the most masterful man in the world, and he means to have his own way.'

'Still, to marry a girl against her will——'

'How do I know that it is against her will? To be sure, she's a little afraid of him—many women are afraid of the man before they marry. Afterwards it's different, and let me tell you, sir, that most women like a man to be masterful. They get their own way fast enough; but they like him to be masterful.'

'Perhaps; but this neglect of Robert's——'

'Never mind that. He'll make it up when they do marry. It's all there, only bottled up. These bottles do pour it out when the time comes—in the most surprising manner. You'll see what an appreciative husband he'll make some day. Let things be, Sir George. You've brought her health and roses; Robert, who will be grateful when he notices it, will do all the rest. I dare say she frets and peaks a bit for want of the kissing and the fondling that all girls naturally expect. Let her have a little patience, I say. And don't let's disturb things when they are comfortable, especially the puddings.'

We spoke no more of love. We continued to go about together with free and unrestrained discourse. As the evenings began to close in, we ceased the long journeys to villages and village churches, and took picture-galleries and concerts instead on Saturday afternoon. Or I remained in the evening at the house, while Isabel played and sang to me; she played much better already, and she sang with untrained sweetness. One evening, when the pianoforte was loaded with new music and new songs, and the books she was reading, she laid her hands upon them all.

'You have given me everything,' she said. 'But these things are only alleviations. The future is always before me—dark and horrible. Oh! I pray that it may be postponed so long as to become impossible. I shall grow old and ugly, and then I hope he will take back his promise.'

'Unless,' I said, 'he can be induced to take it back before.'

Then an incident took place which disquieted me very much indeed—a very dangerous incident. It was this:

Robert was in his study after dinner forging an oration. Isabel was in the parlour practising. On the table was a bundle of papers and certain blue-books. He took up the books and began to turn over the leaves, marking passages. He wanted these passages copied, to be

used in his speech.   He took paper and pen and began
to copy.   Then Isabel's playing reminded him of her.
He got up, opened the door and called her.

She came obediently.   That afternoon she was dressed
in some light blue summer stuff with a ribbon and a
flower, because she now loved a little touch of finery.
The soft cheek, the depths of her eyes, her light, feathery
hair, her ethereal look, might have moved the heart of
St. Anthony.   So far they had produced no impression
at all upon her lover.

He nodded when she appeared—nodded pleasantly ;
he had a very fine speech nearly ready ; he had learned
it by heart ; it was certain to carry the people away ;
he only wanted these extracts copied.

'Take these blue-books,' he said, with the old tone of
command.   'You will find the pages marked with a red
pencil.   Copy out all the passages marked, and let me
have them by to-morrow morning.'

'I am no longer your clerk, Robert.'

'What ?'

'I say that I am no longer your clerk.   You released
me three months ago.   Had I continued, I believe I
should have been dead by this time.   I will not copy
passages for you.'

'Isabel !'   He was amazed.

'Let us understand each other.   I am your housekeeper. I will do for the house anything and everything. I am not your clerk or your private secretary or your accountant. You must get someone else to do that work for you.'

' Isabel !'

' I am grateful to you for taking us in and keeping us all these years. If you think I ought to do more for my father's maintenance and my own, I will give up and try for another place.'

' You are a fool, Isabel !' he said roughly.

' Very likely. Is it polite to tell me so ? You have learned a great deal about the world of late ; Robert— do you think it is polite to call the girl you are engaged to—a fool ?'

' No, no, no ! of course I didn't mean that. But— Isabel—what in the world has come over you ?'

He actually saw the change at last, or something of the change ; not all of it, otherwise the subsequent history would be different. It was the very first time that the girl had ever refused work, or objected, or complained. For four or five months there had been slowly going on under his eyes the transformation of which you have heard ; but because it was so slow and gradual, and because he was always completely absorbed in himself, and because he had never thought it necessary to consider the appearance of the girl at all, having still

in him so much of the working man as not to desire
beauty in his wife, and not to think about it—he had
observed nothing. Now, however, when the word of
resistance and refusal opened his eyes, he was amazed to
see standing before him, in the place of the mild, meek
maiden, who humbly took whatever he gave, and humbly
executed whatever he commanded, always with down-
cast eyes and hanging head, a lovely, airy, fairy creature,
too dainty altogether for such a man as himself, a
beautiful, bright, sunny girl, a head held upright, and
steady eyes that met his own without the least fear or
show of humility.

'Isabel!' he repeated, 'what in the name of wonder
has come over you ?'

'I don't know. You have been thinking about your
own affairs, I suppose. But oh—it is nothing.' She
turned to leave him, being, in fact, frightened at the
admiration expressed in his eyes for the first time—it
was quite a new expression, and it terrified her
horribly.

'No, no; don't go, Isabel.' He leaned back in his
chair. 'You are looking so wonderfully well, and—
and pretty this afternoon.'

She began to tremble. Robert to say things compli-
mentary !

'There is nothing more to say, is there ?'

He leaned his chin in his left hand, and replied slowly : 'I remember now. George talked to me about you, Isabel, when he first came. He said you were overworked. I don't always remember, perhaps, that you are only a girl. I may have given you too much to do.'

'I am only housekeeper now.'

'Very well, then. I don't mean to be unkind, you see. But, of course, I can't be always thinking about your health and your whims, can I ?'

'Of course not.'

'George said you wanted fresh air, and a change and exercise, and all kinds of fiddle-faddle stuff, and to see how other girls carry on—so as to take your proper place when I have advanced myself. Well, I told him I wished he would take care of you, and take you about a bit, seeing that I couldn't afford the time myself. Has he taken you about ?'

'Yes ; all the summer. He has been most kind and generous.'

'George is that sort of man, I believe, ready to waste any amount of time in dangling after a girl. Well, Isabel, as I could not dangle after you, I am very much obliged to him. And I must say that the change is wonderful. You look ever so much better. Your face, which used to be too pale, is full of colour, and your eyes are brighter, and—why, Isabel, give me your hands.'

He held out both hands, but Isabel made no response. And there was an unexpected look in his eyes which frightened her. He got up, not hastily, not like a passionate pilgrim, but slowly, and with the dignity of possession and authority. Isabel trembled as she realized this phenomenon. Between herself and the door stood Robert. She could not run away. She thought of crying for help—her father was in his own room—but a girl can hardly call out for protection against the threatened kiss of her engaged lover. And perhaps he didn't mean it, after all. Yet his eyes looked hungry.

In the corner beside the fireplace stood one of those revolving bookcases filled with books; a heavy thing which turns round when it is pushed with zeal and vigour. Isabel retreated behind this bookcase. 'Let me go!' she cried. 'Do not touch me!'

'I don't want to hurt you,' he said. 'Come out of that corner, Isabel. Why, you are not a baby; and you are my girl. Come out quietly, and don't be silly.'

'No—you promised—you said that there should be no—no——'

'Oh yes: stuff and nonsense! I said so, I dare say. I couldn't interrupt work and distract my thoughts with fondling and kissing. Not to be expected. Be-

sides, that was a year ago and more, and you were not
the girl then that you are now. Come, Isabel, don't
be shy.'

'No, no, I won't have it! I couldn't bear it. Oh,
horrible! Let me go!' She gave the bookcase a
vigorous shove, and it revolved ponderously with its
weight of a hundred books. Robert fell back.

It is not pleasant for one's sweetheart to speak of a
threatened kiss as horrible. His face grew dark.

'You are going to marry me, Isabel, I believe?'

'Not yet—not for a long time yet; not till you are
an Archbishop of Canterbury, or something. And
until we do marry, Robert, I will take you at your
word. There shall be no fondling, as you call it.'

'When you marry me you will have to obey me.
There can only be one master in one house.'

'I am not your wife yet, remember. I am not at
your orders except as your housekeeper. Pray do not
imagine that you have any right to command a woman
because she has promised to be your wife. After I am
your wife—if ever I am——'

He wavered. 'Of course,' he said, 'I cannot command your obedience so long as you are not my wife.
But come out from that retreat, and sit down and
let us talk. I will not attempt to command you in
anything. Perhaps we need not wait so long as

first we thought. Perhaps—as soon as I am in the House——'

'No,' she replied ; 'you must promise to let me go, or I will stay behind this bookcase all night.'

'You can go then, Isabel,' he replied, flinging himself into his chair ; 'I will not stop you.'

She passed out without a word.   But she was shaken ; she went to her own room and sat down to think.   Was Robert, too, changing ?   Was his ancient indifference turning into admiration ? and though her experience of the manly heart was small, she felt by instinct that admiration might at any moment leap into passion, and passion into a demand for the fulfilment of her promise. 'Oh,' she groaned and cried, 'I cannot marry him—I cannot—I cannot—I would rather die !'

But she told no one, not even her physician.   And that evening the furrow reappeared on her brow, and the cloud on her face, and Robert, coming in to tea, saw again the maiden meek and mild, and wondered what had become of the princess, and why he had experienced, if only for a brief moment, that novel and singular feeling of admiration.

'George,' said Robert after tea, when we were alone, 'women are queer skittish creatures.   There's Isabel, now.'

'Yes ; there is Isabel.'

'Formerly I had only to lift my little finger and she ran. She'd do just as much work as I pleased to order. To-day she flatly refused to do anything.'

'Quite right.'

'And when I told her—a man may surely say as much to his own girl—that she was changed and improved—which she certainly is, thanks to you—she wanted to run away.'

'Did she?'

'And when I offered to kiss her—a man may surely kiss his own girl—she shrieked out and ran behind the revolving bookcase.'

'Oh, did she? But, I say, Robert, hadn't you promised that there was to be no kissing, and fondling, and stuff?'

'Well—well—I had, I dare say. But who wanted to kiss the girl a year ago? It's different now. She's become an amazingly pretty girl. If it wasn't for this election business I would—I certainly would——'

'Better not,' I said solemnly. 'Much better not—yet.'

And now you understand how disquieting this incident was.

CHAPTER XVI.

DISSOLUTION.

WHAT might have happened after this act of open
rebellion I do not know. Perhaps these terrifying
overtures were the first signs of a real but as yet un-
conscious passion, just called into existence by some
unexpected charm of a girl whose charms he had never
understood. Certain I am that a man so complete in
all his faculties could not lack the universal faculty of
love ; it is only dullards who are cold to Venus. The
greatest men have always been the most open to the
charms of women ; subsequent events proved so much at
least in Robert's case. Equally certain it is that had this
sleeping lover been awakened completely, he would have
paid small attention to any obstacle or resistance offered
by his mistress. She would have been ordered to put on
a white frock, and she would have been dragged to the
altar. The bells would have rung once more at the
parish church of Wapping for the wedding of another

Burnikel, a boat-builder, like his ancestors. Providence interposed to avert this calamity, and, in order to make it impossible, provided earthquakes and convulsions. Proud indeed should that maiden be, for whom, in order to prevent her own unhappy marriage, the whole nation should be thrown into agitation.

It came the very next morning—the day after this lovers' quarrel. The thing happened which Robert had been expecting so long. You all remember how everybody said it was coming—coming—coming. And it came not. The Government, with its narrow majority, still hung on ; it still discussed and passed Bills. All the papers on one side declared that the Dissolution must come ; they said it must come in a month—a week—the day after to-morrow at latest. How could a Cabinet go on with their absurd little majority ? The papers on the other side declared that the Government could go on for ever if they pleased, even with a majority of one ; but their confidence was weakened by the rumours published in the same columns, and by the reports of movements, the appearance of candidates, and the active work already beginning among the constituencies. And the by-elections, one after the other, were going against the Government. And outsiders like Robert daily saw more reason for believing that there must be, before long, an appeal to the country.

But still the Government continued. Then, lo! the thing came—and it seemed to burst upon the world as quite an unexpected thing. We received it as if we had no idea of its possibility.

Robert took his paper, like most of us, as a part of his breakfast. This morning he opened it with less eagerness than usual, because his mind was disturbed by that little rebellion in the study. He was uncertain, I believe, how to comport himself with the culprit, who now sat opposite him with looks still mutinous. But the thing that he read in the forefront of the paper drove all other thoughts out of his head. And so far as concerned Isabel, they never came back again, as you shall hear, if you have patience. There it was, in big letters, DISSOLUTION.

He read the announcement, and the lines that followed, first swiftly, as one always reads things that are surprising. The plain, bald intelligence of an event can be mastered in a moment. The bearings and meanings and possibilities and certainties and doubt-fulnesses of the event take a second and a third reading for fuller comprehension. It is a strange power, that of reading a whole column of news in one glance down a column. We all have it in moments of excitement. The first time, then, that Robert read the news he grasped it all at that one glance; the second time and the third time he read it more slowly, turning over in his mind at the same moment the possible relation of the Dissolution of Parliament to himself.

Nothing national has ever much affected me, nor is it likely to affect me now, unless it makes the price of materials prohibitory.

Then he laid down the paper, and gazed across the table at Isabel, who was still under the terror of yesterday, and feared new developments. There was no cause for any such anxiety.

'It has come,' he said solemnly. And then she knew that she was safe for the moment, because she divined what had happened.

'What has come?' asked the Captain, astonished, looking up from his plate of bacon.

'What I have been looking for, what is going to make my fortune—the General Election—has come. That's all. Only the General Election! At last!' he sighed. Then he threw the paper across the table. 'You can have it,' he said. 'Anyone can have it. There's no more news in it so far as I care. The dissolution of Parliament! There's news enough for me—quite enough.'

He swallowed his tea, and retreated to his own den without more words.

'Oh,' said the Captain thoughtfully, 'it's a General

Election, is it? Then, they'll have an election at
Shadwell, I suppose. Ah! and Robert will get in.
They all tell me he'll get in. And they say he'll work
wonders when he does get in. Very likely. I don't
know much about these things, Isabel, but I've lived
for sixty-five years, and they've been looking for wonders
all the time, it seems to me. When I used to come
home—which was once in five years or so—I used to
say. " Well, what are you doing—looking for wonders ?"
That's what they always confessed that they were looking after. And the wonders never came, and, what was
more wonderful, we got on quite as well without them.
One after the other I remember them all. There was
Palmerston and Johnny Russell, and John Bright and
Gladstone, and Bradlaugh and Balfour — but the
wonders never came. Next it's going to be Burnikel,
if he's lucky and can make 'em believe in him. Well,
well, Burnikel and Wonders ! Robert's as good as
any of 'em, you'll see. Give me some more tea, my
dear.'

'Since Robert wants to get into the House, I hope he
will. I don't understand why he should want it.'

'I hope so, too. Because you see, Isabel, since we
are alone—it's a delicate subject to talk about ; but, as
I say, since we are alone'—the Captain approached the
subject with some difficulty—'we may talk a bit about

what we can't talk about very well either with George or Robert.'

'What is it, father?'

'Well, my dear, it's about this engagement of yours. I confess I don't like the way it's going on—there!'

'Oh, don't vex yourself, father, about my engagement. You can do no good by interfering.'

'I don't want to interfere, but I don't like it, I say. Robert a lover? Why, he takes no more notice of you than if you were a log.'

'Never mind, father; it is his way.'

'And you the prettiest girl, though I say it, within a mile all round—that is, the prettiest girl since George came and put a little colour into your cheeks, and made you sit upright. Why, you are not the same girl. I shouldn't know you again. You are twice the girl you were. George has done it all—and all for Robert. And Robert sees nothing.'

'It is his way, father,' she repeated.

'George don't like it, either. He told me as much. He wants me to break it off, and let Robert go free. Says Robert ought to cruise about in search of an animated iceberg in petticoats, who would suit him. Nothing short of an iceberg would suit him, that's certain.'

'Pray do not say or do anything, father, I implore

you. Remember what we owe to Robert. The least we can do in such a matter as this is to respect his wishes. If he wants to put off his marriage, he must.'

'I do remember, child. I wish I could forget,' said the Captain gloomily. 'I live upon his bounty.'

'Never by word, or by action, or by look, has he made us feel it, father.'

'I'll be as grateful as you please, my dear; though somehow gratitude isn't one of the feelings which make a man cheerful. It's a gloomy kind of dish to eat, is gratitude. Come back to the engagement. You've been engaged for four or five years—since you were seventeen, and now you are twenty-one. Have you any reason to believe the time is coming?'

'I don't know,' said Isabel. 'He has said nothing.'

'Four years is a terrible long time for a young man to wait. It isn't natural for a young man to wait so long. Do you suppose I would have waited four years?' The Captain laughed. 'Four days was nearer the mark. Isabel, do you suppose there's—there's someone else—up the back-stairs—some other girl—another wife in another port?'

'If Robert was in love with some other girl he would very soon make an end of my engagement,' said Isabel.

The Captain shook his head dubiously, as one loaded

with sad experiences, but refrained from pursuing that branch of the subject.

'To be sure,' he went on. 'Robert's a bookish man; he reads a good deal, reads something every day. It's the only use many of them get of their eyes. But even the readingest of young fellows can't be always thinking about his books. Then he speechifies a good deal—makes 'em up, learns 'em, and fires 'em off; but a young fellow can't be always thinking about his speechifying. Mostly the young fellows of the present day are like those of my day. They are fond of a song and glass, and they like to shake a leg now and again, and to kiss a pretty woman.'

'Robert is not one of that kind. He never wants either a song or a glass. And as for shaking a leg—oh!'

'But to wait for four years—four long years. To go on waiting as if he liked it. It sticks in the gizzard, my dear.'

'I am in no hurry, please.'

'I'm not thinking about you, my dear. No one expects you to be in a hurry. I'm thinking about him. A woman always likes courtship better than matrimony.'

'I know as little of one as of the other,' said Isabel.

'Yes, my dear, and it's a shame and a wonder. What is the man made of? That's what puzzles me. Well

—but now—when Robert gets into the House of Commons, which I've always understood that he desired, I suppose his ambition will be satisfied, and the thing will come off.'

'I am in no hurry,' said Isabel. 'And I do not know —and I shall not ask him.'

'Hang it! 'tis the man's part—the man's part, my dear—to be in a hurry. So, I say, we may expect——'

'Do not expect anything, father. Let us go on in silence. I am to marry Robert when he is willing. Till then I wait.'

'It was to come off, he told me, when he had done something or other. Well, a man can't be engaged for ever. The election, I expect, was what he meant.'

The Captain took up the paper again and read the leading article in the paper twice over, slowly.

''There is no doubt, I suppose,' he said, ' though the papers do reel off lies every day, that they have got the right end of the stick this time. There will be a General Election, and Robert will get in, and——'

' Father, do you suppose he really meant the Election?'

' What more could he mean? And, as I said before, no man likes to go on being engaged for ever. Wedding-bells will be ringing, Isabel—wedding-bells, my dear.'

She rose and fled.

When I arrived at ten o'clock, Robert was still in

his study, pacing the room in uncontrollable agitation. 'The time has come!' he cried. 'It has come! My chance has come. I feel as if it was my only chance.'

'I congratulate you, Robert. As for your only chance, that is rubbish. You are only twenty-six at the present moment. Applying the arithmetical method, you may stand for nine Parliaments yet; probably there will be many more chances between this and your seventieth birthday.'

'No, no. It could not be the same thing. I've thrown all my hopes, all my powers of persuasion and argument, into this election. I could never again be so fresh and so strong, or work so hard. I must succeed this time. I am carrying the men away against their convictions—if they've any—I am making them follow me. That means work.'

'All right. You shall get in. I know nothing whatever about the matter, because I never assisted at an election before; but here I am; take me; take all my time; I will live here, if you like; I will look after the yard for you. I have heard of Nottingham lambs being wanted. I will become a lamb. Platforms are sometimes rushed and candidates hustled off. I will get up a stalwart party of hustlers, if you like. Candidates are heckled out of their five senses. I will become a heckler of the most venomous kind for your opponents.

I can't write epigrams and verses, because that part of my education has been neglected. But here I am, Robert—one man, at least, at your service.'

'Thanks, a thousand times. You shall join my committee, to begin with. I must make haste to get my committee together; they shall all be working men except you. I must sit down to prepare an address. I shall have to arrange for an address somewhere or other every night till polling-day. It's going to be a splendid time—a magnificent time. By ——' He swore a great oath, for the first time in his life. 'My chance has come—my chance has come!'

His voice softened; he sank into his chair and leaned his head upon his hand. Robert was, for the moment, overcome. The spectacle of this emotion pleased me. I suppose no one likes to think of a man as altogether composed of cast-iron. When any ordinary human being sees the thing for which all his life long he has worked and longed actually within his reach, that ordinary or average human being is generally a little overcome. Remember that in this case ambition had devoured nearly all other passions. The man had had no youth; none of the delightful freaks, fredaines and frolics of youth could be recorded of this young man; the unfortunate Robert had never kissed a girl to his subsequent confusion; nor scoured the streets; nor

painted Wapping red; nor passed his midnights over
cups; he had worked and trained himself for this end
and none other. He would have been more than human
had he shown no sense of the crisis or juncture of
events.

While he sat there, head in hand, Isabel stole in softly
like a ghost, and stood beside his chair. I made as if I
would go, but she motioned me to stay. By the two
red spots in her cheeks I was made aware that something
decisive would be said.

He seemed not to observe her presence. She touched
his shoulder. 'Robert!'

'Isabel!' He started, and sat up, with a quick frown
of irritation.

'I have come to congratulate you, Robert,' she said
timidly.

'Yes, thank you, Isabel. Thank you. Don't say
any more.'

'When the General Election is over, you will have
done what you proposed to do, I suppose. I thought
it would be years first. Your ambition, I mean, will be
achieved.'

'Achieved? Why, Isabel, you understand nothing.
That is only a beginning.'

'Oh! Only a beginning?' She looked rather be-
wildered.

' Why, what else should it be ?   No one would want
to be a member of Parliament only for the pride of it,
I suppose.'

' Oh !   I thought——'

' Look here, Isabel, I'm glad you came in.   After the
little misunderstanding of yesterday, it's as well to have
a talk.   You won't mind George ; he knows all about
it.   Sit down there.'   Such was the improvement in his
manners that he actually got up and placed a chair for
her.   As for me, I retired to the seat in the window,
not proposing to interrupt the conversation.

' I will just tell you exactly what is the meaning of
the situation.   I have told no one—no one except
George, so far.   I didn't tell you, because you wouldn't
understand.   It isn't in your way to see.   You've
changed a bit since you took to going about with
George '—there was not a touch of jealousy in his mind
—' straightened yourself, and filled out and improved
so, that I hardly know you any more.   You're bigger
than you were, Isabel—I like a woman to look strong
—but, still, I don't think you can quite understand.'

' I should be glad to hear all your proposals, Robert.'

' I am astonished now to think of it, how I dared, in
my inexperience and ignorance, to form such an ambition.
If I had known, six months ago, what the thing meant,
I should have been afraid.'

'No,' said Isabel; 'nothing would ever make you afraid.'

'You think so, Isabel? Perhaps. In a general way I am not a coward.'

'I suppose you want to do something great in the House of Commons?'

'Put it that way if you please. I will give you details and particulars.'

Isabel sat facing him. There was no look of passion or admiration on his face. The hungry look had left his eyes, which were now filled with the eagerness of the coming struggle. There was nothing to fear from him. Indeed, at such a moment as this it is not of love that a man can be expected to think: he may most lawfully and laudably think of nothing but himself, even before Helen of Troy herself. But I thought, looking at the two of them, What a strange pair of lovers! The man who had never said a kind word—the girl who looked forward to her marriage with terror!

'Now, Isabel,' he said, 'I will tell you. I am going to enter the House as a plain Master Craftsman, not a gentleman, except that I know their tricks and phrases —I shall be a man experienced in industrial questions and in everything concerned with work practical and theoretical. They want such a man badly. I am going in as an Independent Member, like John Bright. When

I have made my mark in the House, and am a power in it, as John Bright was, I shall perhaps join a party in order to enter the Cabinet. And not till then. And perhaps not at all. As for being one of the rank and file, saying what one is told to say, put up to defend the incompetence and the blundering of the commanders, calling the Irish members, for instance, all the names under the sun one day, and all the opposite names the next day, just to catch votes—to be everything and all things for votes—votes—more votes—I won't do it. That kind of work will not do for me.'

'Well?' Either Isabel did not understand the point, or else it had no interest for her. She looked unconcerned, and spoke coldly.

'I told George at the outset. I called upon him on purpose to tell him all this when he was a stranger, and he managed to fall in with it as soon as he saw that I meant business. At the first go-off he thought I was a conceited windbag—one of the ignorant lot turned out by every local Parliament. I could see very well what he thought. When he saw that I was a determined kind of chap he fell in with it, I say, and helped me all he could.'

'Yes?' Isabel showed no manner of interest in this revelation of political ambition.

'And thought about this and about that thing

wanted. Oh, the essentials of the thing were all right
—the knowledge, and the appearance, and the power of
speech; but there was one thing wanting. I had never
thought of such an omission, and without him I could
never have repaired that omission. I'm not ashamed to
say, not as things have gone, that what I wanted was
manners.'

'Manners!' cried Isabel, showing interest at this
point. 'You to want manners!'

'Just what I said myself. But George was right.
There's a thousand little ways in which the fellows at
the West End are different from us. They are mostly
tricks invented to show that they are a superior race.
I've learned these tricks, and now, I believe, I can
pretend to be a gentleman.'

'You never were anything else.'

'There are gentlemen and gentlemen, Isabel. Have
you noticed any change in me?'

'Well, Robert,' she replied timidly, 'I have thought
that you were gentler.'

'Of course. One of the things is to repress yourself, and
pretend not to care. That's what you call being gentle.'

'Oh, but to learn manners!' said Isabel.

'I would do a great deal more than that for the sake
of getting on. Well, now you know what we did when
I went away with George every evening.'

' And when you get on in the House ?' She returned
to the main point.

' I say that, when I have made my mark, I may take
office ; but I don't know quite what I shall do. It may
be best to stay outside.'

' Best, you mean, for your power or for your reputa-
tion ?'

' For both.'

' Power is what you desire more than anything else in
the world, Robert. You have always desired it.'

' Always. There is nothing in the world worth having
compared with power, Isabel. I want to be a leader—
nothing less than that—mind—is my ambition. I
understand now how it must seem to other people a
wild and presumptuous dream for a man in my position.
I don't care a straw what it seems. I realize how great
a thing it is, and I am just all the more confirmed in my
resolution.'

' And when you are a leader !' It was quite impossible to make Isabel understand the audacity of
this ambition. She thought that Robert would simply
stand upon the floor of the House of Commons in order
to receive the distinctions that would be showered upon
him ; that everybody would immediately begin to offer
him posts of honour, because he was so strong and
masterful a man.

'Well, one thing, Isabel: as soon as I am in the Cabinet—say Home Secretary—my first ambition will be achieved. Then, as regards a certain promise——'

'How long,' she interrupted quickly, 'do you think it will take before you arrive so far?'

'No one can say. A party gets turned out or keeps in. At the quickest time possible for a new man to work his way and be recognised, and put over the heads of other men, one can't very well expect such success in less than five years.'

'It can only be done in five years,' I interposed for the first time, 'under the most favourable circumstances possible—if the present Government gets returned again, if it stays in five years, if you meet with immediate success, if vacancies occur among the chiefs, if you are able to serve in some subordinate capacity. If I were you, Robert, I should say ten years.'

'Well; in ten years,' he replied cheerfully. 'A year or two is neither here nor there if a man is advancing all the time.'

'And a woman is waiting,' I added.

'Ten years!' said Isabel. 'But your side may get turned out.'

'They may; then it might be longer. Of course, if a man once becomes a power in the House, he becomes also a power in the country. His influence may go on increasing.'

'Ten years! That is a very long time. There will be many changes in ten years.'

'Changes? I dare say—I dare say. I hope so. I shall make some changes myself.'

'Changes in your own mind, Robert.'

He saw what she meant. 'I think not, Isabel. A promise is a promise. When my word is passed the thing is as good as done.'

She got up. 'I won't waste your time any longer, Robert. I am glad to hear what your ambitions really mean. It was about that—promise—that I came to see you. I thought the time was come when you might want to fulfil that promise.'

'Not yet, Isabel.'

'Not yet. I came to set you free, if you wished to be set free.'

'To set me free?'

'Because a man like you should not be hampered by an engagement, especially with a woman whom—I mean —you ought to be free. So, Robert, I do set you free —if you desire it.'

'What makes you think that I desire it, Isabel? I don't desire it.'

'That is because you don't know other women. So,

Robert, it shall be always and at any time as you desire. We owe so much to you that this is due to you in return. I will wait for the fulfilment of that promise for ten years, twenty years, all my life, if you please. I will cheerfully set you free whenever you desire to be released. That is all, Robert.'

'Why,' said Robert, 'there spoke a good and reasonable girl. But you've given me quite as much in work as I've given you in board and lodging. You owe me nothing. As for being released, ask me if I want to be released when I am the Right Honourable Robert Burnikel, Secretary of State for India. And now let's make an end of thanksgivings and explainings, and get to business; there's lots of work before us.'

'Let me help you, Robert. My shorthand and type-writing ought to be of some use to you.'

'I wouldn't ask you, Isabel; but you can be of the greatest use. I take it very kindly of you after yester-day.' He held out his hand in token of forgiveness. Isabel accepted it, smiling graciously. 'I do indeed, Isabel, after yesterday's little misunderstanding.' He held her hand and looked her straight in the face; and not one touch of softening in his eyes, not the slightest look of love.

It was just what I expected of Isabel. She offered Robert his release if he would take it; if he would not, she remained bound to him for life, if need be, by promise. A barren and a hopeless engagement, miserable in either event—fulfilment or waiting. And for myself—— But just then was not a moment propitious for thinking of one's own broken eggs and shattered crockery. Besides, I was always quite sure that there would be a way out of it.

Then Isabel took her old place as shorthand clerk, and Robert walked about his room dictating to her and talking to me. I understood for the first time how a man may come to regard a woman as a mere mechanical contrivance for working purposes. He spoke to Isabel, once more his clerk, as if she were a senseless log. He ordered her to write this, to write that. I think that I could never bring myself to forget the sex or the humanity of a girl clerk.

That day, the first of many busy days, we arranged a great many things. During the dinner-hour we adjourned to the Yard, and turned that into a reception-room for the working men, who came in crowds. We arranged for addresses; we got together our committee; we opened our headquarters; we prepared our address to the constituents; we wrote our placards and our hand-bills; we started our election cries; in a word, we lost no time. And in order to be on the spot, I took up my residence in the house, being assigned the old

four-poster of the ancient John Burnikel, Master
Mariner.

'My career is beginning,' said Robert at eleven
o'clock, after the first great speech had been delivered
—'it is beginning. Well, I am not afraid—I am not
in the least afraid. The House of Commons is no more
difficult to move than the music-hall of Shadwell.
There's only one way to move any class of hearers : you
must first talk to interest them ; that's grip. I've got
the grip of a bull-dog. Then you must talk to make
'em cry. I can make 'em cry.'

'If you make the House of Commons cry,' I said,
' they'll shove you up into the House of Lords.'

'And you must be able to make 'em laugh. I can
make 'em laugh.'

'If you can make the House of Commons laugh,
Robert, they'll never let you go up to the other House
at all.'

CHAPTER XVII.

GENERAL ELECTION.

DESPITE the changes, suppressions, repressions, and new conditions which have been imposed upon the good old election, there is still some excitement left. We may sigh and pine for the brave days when an election lasted six weeks; when everybody marched up valiantly though clubs were shaken in his face and might be broken over his head, and gave his vote openly before all the world; when the people who had no vote contributed their share in the representation of the country by free fights, hustling and belabouring the voters; when drink flowed as freely as when Wat Tyler held the city; when everybody had to take a side, and behaved accordingly; when the chairmen brought their poles, and the sailors brought their clubs, and the butchers brought their marrow-bones and cleavers—and all for use, and not for fashionable display; when none thought shame to take a bribe; when the air was thick with showers of epigrams, libels, and scurrilous accusations; when the Father of Lies held his headquarters, for the time, in the borough; when the whole of a man's record was exposed to view, with trimmings and additions, and the most ingenious and diabolic perversions of the truth; when the public-houses were open to all electors free, and beer and gin and rum were attainable by the humblest; when every elector knew his value, and proudly appraised himself to its full extent; when the candidates stood upon the hustings courageously facing showers of dead cats, putrid rabbits, addled eggs, and cabbage-stalks—about a fortnight before an election all the cats in the country died, and all the dead rabbits became putrid, and all the eggs were addled, and all the cabbage-stalks went rotten. Thus doth Nature accommodate herself to the ways of man. Those of us who read of the good old days may pine for them; those who have not read of them will find little at the present day to remind them of former customs.

At Shadwell there were none of these things. A fight there was, but only one. None of the ancient customs were observed; only those humours of an election which still survive were with us; and these are mild.

It was an active time for those who, like me, went electioneering. The papers spoke of nothing else;

certainly at our house no one talked of anything else.   I
suppose that something went on as usual in the yard ;
but no one heeded the building of boats.   Everybody
told everybody else that business was completely stopped.
That may be.   In the High Street, however, the cranes
on the third-floors of the warehouses continued their
activity, and the waggons full and empty rumbled along
the street.   They didn't mind the General Election,
and the ships went in and out of the docks without
minding the General Election in the least.   Also the
working men went backwards and forwards.   And they
didn't seem to mind the General Election in the least.
Everybody said, however, that the world thought of
nothing else.   We made our own racket, I suppose, and
thought that all the world was joining in.

And we worked—heavens ! how we worked !   Of
course we were Robert's servants—his slaves, even.   He
issued commands.   At his committee he did not consult
his friends ; he commanded them.   And, of course,
everybody obeyed.   He ordered me to speak for him in
the less eligible districts, and when he was speaking
elsewhere.   Well, I, who had never before spoken, obediently went to speak.   I prepared speeches : I found
freedom of speech.   I even arrived at some popularity.
'We'd send you to Parliament,' they told me, 'if it
wasn't for your cousin.'   I harangued on Robert's lines,

as zealously as a Party man who hopes for office ; I pulled
the enemy's addresses and manifestoes to pieces ; I showed
their abominable inconsistency ; their delusive promises;
their wicked self-seeking ; their shameful ambitions.
Oh, the wickedness and the foolishness of the other
side ! The world will never be righteous, mind you, or
generous, or just, till the other side gives up its self-
seeking and its pretences. And then I canvassed—yes !
I walked through all the streets of Shadwell Borough :
they are mostly streets with a full-flavoured fragrance
hanging about them—the frying of fish in oil is an in-
dustry much practised ; I solicited the votes of all the
voters ; I was received with contumely and with sar-
casms, and even with open abuse, in some parts, and
with a free hospitality in other parts which was almost
worse than the abuse. I also manufactured some lam-
poons which I thought were rather effective. I sent
them to Frances, who told me that I ought to be standing in my cousin's place and doing all this work for
myself. She was good enough, however, to express a
hope that so strong a speaker and so vigorous a speaker
as myself might get into the House, where, she added,
he would very quickly find his own level.

Robert's committee was composed almost entirely of
working men. The employers and shopkeepers, and a
good many of the working men, understood two things

only, Liberal or Conservative. Politics must mean one thing or the other. That a candidate should be neither Liberal nor Conservative, but only himself, they could not understand.

There is no local press at Shadwell, but the London papers, when they spoke of our election prospects, ignored Robert as a mere outsider. The seat, of course, was for the Liberal candidate, or for the Conservative, one or the other. No one knew, or guessed, what Robert had done in the borough by his three months' course of speeches and lectures. The newspapers spoke of him as merely a local man without local influence. He was called a Socialist, being an Individualist of the deepest dye, and a demagogue, being a man who sought to teach the people, but not to flatter them. It was said that he had no importance except that he would take away a few votes from this side or that. The newspapers understood nothing about it, as you shall see.

Before many days were over, I was as much absorbed in the election as Robert himself. I lived altogether at Wapping. We began work early in the morning, at seven, and we ended it at midnight. The committee sat all day long; that is to say, the only man among them who was not a working man—myself—sat all day long. We issued our candidate's address, which was a bold appeal for election on the ground of knowledge

and personal fitness. As for burning questions, we dismissed them. Abolition of the Lords? Not possible.
What was the use of discussing for election purposes a
question not yet within the reach of the Commons?
The Disestablishment of the Church? Whether that
would do any good to the people of the country or not
was an open question. Meantime, was the measure even
possible at the present moment? No. Then why consider it? Was there to be an Eight Hours Bill? Then
there would have to be an eight hours' pay, with reduc-
tions, otherwise the employer would be ruined. And so
on. Our independent candidate would promise nothing,
except the support of such measures as he himself, exer-
cising his own judgment, might think calculated to
advance the whole community. He said that he would
vote for no interest; that he would not needlessly disturb existing institutions; that old things, grown up in
the course of centuries, meant things befitting the mind
of the people, and so far should be respected. He
offered himself as a man who knew things. He reminded the electors that they had heard his addresses,
and had learned his views. If they approved of him
and his opinions, they would send him to Parliament,
where they would find him able, at least, to set the
House right on a good many matters of fact. 'I am
not,' he said, 'and never shall be, a Socialist. Any

attempt to destroy the Individual must inevitably fail, because all work—every enterprise—every invention— every advance—is caused by the individual acting for himself at the right moment, and not by the Society, which can never act at all.   But I want every way open to the man who has the ability and the courage to rise. And I would have the relations of employer and work- man to rest upon some method recognised and adopted by both sides.   I shall always speak, and vote, on the side of the working man, though I am an employer, until such an understanding has been arrived at.   My dream of society is of such an organization as will pro- vide order and liberty for every man to work as he can, and protect him against tyranny ; which will give every man such a wage as the conditions of his trade allow ; which will leave the door wide open for all who are strong enough to pass through and to climb up.'

When one contrasted this address, strong and manly —we called it—with the conventional phrases—we called them conventional—of the other candidates, it seemed marvellous—to ourselves—that anyone should vote for them at all.

Every evening the canvassers went round and brought back their sheaves of promises with them ; every day it became more and more certain that we had the people with us.   At the end there was no doubt possible.   But the other candidates still believed in the 'merely local' theory, and they spoke of him with scorn as the working man's candidate.

Every evening for four weeks Robert spoke. On Sundays he spoke at the working men's clubs, in their own club-houses; on Mondays he spoke in such halls and big rooms as can be got in this neighbourhood. It was one evening just before the polling that the fight happened which has been mentioned above.

We were in the same music-hall to which I had brought Frances on a certain memorable occasion. Robert would still have no chairman or committee-men on the platform. He stood alone; with some of the committee I was in the stage-box. Now I observed, when we took our places, a lot of fellows whose faces were unfamiliar to me—yet by this time I knew all Shadwell; they were standing gathered together in the orchestra. They talked to each other, and nodded their heads, and stuck elbows in each other, with a good deal of earnestness, as if they designed something; they all carried sticks; and they looked inclined for mischief. Well, at election time there is still something left of the old leaven. It looked to me as if they meant to rush the platform. Robert would be alone there; if these fellows should try to rush it, how would he defend it by himself? I mentioned my suspicions—we resolved to jump down to the stage if there should be any need.

Well, our candidate came on: he was received with a storm of applause; but the men in the orchestra did not applaud: they only whispered and nudged each other. Robert began his address. The company in the orchestra continued to whisper; they did not pretend to listen. After the speaker had gone on for a few minutes the house became perfectly silent, carried away by the current of the speech flowing full and strong and clear. The voice of the man was magnetic; it would be heard; it recommended silence. Then suddenly one man blew a whistle. Instantly the men in the orchestra at either end climbed up on the platform, shouting and brandishing their sticks.

The whole house rose, crying ' Down! down! Off! off!' And then followed the finest display of physical strength and bravery that I have ever seen. There were at least a dozen of them, equally divided. Robert seized the chair beside him, and with this for weapon he fell upon the party on the right, and literally broke the chair to pieces over their heads. We might have leaped down and joined him, but there was no need ; the battle was over as soon as it was begun ; the assailants fell back one over the other; their heads were broken, their teeth were knocked out, their collar-bones were broken. Robert wielded his chair with the lightning-like dexterity of a skilful player in the olden time who wielded his quarter-staff. It seemed but a moment before the fellows of the right-hand party were down again, broken to pieces, with no more courage for the fray. Robert kicked the last of them over the foot-lights into the orchestra. He then turned to the second party. But they had seen enough; they were now tumbling over each other to the place whence they came in much greater haste than they had shown to mount the stage. Then Robert stood alone. A streak of blood lay on his white shirt-front: it came from his lip, which was cut, but not badly; his table was upset, his water-decanter broken, his chair lay about in frag-ments. And then, oh! I have never heard such a splendid tumult of applause. From every throat it came; from every man and woman present there arose such a storm and rolling, roaring, continuous thunder of applause as I have never heard before or since. Who is there among us that does not rejoice to see an act of bravery and strength? One man against a dozen, and where were all the rest? Again—again—again—will it never stop?

A hand was laid upon my shoulder. I turned quickly. It was Frances.

'I came to hear your orator again,' she whispered;

'but I have seen him as well. George, it was splendid! Oh, the great, strong, brave creature! He must get in—he must!'

Then Robert, advancing to the front, held up his hand for silence, for the people, having tasted blood, wanted more fighting, and were now roaring for the disturbers of the peace to be thrown to the lions; and the ill-advised rushers, caught in a trap of their own making, were looking at each other with rueful countenance, expectant of a troublous five minutes. Imagine the Christian martyrs going to be let out into an arena full of lions, all hungry. And these poor fellows had not, it was clear, the support of faith. They had been paid to make a row and break up the meeting, and now it looked as if they had achieved martyrdom.

Silence obtained, Robert pointed to the orchestra below him. 'I think,' he said, 'that before we go on, these gentlemen had better be removed. If they do not go quietly, I will go down among them myself with all that is left of the chair. In taking them out, remember that there are, perhaps, a few ribs and collar-bones broken. Please not to kick the men with the broken bones down the stairs!'

The house roared with joy; the men jumped up and poured to the front. They summoned the rushers to come out of that, or—they promised truly dreadful things as an alternative. But these misguided young men surrendered; they climbed ruefully over the pew. As each descended he was escorted between two of our fellows to the stairs, and then, one had reason to believe, he was assisted down those stairs by strange boots. The unfortunates on whose skulls and ribs the chair had been broken came last, all the conceit out of them, with hanging heads, and the exhibition of pocket-handkerchiefs. They were received with cheers derisive.

'And now,' said Robert, when they were gone, 'let us go back to business.'

And I really believe, so great is the admiration of the crowd for personal bravery and a man who can fight, that this little adventure brought him as many votes as all his speeches. For once the people were presented with evidence conclusive that they really had a very strong man before them.

'I am glad I came,' said Frances, when the meeting was over. 'I never saw a brave man before. Oh, what a thing it must be to be a man! And you go and throw it all away. Take me down now. My carriage is waiting by the door, I believe.'

I led her down the stairs, in the splendid dress which was always part of her, through the people, who made way for her right and left—the poor women with their pinched and shabby shawls, and the working men in their working dress.

'You people all,' she said, standing at the top of the staircase, 'I have heard a splendid address' to-night, and I have seen a splendid thing. If you don't send that splendid speaker and that splendid man to the House of Commons, you deserve to be disfranchised.'

'Don't be frightened, lady,' said one of the men, whom I knew to be a rank Socialist; 'we'll send him there fast enough, especially if you'll come here and speak for him.'

So she got into the carriage and drove off, while the crowd shouted after her.

And this was the nearest approach to the old-fashioned humours of an election that we had to show.

When the day of polling arrived we had no carriages. Robert would not pay for any, and no one offered to lend him any. The carriages of Liberal and Conservative ran about all day long, but our voters had to walk. In the evening they came by companies, among them all the costers of the quarter with their barrows. What made the costers vote for Robert, if it was not that very noble battle on the stage?

And when the votes were counted, Robert was head of the poll by 754 votes.

So he had got the desire of his heart, and was a

Member of Parliament. He had worked for it for seven years; he had even descended so far as to learn manners, which was at first a very bitter pill. He had trained his voice, and taught himself the art of oratory : he had studied economics of all kinds ; he was patient, courageous, tenacious, and he was ambitious. What would he do after all this preparation ?

CHAPTER XVIII.

IN THE HOUSE.

THEN followed the meeting of the newly-elected Commons. Our own member went off with a quiet air of self-reliance, not arrogance. 'I am not in the least afraid of my own powers,' he repeated. 'I have tried and proved them. I shall speak to the House first, and to the country next.'

'Don't be in a hurry to begin, Robert.'

'Certainly not. I shall wait until a question arises on which I can speak with authority. And I shall not speak often. My first ambition is that, when I do rise, the House may look for a solid contribution, not for talk. Let me be considered as a man who knows. Don't think that I shall throw away my chances by chatter.'

'We shall look out eagerly.'

'You will, I believe.' There was just a little touch of disappointment in his voice. 'You will; Isabel will not. She cares nothing about it. I suppose that women never understand ambitions or politics.'

'Some women do.' I thought of Frances, who understood nothing else.

'I wish I knew them, then. Not that it matters. Men don't want the sympathy of women in their work ; we want power and authority. All a woman wants is comfort, and to sit by the fire. If you had had a woman for a shorthand clerk, as I have, your opinion of the feminine intellect would not be quite so high, perhaps.'

So he went off, the strong man armed, to begin the fight ; and we looked after him as he strode down the street, for my own part always with the feeling that we had somehow changed places.

'Robert will get, I suppose, some day, the desire of his heart,' said Isabel. 'I wonder why men desire these things ?'

'They are very grand things,' I told her. 'Robert wants to be a leader of men. Is not that a great thing to desire ? What greater thing can there be ?'

'Yes, if he is fit for it, and if he be a wise leader. But Robert puts the leadership first and the wisdom next. He only desires the wisdom in order to get the leadership.'

'Nay, Isabel ; we must think exactly the contrary.

Otherwise, how is the world ever to respect the leader?'

'I cannot think anything except what I know.'

'Well, then, power is a very great thing to have. Every man in the world, except myself, ought to desire power. I don't want it, I confess, because I am not ambitious. Perhaps that is philosophy. Give me a tranquil, an obscure life, if you like, with private interests—boat-building, for instance—and—what it seems I shall have to forego.'

Isabel paid no heed to the latter sentence, but went on talking about Robert. 'Always to lead, always to command—that is Robert's single thought. If he was King, he would not be contented unless he ruled the whole world.'

'A noble ambition, truly.'

'Sometimes I wonder whether all the great men of history have been self-seekers as well as masterful.'

'I should say all. The personal motives, desire of place and authority, must underlie everything else.'

'Then, how can any woman love a man who thinks of nothing but himself? I could not, George; but you know it—you—I cannot.'

'Well, Isabel, a woman may love the greatness and strength of the man, first of all. Besides, she may call that a noble ambition which you call self-seeking; she may call that tenacity which you call selfishness; she may lend her whole strength'—I thought of Frances and what she would do—'to advance the career in which her husband is absorbed without asking for thanks or recognition from him at all.'

'I could not do it, George. The thought of devotion without thanks or recognition makes me wretched. I could never love a man who would accept such work. Besides, I could never love a man unless I filled his heart, and made him think of me.'

So she spoke, telling me all her thoughts in sweet confidence, knowing that it would not be abused. Well, some women differ. Frances would be contented, if only her husband became a great man, with neither thanks nor recognition. Isabel cared nothing about the greatness. And I suppose that some women are contented with the ideal they have set up. They love not the strong man for his strength, nor the weak man for his weakness; they love an imaginary man. In this way the noblest woman may love the lowest man, seeing her ideal even through the matted overgrowth of animalism. Isabel had no power, unfortunately, of setting up an ideal. In this case she knew the real man in his workshop, without his coat—so to speak, in his shirt-sleeves. I said so. 'You worked with him, and for him, Isabel; that destroyed the ideal. No man is a hero to his type-writer.'

'Perhaps; but love and mastery cannot go together. Well, Robert is now beginning the career of which he has thought so much. It will be ten years, you say— ten years—ten good long years—before he succeeds. Ah! a great deal may happen in ten years. He will grow tired; I shall grow old. I hope I shall grow old and hideous.'

'A great deal may happen in ten years. Yes. Men may ask to be released from hasty promises. Anything may happen. Perhaps, again, he will never succeed.'

'We must not dare to hope that he will fail. It would be like hoping that he was dead.'

'If he were any ordinary person I should say that his ambition was wildly presumptuous. Seeing that he is Robert, and seeing what Robert stands for, I do not call it wild. Yet there are many things in the way far more than he understands as yet. Let us be patient, Isabel. If you are waiting, I am waiting too. When you promised to wait his will, you passed that sentence upon me as well.'

For three weeks nothing happened. At the house we went on as usual, but without Robert, who remained at Westminster, living in my chambers, while I took over the work of his boat-yard all day, and the care of his mistress every evening. We were loyal to him; there was passed between us no word or look of which one need be ashamed. Isabel had repeated her promise; she had renewed the oath; one could only wait.

One morning, however, I found a letter lying on my plate. It was from Frances. I opened it. A long letter. I laid it aside. With my second cup of tea I began to read it leisurely; but over the second page I jumped with interjections.

'My dear George' (she began),

'I was in the House last night looking down upon the new lot. They seem to be rather a mixed lot. We have had losses. However, a good many of our old friends are back again, and the majority is assured, and is large enough if the Whips do their duty. Alas! if my mother were still living, with her salon and her dinners, that majority would become a solid block growing every day. I might myself have such a salon, if there was a man anywhere for whose sake I could take the trouble, and make myself a leader. But, George, as you know very well, there is not.'

I laid down the note. I could see in imagination Frances writing these words. She would throw down the pen and spring to her feet in impatience—in queenly impatience—because among all her subjects she could not find one man strong enough. Yet to one strong and ambitious she would give, not only herself, but also such help in his career as few, very few, men could hope for; the help of a very long purse, very great family influence, political experience, and social power. She wanted to find such a man; she desired above all things to be a political lady, the wife of a great political leader. She would exact from him in return for all she gave nothing but devotion to his career; she would acquiesce in his working and thinking for no other object.

On the other side of the table sat the other type of woman—one who wanted nothing of life but love, with sufficiency and tranquillity; one who would be perfectly contented with a life in the shade, and with a perfectly obscure husband.

As for myself, it seemed then, and it seems now, as if no distinctions—which do not distinguish—were worth the struggle and conflict, the misrepresentation and lies and slanders of the party contest. Whereas, to live in obscurity beside a babbling brook, or Wapping Old Stairs, for instance; among thick woods—the burial ground of St. John's, Wapping, for instance; in country lanes with high hedges on either side—say the High Street, Wapping; with love and Isabel . . . I resumed the letter:

'The questions do really grow more tedious every
day. At last the adjourned debate began again—at
half-past nine. You never take interest in anything
really interesting, my dear George, so that it is useless
to tell you that the Bill was a Labour Bill, and that
everybody thought it a very useful Bill—even the
working men Members until to-night. The Bill, everybody says, will have to be abandoned. In other words,
your cousin, in a single maiden speech, has done the
Government the injury of making them withdraw a
Bill. It is equivalent to a defeat. But I am antici-
pating. My dear George, your cousin's speech is talked
of by everybody.'

' Where's the paper?' I cried. ' Give it to me, Captain.' I tore it open and looked at the debates. Yes,
there it was ! Robert had made his first speech. ' Look,
Isabel !' I cried. ' Look ! he has succeeded with a
single speech.' I threw the paper across the table and
went on reading :

'I dare say you will have seen all about it in the
papers. Now, it is very curious ; I had almost forgotten
that your cousin was a candidate. They told me that
he had no chance whatever, and I left off thinking about
him as a candidate. Of course, I could not forget the

fiery orator of Shadwell, or the hero of the splendid fight that I witnessed. So that when he got up to speak I was quite unprepared for him. Of course, I remembered him instantly; he is not the kind of man one forgets readily. I think he is quite the handsomest man in the House; not the tallest, but what they used to call the properest man and the comeliest; he has not the least air of fashion, but he has the look of distinction.'

'Good,' said the Captain. 'I always said that he looked like a Duke.'

'Read the speech, George,' said Isabel, 'and then go on with the letter.'

I read the speech aloud. The oblique narrative makes everything cold. Even in direct narrative one loses the voice—in this case so rich and musical a voice—and the aspect of the man, the personality of the speaker—in this case so marked and so distinguished. Now, the House of Commons may be cold—how can that unhappy body, doomed to listen day after day to floods and cataracts of words, be anything but cold?—but I was sure even from this dry précis that the members must have listened with surprise and delight. The close of the speech I turned back from the oblique to direct narrative, and read it in the first person.

'Oh!' said Isabel. 'I think I hear him speaking.

Those facts I copied for him myself from a Blue-book.'

'Robert will be a great man,' said the Captain. 'My dear, they will make him something. He will be a nobleman, and you will be my Lady.'

'You read it just as Robert would speak it,' said Isabel. 'Your voice is like his, only not so strong. But you are like him in so many ways.'

'It is a noble speech, Isabel.'

'It is his first bid for power,' she distinguished. 'I dare say it is an able speech. But I feel as if I had been behind the scenes while he was preparing the show. To me, George, it will always be a show.'

'You are like the child who wants to go beyond the story, Isabel. Why not be contented with the things presented?'

Why, indeed, not be contented with the show? If one were to analyze things and to discover the real motives and the springs of action, what would become of the patriot, the statesman, the philanthropist? What worth are the tender words of the poet? What consolation is left in the sermon of the preacher? No man, I said, is a hero to his type-writer: Isabel was the type-writer. There must be rehearsals and stage management, even for the effective conduct of a martyrdom. One may be filled with pity for the poor, with enthusiasm for a cause; but consider how emotion is stirred into action when the personal ambitions and the private interests lie in the same direction. 'It is the first bid for power,' said Isabel. So it was; and yet that speech, while it revealed the speaker, killed a Bill which might have involved mischief incalculable. The perfect private secretary—a very, very rare creature—is able to forget the rehearsals and the stage management.

I laid down the paper and took up the letter again, and read it aloud:

'I told you, George, in that East End den, that the man was a born orator. He spoke better to-night, in the House, than before those working men—perhaps because he was more careful. He is one of those speakers, I mean, with whom repression increases strength. He spoke consciously, I am sure, to the country as well as to the House. His voice is magnetic in its richness and fulness; his periods are balanced; he spoke without the least hesitation, yet without the fatal fluency. He was not embarrassed; he spoke with authority. The effect of his speech upon the House was wonderful; the members were dominated. They listened—compelled to listen. When he sat down there was a universal gasp, not of relief, but of astonishment.

'Of course I do not know what your cousin means or

wishes by going into the House. Probably nothing but a vague ambition. What should such a man understand of the political career? Yet, when I say "such a man," I think of his trade, not of his appearance or his manner. He looks like a king, and has the manners—in the House, at least, whatever he might have in society—of one accustomed to the best people. Come and talk to me about him.

'Of course, also, one must never judge by a first speech. It is always interesting to hear the maiden effort. Very likely your cousin prepared every phrase and every word of it, and he would break down in debate. I wait for his second speech, and for a speech in reply.

'The member for Shadwell, as I told you before, is absurdly like you in face and in general appearance, but he is a bigger man. Perhaps he resembles the Judge, who was a very big man, more than you. Well, George, for your sake I shall watch his movements and read his speeches. He may do something considerable; he may not. Many a man makes a good beginning in the House who cannot keep it up. The floor is knee-deep with the dust and bones of dead and gone ambitions. They take the place of the rushes which they formerly strewed on the floor. I was looking at the faces of the members last night. There were the old stagers who

have long since parted with their ambitions, and now
sit quiet and resigned, and vote like sheep. Why do
they do it? What is the joy of remaining all their
lives among the rank and file? Then I saw the faces of
the new young men. I made them all out, one after
the other, those who are ambitious and those who are
not. Oh, George! what an interesting place the House
of Commons is, and why—why—why have you left it
to a tradesman cousin to have all the ambition in the
family?'

I read all this aloud.

'Who is your correspondent, George?' Isabel asked.
'I suppose it is your friend, Lady Frances. Why is
she so contemptuous about tradesmen?'

'She only thinks that I ought to have gone into the
House, Isabel. It is her way of expressing herself.'

However, the rest I did not read aloud:

'You may bring your cousin to see me, George. I
am at home this day week. You so seldom come to see
me that I am almost tempted to come over to Wapping.
But it would be too dreadful to see you among the
chips, with your coat off and your sleeves turned up,
and an apron, and, I dare say, disfiguring callosities
already appearing on your hands. When you are sick

and tired of it, come back to the world. Lord Caerleon will soon want a private secretary. The post would suit you entirely. He is a man of the world—not a politician only. And there are still things to be had worth the having, and in the gift of Ministers, which are not awarded by competitive examination to candidates who certainly have no more merit than you yourself. Come back. Great Donkey, it is dull without you.

'Your affectionate sister—by adoption,

'FRANCES.'

CHAPTER XIX

LADY FRANCES AT HOME.

I FOUND Robert satisfied—he used the word himself—with his first success.

'I could have desired nothing better,' he said, ' than such a chance. So far as I can learn, there will be a good many more such chances before long. What does Isabel say? But, of course, she takes no interest in the subject.'

' Would you like a woman's opinion, Robert?'

'I don't know. Women don't count for much in politics, or in anything else, as far as judgment goes.'

' The woman I know counts for a great deal. She is an old friend of mine—a friend from childhood. She is the daughter of a Prime Minister, and the widow of a Secretary of State, and she is an ardent politician. Well, Robert, she is a very charming woman, too. I took her to Shadwell to hear you speak. She came again that night when you fought the rushers, and she was in the House last night. And she commands me to bring you to her next "At Home."'

'Oh,' said Robert.

'You are quite wrong—absurdly wrong—in your views of women. They may be extremely useful in politics; they have often played a great part. A certain Delilah was a politician, I believe. She coaxed a giant out of his sense and his secret.'

'Are you going to get me coaxed out of my strength?'

'Not a bit. I am taking you to a woman who will add to your strength if you are so happy as to win her interest.'

'A party politician.'

'Certainly—a party politician, as you will be before long.' He shook his head. 'For the rest, the less important affairs, she is a most delightful person, handsome and rich. The way to her friendship is to be strong, capable, and ambitious. You are all three. She is prepared to welcome you. Of course you will come?'

We were dining at my club. I do not think that there was anything in the quiet, assured manner of my cousin Robert to make anyone suspect that three months before this man had never even possessed a dress-coat, had never seen a dinner properly served, had never tasted claret, and had never dined after one.

'Of course, I know,' he said slowly, 'what you mean by this invitation; it means that you think I may now enter a drawing-room.'

'Partly. You can never be taken for a man born and brought up in the Eton and Trinity way. You don't desire such a thing. But you are now one who has the bearing and the speech of a gentleman.'

'I will go with you; I am not afraid of being dazzled either by a woman's face or by her finery, or by a man's titles, nor any airs and affectations, nor by the languid superiority of some of your fellows. I know my own value, and that, I take it, is the best foundation possible for courtly manners. And so you think I am polished enough for a drawing-room, do you?'

'Not polished, but finished. If you went farther you would lose your natural manner. You could never lose the form and figure which proclaim your strength. Your big head, your broad shoulders, your short, curly hair, your square beard, your deep-set eyes—I swear that you are just the strongest-looking man in the world.'

Robert laughed. No one, not even the strongest-looking man in the world, dislikes being described as looking what he most desires to be.

* * * * *

Lady Frances's rooms were already well filled when we arrived; later they were crowded. She welcomed me with her customary kindness. 'I shall never cease to reproach you,' she said; 'but I have forgiven you.'

She was dressed in all her splendour—a blaze of diamonds, a vision of silk (if it was silk), of velvet (if it was velvet). She might have stood to Robert for some great Court lady. Her queenly stature, her noble figure, her large head and ample cheek, set off her splendid dress. She looked as if this was the only dress she ought to wear; she looked indeed a *grande dame de par le monde*.

I presented my cousin. For the moment Robert was staggered. I saw upon his face an expression of weakness quite new to him. It was the weakness of the strong man in the presence, for the first time, of the queenly woman.

She received him with gracious courtesy.

After a few words, I left Robert to talk a little with his hostess. While they stood together, there entered a little old man with shaggy white eyebrows, keen eyes, and a white mane and a big head—a leonine person. Frances shook hands with him, and then turned to Robert.

'Mr. Burnikel,' she said, 'let me introduce you to

Lord Caerleon. Mr. Burnikel is Member for Shadwell, and a cousin of your friend, Sir George.'

Lord Caerleon shook hands with him. 'On our side, Mr. Burnikel, I hope.'

'I have entered the House as an Independent Member,' said Robert sturdily.

'Oh!' Lord Caerleon replied dryly. 'Yes, I have known several young men announce that intention; but they change it—they change it. There is a good deal to be got out of the House by an ambitious man who goes the right way to work—a great deal : distinction and recognition, that is something ; place and power, that is something. You are a lawyer, perhaps.'

'No ; I am not a member of any learned profession. I am a Master Craftsman—by trade a boat-builder.'

'Oh!' Lord Caerleon refrained from the least expression of surprise. 'But one may imagine that every young man who goes into the House is actuated by some ambition.'

'My ambition is to make a mark in the House—and out of it,' said Robert.

'Then, sir, I wish you every success; and you will speedily discover that, in order to make that mark, you must join a Party—that is, our Party—my Party.'

Lord Caerleon left him and walked over to me. He

was a former friend of my grandfather, the Judge. 'Is that your cousin, George?' he asked—'that tall, good-looking fellow over there, Member for Shadwell?'

'He is my cousin, certainly, though rather distant.'

'Oh! He said he was a—a—a boat-builder. Did he speak some kind of allegory?'

'A hundred years ago my great-grandfather and his great-grandfather were partners in a boat-building-yard. At the same time, if I remember rightly, your great-grandfather, Lord Caerleon——'

'Was unknown. Certainly. Yet one does not expect to see an actual boat-builder in a place like this, and looking and talking like a gentleman. You and I, Sir George, belong to the third generation of those who were born in the purple of gentlehood. This man says he is a Master Craftsman. Do we receive the man with a plane and a chisel in our drawing-rooms?'

'He is a master of labour; he employs many men. I believe he will prove himself to be a Master Crafts-man in the craft of oratory and debate. He is the strongest man, Lord Caerleon, the most courageous man, and the most finished man, that I know. You can't dazzle him. You can't frighten him. And I am quite certain, from his first speech, that he will carry away the House as he carries away his constituents. Look after him, Lord Caerleon. Don't forget to reckon with him as soon as you can.'

Lord Caerleon looked at me thoughtfully, but made no reply. Half an hour later I saw that he was again talking with Robert.

Thinking of what the man was when first I knew him; how contemptuous of social conventions; how determined to go into the House as a rough craftsman; to set everybody right on all questions of labour and employers, knowing nothing whatever of the ways and manners by which alone anything real can be accomplished; and seeing the man in this salon, quiet and assured, yet strangely unlike the ordinary young man of the West End, I was elated to think of my success. To be sure, I had a pupil who was determined to learn. But, then, a well-bred manner is to some people impossible to learn, or to assume, if they work at it all their lives. To Robert the manner came easily.

'He has the air,' said Frances, reading my thoughts, because I was looking across the room, 'of a man who has lived in the best society, but not our own. Has he lived in New York?'

'No; he has only lived in Wapping—a distinguished suburb near the place where you heard him speak.'

'Wapping has, then, I suppose, a curiously distinguished society of its own. Has Wapping a nobility, an opera-house, ladies of the world? Seriously, George, how did this man arrive at a distinguished manner as well as a distinguished look? You know—I told you—when I heard him speak. I made up my mind that he was a born orator.'

'Well, Frances, he has practised a very honest trade; that prevents meanness; and he has read enormously, so that his level of thought is elevated; and he takes himself very seriously, so that he is self-confident; and he is quick to observe; so that, altogether, I think you may understand how he has arrived at his present manner.'

'He is not a young man for a young lady. I introduced him to one just now, and they separated five minutes afterwards with a lively look of mutual repulsion. Perhaps he began by telling her, as he told Lord Caerleon, that he was a boat-builder.'

'Very likely.'

Then I retired into a corner and looked on. I saw that Frances looked after this guest with a care which she seemed to bestow upon no others. She talked to him, she introduced him to people, especially to members of the House; and I saw that he was not dazzled—not in the least dazzled—by title, or by fine dress, or fine manners. It was impossible to condescend with such a man; most likely he condescended to the condescender.

'I like it, George,' he said, when we found ourselves together. 'I like the crowd and the fine dresses and all. It is amusing. I don't belong to it in the least. That makes it all the more amusing.'

'And the women—how do you like them?'

'Lady Frances is splendid! I do not see any other woman in the place.'

It was filled with women: some young and beautiful, some old and no longer beautiful; all well dressed, and most of them animated. But he had no eyes except for Lady Frances.

Presently all were gone; I alone remained behind.

'Let us sit down, George, for a few minutes' quiet talk. Come into the little room. You may have a cigarette, if you like. Now about that tall cousin of yours. Do you really think that he has the qualities necessary for success? It is not enough to fire off a speech now and then, you know.'

'Well, he says he has these qualities. Whatever he says is always true. Quite a man of his word, you know. I think he has these qualities. The House loves a strong man beyond anything. Remember how they all turned round about Bradlaugh. Well, Bradlaugh was a strong man, if you like; and Bradlaugh knew a lot; but Bradlaugh in all his glory wasn't, I really believe, a patch on my cousin Robert.'

Frances became thoughtful. 'You know, George,' after a pause, 'I was bitterly disappointed that you did not go into politics. You would have had every kind of help. I cannot tell you half the dreams I had nourished about your success. Everything is possible for such a man as you. And you basely deserted us and went off boat-building. Oh, heavens! — boat-building!'

'I did, Frances. I am a wretch.'

'Well, the Party wants a few young men — good young men. If I can get that big, strong man, your cousin, to throw himself heartily into the Party, he may prove himself worthy of being looked after. Help me with him, George.'

'What am I to do?'

'Bring him to dinner with me. I will have a little dinner of you two first; then a little dinner alone with him; then a little dinner with one or two of the chiefs thrown in. Then—but you understand how a woman works in such a case. I want him for the Party.'

'What will you offer him?'

'I don't know yet; we must see first what he is worth, and next what he wants. An ordinary young man would be contented with dining with me. He would then go home and dream of making love to me— they all do. Then he would come here and try to make that dream a reality. But a young man with a great future before him would want more than that. What would he want?'

'One thing, Frances. Don't speak to him just yet of place or salary. The man thinks nothing about money. Later on, when he discovers that his few hundreds a year won't buy all things he wants, he will, perhaps, modify his views.'

'What will tempt him, then?'

'Power. He wants Power. He would be another Gladstone, another Bismarck. He desires Power about everything. The greatest presumption—the greatest audacity.'

Frances sighed. 'Oh!' she said, 'if they had only made me a man! George, there is but one thing in the world that I desire, and that is Power. I could get it easily, even though I am a woman, if I had a husband strong and able and ambitious, and worth working for. Where is that man? You ought to have been such a man, George, but you're not. You are only a common carpenter. Oh, the grovelling of it!'

'I will become a cabinet-maker, if you like, Frances, and make the Cabinet in which my cousin is to sit.'

CHAPTER XX.

AT THE YARD.

A few days afterwards Robert came over to the yard. He came during the men's dinner-hour, when a delightful calm settles down upon Wapping, and even the cranes and the donkey-engines are silent; when the waggons rumble no longer, and there is no ringing of bells, and no hammering of hammers, and no grinding of machines. And we sat upon two workmen's benches opposite each another and talked.

'I saw Lady Frances yesterday,' he began; 'she was good enough to invite me to call, and so I did call, and had a long talk with her.'

'Good!'

'She's a splendid woman! That's the kind of woman to back up a man. I used to think that a man wants no help from any woman. I now see that a clever, sympathetic woman who understands things may be of the greatest use.'

'Undoubtedly. Lady Frances could help a man very much in politics if she chose. She might help you—but it must be in her own way. She is interested in you already.'

'Of course she's all for Party. She says I must join her Party, or else there is no chance.'

'You've heard that before, haven't you? Well, there is no chance outside the grooves; I am certain of it.'

'Anyhow, I won't join a party. I went in an Independent Member, and I'll continue an Independent Member. Nothing whatever shall induce me to join the rank and file of Party, to run about and say what I am told to say—nothing, mind you. Not even to get the assistance of that woman.'

He spoke with the determination of approaching submission. His words had a forced ring in them; their exaggeration showed weakness. He was under temptation.

'Then, Robert, farewell, a long farewell, to dreams of greatness!'

'We talked about my speech, and she spoke highly of it. Well, why not? A very good speech it was. When we came to read it next day, how it stood out from the windbags and froth of the rest!—you noticed that, George?'

'I did. A very fine speech—full of solid stuff.'

Robert never pretended to any modesty as regards his own work. He honestly thought it a great deal better than the work of anybody else, and he said so, without any affectation of inferiority. This candour impressed people. Other men it might injure, but not Robert. Very few men, indeed, do really possess a sincere, unaffected admiration for their own powers. Most of us are spoiled by diffidence. It is not everyone who realizes his own value.

'Of course,' he added, 'she admired the speech.'

'She admired your speech. What else did she say? What did she advise?'

'Well, of course, criticisms are not always pleasant, but she has a large experience. She says, to begin with, that I must not be too earnest. You always said that, and I believe she's right. The Members don't like a preacher nor a funeral sermon. Everybody used to get up and go out in the old days when John Stuart Mill lectured the House. I've got to cultivate a lighter vein for ordinary occasions. Well, I believe I can do that; only I was anxious for them to learn the facts. I had to teach them the facts. Don't they want the facts, then?'

'They don't want the trouble of learning them.'

'She advises me very strongly to follow up the success of the first speech. This time I must answer someone,

and prove that I have the power of debate.   Well,
George, though I now see very plainly that our
little mock Parliament was conceited and cocky and
shallow——'

'Isn't that almost enough in the way of adjectives for
one little mock Parliament?'

'Yet it did give me certain power of reply and re-
partee—as I mean to show the House at the earliest
opportunity.'

'Very good.   Next.'

'Oh, then we began talking about other things.   It
seems odd that I should be taking advice about my own
affairs from a woman, doesn't it?'

'It would have seemed odd three months ago.'

'But, of course, Lady Frances isn't an ordinary
woman.   She's got the brains of fifty women and the
experience of a hundred put together.   What a woman
she is!'

'How did she advise you about your own affairs?'

'She asked me about myself.   Of course I told her
everything there is to tell.   Why should I conceal
things?   I even told her how you have given your
evenings for three months or more to show me what the
West-End world was like.   She strongly advises me to
go into society.   "Become one of the world," she says.'

'Did she tell you how to get in?   The gates of what

she calls the world do not exactly stand open to everybody.'

'Exactly. What they call Society is divided into
circles, and there are circles within circles. There are
art circles, literary circles, musical circles, rich circles,
exclusive circles, dramatic circles—all kinds, overlapping
each other. And there are political circles; and in
them she could launch me—of course on the usual conditions.'

'Party, of course.'

'Party. No room anywhere, it seems, for the Independent Member.'

'And you are an Independent Member. It is unfortunate, isn't it?'

'Says I must join a political club. But there are
none for us Independent Members.'

'No; it is unfortunate.'

'Then we talked about the way in which men get on
nowadays. No one, not even you, ever before understood my position so perfectly. Whatever I tell her,
she catches it in a minute. One would think she had
lived next door. And about the ways of men—they
don't climb, George, they wriggle—they wriggle, most
of them.'

'So I have heard. That is partly why I came here.
I don't like wriggling.'

'Wriggling and advertising. One must be like the man who advertises his soap, always before the world.'

'That is, in fact, the first thing, and the second thing, and everything.'

'She told me about one man who has certainly got on remarkably well, yet not so well as I mean to do, because he hasn't the same ability. This man, who, like me, had no family influence, got into a political club, wrote a paper now and again for one of the magazines, spoke frequently at public meetings, was seen everywhere at private views, and first nights, and at private houses, went into the House, spoke on occasion and with weight, published a volume of essays, was accepted as a man who went everywhere long before Society received him at all, and is now married to a woman whose wealth and connections will advance him rapidly.'

'That may be your fate.'

'But the trickery of it!'

'If you want to achieve a definite object, you cannot always choose the way. Nobody but yourself, remember, knows your own motives. What you call trickery may appear to the world as the natural rewards of ability.'

'Well—but—I don't know.' He walked to the edge of the Quay, looking up and down the river. 'It is a world so different from anything I ever imagined,' he said. 'You have opened out the world to me. I confess that I hesitate to venture in upon this kind of path.'

'You don't think that you are the only ambitious man in the world, do you? My dear boy, everybody there is ambitious, except the men who have got up as high as they can. And even then they all want something—a little more social consideration. Everybody for himself, anywhere. Nowhere so much as there, in the City of the Setting Sun—in the West. In other words, you have discovered that your old dreams must be abandoned.'

'I am beginning to understand that it is so. I have been plunged in ignorance. But it is difficult to give up the old ideals.'

'You are a more human creature than I thought you, Robert. I don't believe you will ever be so happy over there as you have been in this old shed among the shavings.'

'It isn't happiness I want; it is success and power. Well, George'—he came to the bench and sat down beside me—'I shall not give up because things are different from what I expected. I mean to go on, though perhaps in another way. I mean, I say, to go on.'

'With a wriggle and a twist?'

'I shall wriggle as little as may be. Now listen care-

fully, and don't interrupt. I am going to make a proposal to you of the greatest importance.'

'Go on; I will not interrupt.'

'Well, I see very plainly, to begin with, that the
way open to me means a good deal of expenditure. I
must have good chambers, some place where I can receive people. I must keep myself well groomed.'

'Both points are important.'

'I must have a club. I must cultivate people.
There are already plenty of men in the House who
want to know me. I must be able to give a dinner
occasionally, as Lady Frances advised; and there are
the daily expenses, which in the West End run away
with so much money. One must go about in cabs; it
isn't possible to go without cabs. Why, here I used to
spend nothing at all from day to day except our modest
house-keeping money. It means money. I must have
money, George.'

'Yes, if you are going to live over there. But you've
got your business here.'

'I can't live in two places. There you have it. If I
am to get on, I must live in the West End; and I
can't carry on this business from Piccadilly Chambers,
that's quite certain.'

'I'm afraid it's impossible. Shall you sell this business?'

'No, I can't afford to sell the business. But I've

thought of a plan, and I'll lay it before you to turn
over in your mind. First of all, are you perfectly
serious and in earnest about the boat-building trade?
Mind, I never believed it. Do you really and truly intend to go into the trade as a living?'

Put in that way, I was staggered, because, you see, I
perceived at once what he was driving at.

'What I thought,' I replied slowly, 'when I came
here was that I might learn the business from you, and
that I might then take my small capital, which is no
more than three thousand pounds, and start as a boat-
builder in one of the Colonies—British Columbia, for
example—wherever I could find an opening. That was
my plan, subject to my mastering the mysteries of the
craft.'

'You have mastered most of them, and you are a
first-class hand already. But you can't be trusted yet
in the buying and the selling.'

'Since I've kept the books for you I've learned something of them as well.'

'Yes; but you can't run alone yet. However, that
part of it might be managed. Now for my plan.
You've got a good pile, though you call it so little.
It's a good deal more than I shall want. Give up the
idea of a Colony. Settle here in the old place—you
can go on living in the old house, if you like—and be-

come my partner—the managing partner. You shall
buy your share. Don't think that I want only to get
your money, though that will be of the greatest use to
me just now. You will make your solicitor examine
the books—for that matter, you have the books already
in your hands—and he will tell you what you ought to
offer, if you entertain the proposal. Come! Burnikel
and Burnikel it has always been called. There were
once two cousins in it before they quarrelled over the old
man's diamonds. Let there be two cousins in it again.
Robert and George they were once. Robert and George
they will be again.' He got up from the bench. 'You
want time to decide,' he said. 'Don't press yourself.
Take as much time as you like. I will advise you in
any difficulty, but I will no longer think for the business. You will have to do that. Well, turn it over in
your mind, and tell me when you have decided.'

So he got up and left me. Then the men came back
from their dinner, and the work went on again.

The most remarkable part of the proposal was that
we were actually going to reverse the situation, to
change places. I was to give up clubs, chambers,
friends, society, and everything that belongs to the
class in which I had been brought up. As I had no
fortune that was inevitable. But I was to put my
cousin in my place. He would give up his business—

hitherto his livelihood—and take my place, and belong to the world. And I was to take his place down in this deserted city of warehouses, where, except the clergy of the parish and myself, there would be no single resident who by any stretch of imagination could call himself of the gentle class.

Ninety years ago the two cousins, Robert and George Burnikel, were partners. After all these years two other cousins, Robert and George Burnikel, were to become partners again.

Ninety years ago Robert and George parted. Robert stayed at the yard; George went West. Now this situation was reversed: George was to stay at the yard; Robert was going West.

CHAPTER XXI.

THE SECOND SPEECH.

THEN came the second opportunity. It was three weeks after the first. The occasion was the first reading—or was it the second?—of a Bill for the prohibition of more than five—or was it fifty?—hours' labour in the day, or something to that effect. For my own part, I concern myself about Acts of Parliament only when they bring the tax-gatherer to the door with his little piece of paper. It is a remarkable circumstance in this highly political country that our politics are mostly limited to getting one man in, and that we care very little, when he is once in, what he does, or what anyone else does. If you doubt this allegation, listen to the talk in the train, or where men gather together.

However, we knew it was coming, and Robert got me a seat in the Speaker's Gallery, where I sat during the questions with as much patience as I could command. The Gallery was not crowded; the strangers were people up from the country, with a few Americans. They had opera-glasses, and whispered the names of the members whose faces they knew. The House of Commons is one of the sights of London, which is the reason why so few Londoners ever go to it. As for the House of Lords, I wonder how many Londoners have ever seen that august body in deliberation.

The Bill was introduced with a somewhat short and self-excusing speech. I wish I could remember what the Bill really proposed. Not that it mattered, however. As the subject was not attractive, the House rapidly thinned. There, again, we are the most political people in the world; but the moment a subject is introduced which deals with the realities of life, the welfare of the millions, the case of the unemployed, the rule of India, the agricultural depression, the safety of the Empire, the condition of the navy, the weakness of the army, the departure of trade, the silver question, the House is swiftly and suddenly thinned or emptied. I suppose the reason is that the human brain can only stand a certain amount of dull speech, and that these subjects generally fall into the hands of dull and un-interesting speakers. I really do not know what this speaker said. Presently he sat down. Then Robert arose. I think I was more anxious about his success than he was himself. He was perfectly calm and self-possessed.   In his hand he held a small bundle of papers, a striking presence, and he began speaking slowly, with measured phrase, and with his rich musical voice, which at once commanded attention.   Of all the gifts of oratory, the most useful is a rich and flexible voice.   Then his first speech of three weeks ago, now almost forgotten, was again remembered, and the House became quickly filled again.

As I have forgotten what the Bill was about, and as I paid no attention to the first speaker's Introduction of the Bill, and as I concentrated my attention to the style of Robert's oratory and to the effect it produced, without the least reference to the matter, I cannot re-produce for you the substance of his speech.   You may find it in Hansard ; in fact, you are sure to find it in Hansard, if you please to look ; you will also find it worth reading.   He spoke on a labour question, from his own point of view, as one who was at once a crafts-man and an employer.   ' I am myself,' he said, with the pride of a duke and the appearance of a gentleman of ancient lineage—' I am myself a Master Craftsman.'

Then he proceeded, from his own experience, and from quotations from Blue-books, to marshal his facts and to set forth his arguments.   I did not listen ; it was enough for me to let that rolling music of his voice play about my ears, and to watch its effects upon the faces below. Could he grip those faces? He could. Could he move those faces? He could. The average Parliamentary face is singularly cold. One might as well expect that one wave out of all the others would move a hard rock. Yet Robert moved that rocky face. Could he make those faces smile? He could. He had taught himself the lesson—the most difficult for some men to learn—that a speaker should be able to amuse. He related gently humorous anecdotes, so that the House bubbled with rippling laughter, which is far more delightful than the broad roar at more comic strokes. Robert would certainly never become the comic man of the House; but he might become one of the humorists. And this was a new development. Who would have imagined three months before this that the grimly-in-earnest young man, who was going to thunder his gospel into the unwilling ears of the House until he conquered it and laid it at his feet, had become one of those who could treat the most serious subjects from a humorous point of view, and convince by laughter where he would have failed by indignation?

I think, not being a critic, that Robert, like Mr. Gladstone, possessed the wonderful gift of being able to invest the baldest facts and the most intricate figures with interest and charm. Like a novelist, he made them personal. He connected figures with men, and brought facts into touch with humanity. And this he did, as it seemed, spontaneously, without effort or any appearance of lecturing. In the House of Commons a man must not be a lecturer, but an orator. The lecturer is necessarily a critic or a teacher. As lecturer, without imagination, he explains carefully how the orator, the poet, the novelist, the dramatist, produces his effects. He knows exactly, and can tell all the world how it is done—the trick of it. Yet he cannot produce the thing himself. Therefore he is of no use in the House. The orator, poet, dramatist, novelist, on the other hand, produces these effects continually ; yet he cannot tell you how he does it.

Robert, then, had this gift of making things attractive. He spoke for an hour or more. The members remained in respectful silence until he worked them up into producing their signs of approbation, of which the House is never chary when it is moved.

When he sat down it was with the pleasing consciousness that he had at least made the House for the second time ask whether they had actually got another coming man. The speech, in fact, produced a very marked impression. Some of the papers quoted it, and made it the subject of leaders.

A few days afterwards he spoke again, and again as a man of personal experience, as a Master Craftsman.

His experiences were interesting and effective. And a third time, and a fourth, but always when he had something to say that ought to be said.

Lady Frances gave a dinner-party—a political dinner —at which some of the heads of the Party were present. And she invited Robert. Among her guests was old Lord Caerleon, to whom he had already been introduced. It was a large party, and Robert's place was down below among the younger men, who were civil to him. But, of course, in the conversation it was impossible for him not to feel that he was an outsider.

After dinner, however, Lord Caerleon again talked with him apart. He talked as one who knows the game, and as one who has played it, and now looked on rather tired of it.

'I have read your speeches, Mr. Burnikel,' he said, much as a schoolmaster may speak of a boy's set of verses. 'As reported, they were fair. I am told that they produced—ah! some effect upon the House. I am told that you have a good delivery and a good voice. Is that so?'

'It is so,' said Robert calmly. 'I have a good voice by nature, and a good delivery by art.'

'Yes.' Lord Caerleon looked just a little astonished at a young man who thus immodestly claimed these gifts. 'A good voice is a great thing. You have

begun well, Mr. Burnikel. But a good beginning in
the House counts for nothing. The House is filled, to
me, with the ghosts of men who in my recollection made
a good beginning.'

'I have made a good beginning, Lord Caerleon; and,
with your permission, I intend not to become a ghost
at all.'

'Very good—very good indeed. But, Mr. Burnikel,
how are you going to get on? Permit me—I understand, for some mysterious reasons of your own, you
still wish to be considered an Independent Member.
You told me so, if I remember rightly, in this house
two or three weeks ago.'

'That is so. I am returned by my constituents as an
Independent Member.'

'I don't think it matters much what they think.
But I suppose you talked the usual stuff—voting to
order, no conscience, changing opinions, and the rest
of it?'

'All the rest of it,' said Robert quietly.

'Of course you did. Now, then, Mr. Burnikel, let us
go into the question of Party for a few minutes: not
the whole question of Party, on which you have read—
or ought to have read—your Constitutional History,
but that part of the question that affects you personally.'

'You do me great honour.'

'I talk to you, sir, because I think that you may possibly—I don't know—turn out an acquisition to either party. Otherwise, of course, one cannot at my age, and with my experience, pretend to take the least interest in the average member. I take the personal side, then. You propose, I believe, to make a career in politics?'

'I do.'

'Lady Frances tells me—you told me so yourself, if I remember rightly—that you are extremely ambitious. I am pleased to hear it. Well, you cannot be too ambitious. Nothing does a young man so much good. It is impossible to be too ambitious. It was my own great happiness, for example, to be born with enormous ambitions, which have been gratified, yet not satiated— not satiated. Get me a chair; I think I will sit down. So; thank you. Ambition,' he went on, 'the desire for personal distinction, is one of the finest gifts that a boy can conceive. I always had it. You would, I dare say, if we were to compare symptoms, and if you were dissected, present the same phenomena. Therefore, you may suppose that what you were as a boy that I was too—with such differences as the accidents of birth, and perhaps position, may have caused. For your encouragement, sir, I will tell you that my rise in the

House was not due to any family influence. I was the son of a country clergyman, but, like your cousin, Sir George—an excellent young man, if he possessed any ambition—the grandson of a Judge and a Peer. There was very little money in the family, but enough for me to get into the House. And I say, in my age, that my highest ambitions have been gratified, but not satiated. Believe me, sir, the ambitious man enjoys the winning of every step—one after the other. He is never satiated; he can never say " enough."'

'Well, sir,' said Robert, 'you have never had occasion to regret having embarked upon this splendid career.'

'Certainly not. If I were to be offered the choice once again, I would choose the same career.'

'You have led the House,' said Robert; 'you have been in three Cabinets; you have been First Lord of the Treasury. Well, my lord, what you desired and attained, that I have the audacity also to desire. Perhaps I shall attain it.'

'Not if you continue in your present course. The one condition which was imposed upon me is also imposed upon you. You must rise in the customary manner by becoming a faithful servant of your party.'

'That we will see,' said Robert, obstinate and incredulous.

'How, then, do you propose to climb? My dear sir,

before you rises an inaccessible precipice. There are only two ladders. Would you fly?'

'I wish to climb by doing good work.'

'My case, too—exactly my case. I kept on saying that while I was at Oxford. It is really a very fine thing to think, though it is a very foolish—and, indeed, a boyish—thing to say. Mr. Burnikel, you ought to understand by this time that there is only one possible way of climbing, and that is, as I said, by one of the only two ladders. No other way exists, believe me, young man. If there were any other way, it would have been found out long ago.'

'There was the case of John Bright.'

'He had to join the Party at last, remember. John Bright was in every way exceptional; he wanted neither money, nor place, nor power, nor rank. You, I should imagine, want everything.'

Robert was silent.

'So that's settled. If you want to climb, enter by the usual gate, and you will find the ladder waiting for you. Let us pass on to consider the noble work by which you desire to make a mark in history. Noble work, for a politician, means great and beneficent measures. You, as an Independent Member, would never be able to pass any considerable measure—not any single measure of the least importance. Why? Because all great measures are adopted, as soon as it is found possible to pass them, by the Government. As for moving public opinion so as to make these measures possible, that is done by essayists, leader-writers, authors, poets, dramatists, and other intelligent persons, who nowadays prevent a Minister from being original in his ideas. You, as an Independent Member, would have no chance at all—not the least ghost of a chance—even of introducing a Bill.'

' I always thought——'

' Think so no longer. Look about you and face the facts. They are these : An Independent Member, whatever he could formerly accomplish, which wasn't much, will never more be able to introduce or to pass any measure, good or bad ; he can never become a leader in the House ; he can never have the least chance of proving himself a statesman ; all he can hope to do is to get the House to listen to him, and, through the House, the outside world ; and believe me, sir, on the most favourable condition possible, you will never, as an Independent Member, acquire half or a quarter of the influence over your country that is enjoyed by an anonymous leader-writer on a great daily paper.'

Robert made no reply.

' Will such a condition content you, sir ? Does such a position gratify your ambitions ? Why, you have just told me what they are. Pray, sir '—Lord Caerleon looked up sharply with his keen eyes under his shaggy eyebrows—' will this content you ?'

'No ; it will not.'

' Let us go on, then. You have told me that you have been pleased, in the education of your Shadwell constituents, to speak of party allegiance as a slavery, a stifling of conscience, a suppression of manhood, and so on. You did talk like this ?'

' Certainly. It is the only way of talking.'

' So you think. Now let us look at it in this way : There is a party which, in the main, clings to the old things, and only admits change when new and irresistible forces command change. There is another party which is always desiring change, because they think that things might look prettier, or because things would be more logical, or because things might help the people, or themselves, by being changed. In the main, every measure belongs to one or other of these parties. Is not that so ?'

' Perhaps.'

' Every measure which is brought forward by one or other of the two sides has been talked about, advocated, discussed in newspapers, in magazines, everywhere, long before. It is brought forward at last when one party has made up its mind to support it, and the other to oppose it. The House is divided into two camps, in which are the two armies. The Bill is proposed and meets its fate. All is done in order, according to the rules of the game. You understand?'

'Of course.'

'What would you have? A House filled with a mob of six hundred undisciplined, separate individuals, all clamouring together—every one fighting to bring forward some fad and fancy of his own? What a House would that be? What kind of legislation would you expect of such a House?'

Robert at the moment could suggest no kind of legislation.

'Suppose you think over the matter from this point of view, Mr. Burnikel. Construct—that is, in your imagination—the House filled with Independent Members, and see how it would work. Oblige me by doing this.'

Robert bowed gravely.

'I dare say that you have already recognised this view of the question. But there are times when the mind seems more especially open to the apprehension of plain truths. This is, perhaps, one of those occasions. The very name of Lady Frances fills one with the idea of Party.'

'I will, at least, consider your view.'

'Well—and now, Mr. Burnikel, I want to speak quite

plainly, and, I take it, you are not a man to be offended
with plain speech. Very good. You are not a rich
man, I believe, nor a man of family ?'

'I have already told you that I am a boat-builder—a
Master Craftsman—and my income is small.'

'I have heard as much. Well, your birth and
position should be no bar to your ambitions. You
have heard that I began with much the same dis-
advantage. You will very soon find your way about.
You are in excellent hands so long as Lady Frances
takes an interest in you, and I hope that you will find,
as I did, that this is the very best country in the world
for a young man of ability and courage and ambition.'
He rose from the chair. 'So. I have said nearly all I
wished to say.'

'Thank you,' said Robert humbly. He was touched
by the comparison of the man who had succeeded with
himself.

'Not quite all. Some of the people think that you
may possibly be a coming man. I'm sure I don't know.'
Lord Caerleon, who had worked himself up into some
eagerness, became all at once limp and tired. 'There
are too many wrecks. I have had too many disappoint-
ments. But—I say—I don't know. Anything may
happen. I don't think I could have made such a
clever speech as yours of the other day. I don't know.

Anyhow, we are watching you. And—I don't know—it depends entirely on your own ability and common-sense. I believe you may find friends and backers—when you give up nonsense, and are content to play the game according to the rules. But—I don't know. Good-evening, Mr. Burnikel.'

He inclined his head with dignity. The interview was at an end.

'I was very glad,' said Lady Frances, after this con-versation, 'to see Lord Caerleon talking so long and so earnestly with you. It is a sign that he takes a personal interest in you. Believe me, Mr. Burnikel, it is a great honour to have been able to interest that old Parliamentary hand.'

'I am indeed very much obliged to him for the trouble he took to convert me to his views.'

'I will tell you a secret, as people always say when they tell a thing that everybody knows : Lord Caerleon came here this evening on purpose to meet you and have the talk with you.'

'Did he really ?' Robert, who was not to be dazzled, blushed like a girl.

'He did indeed. And, Mr. Burnikel, I understand from your cousin that you are a very masterful man, and that you think very much of your own opinion. Only, remember, you are young, as regards political life. You cannot possibly know as much, or anything like as much, as Lord Caerleon, who is seventy-seven; and as regards the House, you are yet only a theorist, and Lord Caerleon has an experience of fifty years. You are a very strong man, Mr. Burnikel, but strength wants experience. You must not feel shame at the outset to be guided.'

Thus skilfully did this diplomatist play upon the weakness of the strong man. The stronger the man, the more this weakness may be played upon. It is your weakling who has no such vanity.

'Let us talk again about this subject, Mr. Burnikel. I cannot talk freely to-night. Come to-morrow after-noon—it is not my day—and we will consider the thing calmly and from your own personal point of view. Oh, I understand it perfectly; but ambition, Mr. Burnikel —ambition must use the appointed ways. We belong to our own generation; we are subject to the conditions of our time; and, *enfin*, you must not waste what might be—and will be—a great career, for the sake of a visionary scruple.'

Robert went away in a thoughtful mood. The observations made by the noble lord went straight home. If, by remaining an Independent Member, he obtained neither power nor place, nor even the intro-duction of the great, remarkable, never before imagined, measures of which, in ignorance of his powers and possi-

bilities, he had vaguely dreamed, he might as well keep
out of Parliament altogether, and go on haranguing the
working men of Shadwell.

The day after the dinner Frances wrote me a letter.

' I have just parted,' she said, ' with your remarkable
cousin.   He dined with me last night, and heard plain
truths   from   old   Lord   Caerleon.   He   went   home
staggered, and he came this afternoon to consult with
me.   He protested vigorously, of course ; his principles,
his teaching, his convictions, were all against Party.   As
if that mattered with so young a man !   He protested,
however, too vigorously ; the very strength of his pro-
testation showed that he was weakening.   Of course, his
pride, which is colossal, and his self-confidence, which is
unbounded, prevent his giving in without a struggle.
But he will give in, George—he will give in—and we
shall have, I believe, a recruit worth fifty of the men
that the other side can show.   I have never seen any
reason to depart from the opinion which I formed at the
very outset—that your cousin has in him the very
highest possibilities.

' The thing which makes me quite certain of his
conversion is that self-interest, which in him means
ambition, and pride, and desire for conquest, will be
continually prodding and prompting him.   It is like

the dropping of water upon a stone. I am sure there
can be no stronger force, and it is always in action upon
every man. It is especially a characteristic of this man.
Generally self-interest means money. Not so with your
cousin. Dear me! if we take away self-interest, how
many noble patriots and great and pious persons would
be left? Well, it is for your cousin's interest—looked
at from every point of view—that he should join us;
and now that he fully understands it—and understands
as well that he can never get on without joining us—he
swears he will never, never, never do so—standing on
the point of honour—as one who, while she swore she'd
ne'er consent, consented. Oh, he will come in, as soon
as he can square it with his pride.

'You see, he lived alone; he read books; he formed
theories; he did not know how things were worked
practically; he did not know men and women; and so
he got notions in his otherwise sensible pate. He fully
intended—which was a very nice thing to intend—to do
"great and noble" work—what kind of work that is I
cannot tell you—all by himself, which an admiring
world would behold, and for which an admiring Premier
would ladle out rewards. And, of course, he saw in his
dreams the House of Commons looking on, not with
eyes of envy, but of wonder and applause, and he heard
the papers ringing wedding-bells of praise. It is the one

discernible note of his out-of-the-world upbringing and his solitary self-making, that he could seriously entertain this idea, and could imagine himself mounting in this Will-o'-the-wisp fashion to the place of First Lord of the Treasury, and all kinds of sweet things. A most childish dream, and yet in its way the dream of a generous man. He who could imagine a career of this sort cannot be altogether a selfish man. The lower nature, you see, thinks of the reward first and the kind of work afterwards. It does not detract from the higher nature that a man should think of his reward after he has thought of his work. Otherwise he would be more than human. So I do not blame your cousin, but rather respect him the more. A childish dream. I told him so to-day, and I told him why. And an ignorant dream. I told him that as well. He thinks so now; but it shamed him, just for the moment, to confess that he has been all wrong. A man like Robert Burnikel cannot bear to be thought ignorant.

'I had on the table a copy of the *Morning Herald*. It contained a leader against him and his last speech —quite a leader of the old stamp. I had thought the trick of writing such leading articles was gone. Every sentence perverted; every phrase misinterpreted, and made to mean something more, something less, and something different—a masterpiece of party malignity—

a leading article, in fact, that cannot fail to do our friend all the good in the world.

'I handed him the paper; he had not yet seen it. Well, you would hardly believe that a real politician could be so young and so foolish. He actually flew into a rage over it; he lost, for a moment, command of himself.

'"My dear friend," I said, " the thing is so exaggerated that I thought you had written it yourself."

' " Written it myself—myself?"

' " Written it yourself. Don't you understand, Mr. Burnikel, that what the young politician wants is plenty of abuse from the other side. There is a story of a certain aged statesman who very kindly advanced a young man of the opposite bench, in whom he took a fatherly interest, by personally abusing him for a whole twelve months. In five years that young man was Chancellor of the Exchequer. Now, if we could only find some good man on the other side to abuse you. It is difficult, but it might be done."

' " Rise through abuse ?"

' " Certainly ; I will tell you why : First, because it keeps people talking of you, thinking of you, and giving you increased importance in the Party ; and next, because the abuse is always grossly exaggerated, and people compare it with your printed utterances. If you were rich enough, you should pay a journalist so much a year to abuse you twice a week."

'He threw down the paper. "Mean artifice!" he cried. "Does this also belong to Party?"

'"You must not take things so seriously, Mr. Burnikel," I said. "It is true that the abuse will in the long-run end in strengthening your position. As for hiring a man, you ought to understand by this time what we mean in earnest, and what in the language which we use to each other."

'"Oh," he cried, "I am an awkward, stupid log!"

'"Never mind, Mr. Burnikel. You are half a nautical person; you shall be the ship's log, which is very good reading, I believe. Now, let us say no more about this article. You must learn to accept these things philosophically. They are all in the day's work. A man who wants to stand on a pinnacle must expect to have dead cats thrown at him. Force of habit, you see, makes the journalist who used to throw dead cats and addled eggs at the man in the pillory now throw them at the man on the pinnacle. They don't hurt— that is, they don't hurt the man who belongs to the Party—they do him good; they only hurt and defile the man who has no Party to protect him, and no friends."

'Eleven o'clock.

' I have just opened a note from him.   He has joined us.   Yes ; the Independent Member has vanished.

' "DEAR LADY FRANCES," he says, "I have thought over what you said this afternoon ; you have convinced and converted me.   I am now quite sure that the only way of working the machinery of Government is by means of Party.   You have shown me that I have been quite wrong.   I shall join your Party as one of its private soldiers, and I shall set myself to learn the obedience and discipline of which you spoke."

'There, George ; I have converted him.   Now, it was not by my arguments at all, but by those of Lord Caerleon, that he was converted.   There were all the signs of conviction on his face last night after that conversation. I thought, indeed, of inviting him to sit down on the stool of repentance before the world.   But do you think he is capable of confessing himself converted by a man ? Never.   By a woman, perhaps, although he is too much absorbed in his own ambition to think much about women—never by a man.   I am contented, however, with my share of the work.   You made your cousin a gentleman, my dear George.   You gave him manners. At first, I plainly see, he was probably little better than a self-satisfied prig of the boorish sort—a lower middle-class, prejudiced, book-learned, ignorant prig—yet with wonderful capacities. I shall make him a model statesman of the modern kind. What else can we, between us, do for him?'

'Well, my dear Frances,' I said to myself, folding up the letter, 'the next thing you might do for him—if you would, just to oblige me—is to make him a model husband, and so get him out of my way.'

CHAPTER XXII.

A SURPRISE.

AND now I have to relate the occurrence of a very surprising incident. It was not only surprising in the way it happened, accompanied by circumstances that have a kind of supernatural appearance, but also in the time when it happened. Had it been earlier or had it been later, this history might never have been written. Had it never happened at all, what might have become of Isabel? And for myself, I might as well have jumped off my own quay into the flowing river, for all the hope or joy of living that would have been left to me. The wonder of the thing is that it was not found out long before. A hundred times and more the place had been searched; an accident might have revealed the secret; a jar, a fall, might have thrown open the hiding-place; a casual cabinet-maker might have found it out had he looked in the right direction. But kindly fate left the discovery to me.

The room allotted to me for a bedroom was that in which old John Burnikel's bare and naked four-poster was standing. When I was first shown the room, it had no other furniture than the four-poster and the old man's sea-chest. They had now clothed the forlorn bedstead, and put in certain chairs and things, so as to make a habitable room of it. The window faced south, and as it was on the second-floor, it looked over the boat-shed upon the river. Here I slept every night in the bed where the old Master Mariner died, quite untroubled by any thoughts about him or the long-lost diamonds, and unvisited by the ghost of their former owner.

It was in the beginning of August, when the nights are still short. Perhaps it was a hot night; perhaps there was more noise of passing steamers from the river than usual—the Silent Highway is generally much noisier than Cheapside by night, as well as by day. Whatever the cause, I woke up, starting suddenly into wakefulness. It was early dawn, but the light was rapidly increasing. My blind was up, my curtains drawn, my window wide open. I lay lazily watching the sky in the south grow lighter—gray at first, and then suffused with some of the eastern glow—a tender, subdued glow like the colour on Isabel's cheek, which so quickly comes and goes—the tell-tale glow. Perhaps, had I not begun to think about Isabel, I might have gone to sleep again, in which case this thing would not have happened.

The gray hues passed away, the rosy hues passed away; there remained the clear deep blue of early morning before the smoke begins, when the sky may be like the sky of Africa for clearness and for depth, and when the river, with its bridges and its boats, all asleep in silence, save for the wish and wash of the ebb and flow, is an enchanted stream.

Presently I closed my eyes again. Contrary to reasonable expectation, I did not go to sleep again. It was that kind of hopeless wakefulness which makes sleep past praying for. I insist upon this point on account of what followed, which was not a dream, for I was awake; but a kind of vision, and only remarkable because it coincided with the discovery which followed.

Do not suppose that I attribute this vision to any supernatural interference. Nothing of the kind. Neither the ancient mariner, the master mariner, nor the unfortunate nabob of whose existence I first learned in the vision, ever appeared to me or afflicted me with terrors. I have never been in the least afraid of ghosts. Had old John Burnikel come to my bedside, I would have had the secret of the diamonds out of him before I let him go, as sure as my name is George Burnikel.

But he never came; he made no sign. I think he must have forgotten in the other world all about his diamonds; his ghost never once appeared to me. Had it done so, I would have had the great secret, I say, out of him in no time. 'Ghost,' I should have said, 'where are those diamonds? Who stole them? What is the truth about them? If they were stolen, and have long since been dispersed, let me know. If they still remain to be discovered, somewhere or other, tell me where they are. I adjure thee, I command thee, by all the charms and spells that you ghosts are fools enough to dread, tell me where those diamonds are.'

That is what I should have said. But the only man I know who ever claimed to have raised a ghost—and that was also the ghost of a sailor—told me that he was only too glad to let him go back again below, below, below, and that, though as brave as most, he did not dare to ask any questions. I don't believe a word of it. However, ghosts are scarce; perhaps I should have behaved in the same manner. And this, I take it, is the case with most; otherwise we should know more about certain things whose uncertainty is sometimes disagreeable. All you have to do is to raise your ghost and not be afraid of him. There was no ghost, and yet the air seemed this morning full of the Burnikel legend. There was the sound of a ship slowly making her way up the river—a Hamburg or Norwegian steamer, perhaps. One is never allowed perfect calm at Wapping. I lay on my back in the old wooden four-poster, which they had fitted with a spring mattress instead of a feather bed, and I recalled the wonderful story: how the old man one night displayed his bag of precious stones, worth anything you please; how he told the cousins it would be theirs; how, a day or two afterwards, he was found dying, and told them collectively that they knew where the bag was kept; how they did not know, but searched and could not find it, and accused each other, and fought and separated.

I lay on my back recalling this odd story, which was chiefly interesting because it was a story without an end.

Another interest it might have, if one were to consider how John Burnikel got those diamonds, because the old man's romance of the Great Mogul and the invitation to fill his pockets in the Royal Treasure Vaults was clearly too ridiculous; it was so very plainly invented with intent to deceive.

The first thing that happened after this awaking was a vision. It was a very odd vision. To begin with, I was not asleep. To this day I cannot understand how this vision, of all others, came to me. One never dreams original plots of novels; quite new stories never come to anyone; and this story, except for one little half-forgotten circumstance, was quite new. Some novelists have pretended that their plots habitually come to them in dreams, but I do not believe it. Dreams and visions are erratic, incoherent, and unconnected things for the most part. That makes my vision all the more remarkable.

I suppose I must have dropped into some kind of bodily torpor. I am sure I was not asleep, because all through the business I knew that I was lying on the bed, although the action of the piece, so to speak, was elsewhere. However that may be, it is really useless to explain or account for a vision. The one that came to me was, so to speak, a magnified and embroidered piece of work, springing from something that Isabel had once told me. Why, I had quite forgotten it. She was talking about her people, who were no more illustrious in station than my own; and she informed me that once there was a strange man among them who had run away to sea, and come home again in rags twenty years later, raving about a fortune he had lost in India. Nothing more than that. A very slight material of which to construct a vision. Yet it came, and as long as I live I shall believe that the vision was somehow a revelation of the truth sent to me just before the great discovery.

It began by my stepping out of the house—but I

knew all along that I was in the bed—and walking down the narrow lane leading out of the High Street to Wapping Old Stairs. There I found, sitting on the stairs, an elderly gentleman dressed in clothes extremely shabby. He wore a coat of brown cloth, he had worsted stockings, hat frayed and worn at the edge—quite a poor man he seemed to be. From his dress it was evident that he belonged to the eighteenth century, which I like to consider a picturesque period.

He sat upon the top step of Wapping Old Stairs, and he looked across the river; and as he gazed the tears ran down his face.

It is not often that one gets the chance of talking to a man of the eighteenth century, but it seemed not unnatural. I sat down beside him as if it were the most natural thing in the world.

'What, sir,' I asked timidly, 'is the cause of this grief?'

He sighed heavily. 'My diamonds!' he said, 'my diamonds!'

'What diamonds? I am a stranger to your time, worthy sir, and I know nothing of your diamonds.'

'What troubles me,' he said, 'is that I think I must have lost my soul in getting them together, in which case I have thrown away my soul for nothing.'

'Dear me, sir, this is serious indeed.'

'Yes, young man, they were amassed by scraping and grinding, and squeezing and skinning. Never were people ground down more miserably; and it was I who did it in my master's service — in the service of the devil, I think. And now I have lost the diamonds as well. What have I got in exchange for my soul?'

I ought to have thought of John Burnikel at this point, but I did not.

'Tell me more about the diamonds,' I said.

'Once I was a Nabob,' he began, fetching a sigh as deep as an Artesian well.

'Really? A Nabob? I thought a Nabob had a carriage and four, and troops of servants.'

'Once I was a Nabob.' Then he stopped and looked around him suspiciously. The watermen lay asleep in their boats. It was a Sunday afternoon in summer. The ships were moored in long lines down the river from London Bridge, which we could not see for the bend, down to the Lower Pool. 'Is there no one here but yourself?' he whispered.

'No one; and I belong to the next century.'

'So you do. And you can't lock me up in a madhouse, can you? Oh, it's dreadful to be in a madhouse when you are not mad! Horrible! They knock you about! they starve you! they abuse you! they chain you up—when you are not mad at all. Young man, never, if you can possibly help it, lock up anyone in a madhouse.'

I promised him that I would not.

' They put me in on account of these lost diamonds. They said I was mad.'

' What diamonds, then ?'

' Sir, it relieves my grief to tell the cause. I was one of those unlucky youths who cannot remain at home and do what the others do. I had to run away when I was fourteen to prevent being apprenticed to some vile trade—saddlery, I believe. So I ran away and went to sea ; and when we got to Calcutta, because the Captain was a brute, and the mate was a brute, and the bo's'n was a brute, I ran away from the ship, and went up country, and entered the service of a native Prince. And him I served for twenty years and more—served well—squeezed and ground and skinned his people for him. And I got rich in his service, for he gave me great presents. I told you—I was once a Nabob. Great presents he gave me, though he was a devil.'

' Very good, so far.'

' When he let me go I carried down to Calcutta all my treasure in jewels and gold pieces. I bought jewels, of which I understood the value very well, with my money, and put them in a bag with what I had already —a long, narrow canvas bag—and put the bag in a leathern belt, where it could not be seen. And then I took passage in a homeward bound, with all my fortune upon my person, worn night and day, in that narrow leathern belt. Lots of people brought treasure home from India that way. It was thought a safe way.'

'Well?'

He sighed heavily. 'On the voyage,' he resumed, 'I believe soon after sailing, I was taken ill: it was brain-fever, sunstroke, or something. When I came to myself again I was on shore—brought ashore and taken to Bedlam because I was still disordered in my wits with my fever, or my sunstroke.'

'Oh! You were taken to Bedlam.'

'I was taken to Bedlam and kept there—I don't know how long. When they let me go, and I remembered things, the belt was gone—the belt with the diamonds was gone, I say!'

'Who took it?'

'I don't know. Some sailor on the ship, perhaps; the keepers at Bedlam, perhaps. So I went home to my own people, who lived at Canterbury, and were saddlers. And when I went home in rags, they drove me out, and when I raved about my diamonds, they locked me up again in another madhouse.'

All this time I never thought of old John Burnikel at all.

'That was very unlucky. What was the name of the ship?' I asked him.

'I cannot remember; I have never been able to remember.'

'Or of the captain?'

'I cannot remember.'

'What is your own name? Can you remember that?'

'Samuel Dering.'

'Oh! Are you by any accident related to Captain Dering, and Isabel, his daughter, both living in the year 1895?'

'They will be my great-grand-nephew and great-great-grand-niece.'

'Then they ought to have the diamonds, if they were found?'

'Certainly they ought. I give them to Isabel. Please tell her so.'

'And the name of the captain — was it John Burnikel?'

'It was!' He sprang to his feet. 'Captain Burnikel it was! Where is he? where is he?'

'Dead, my friend—dead for nearly ninety years—as dead as you yourself.'

He looked at me reproachfully, and the vision vanished. I was lying in the old man's bed and gazing at the sky. It was an odd trick of the brain, more especially as I had never heard any hint or suggestion of the kind. But at this moment I believe that I dreamed the truth, and that old John Burnikel simply cut the belt from the waist of a passenger gone mad for the time with sunstroke, or some other cause. The passenger recovered after landing, but could not remember the name of the ship or the captain, and he was the great-grandfather of Isabel.

Nothing in the story at all, except for the accident which followed.

My eyes fell upon the sea-chest. It was a large iron-bound trunk—the sea-chest of an officer, not a common sailor, who is only allowed, I believe, a sea-bag.

The more I looked at that chest, the more I thought about the unfortunate Nabob turning all his fortune into precious stones, and tying them up in a canvas bag worn as a belt. The vision, I repeat, was so clear, the words were so plain, that I had not the least doubt about the truth of the thing. John Burnikel had grown rich suddenly by robbing a sick man of his fortune. No one suspected him; no one can trace gems unless they are very large indeed; no one thought that he possessed any precious stones till the last year of a very long life, and then he accounted for their possession by a cock-and-bull story. Had the injured man,

this poor ruined Nabob, found him out, he could bring
no charge against him, for he had no kind of proof.
And then an irresistible desire seized me to search the
chest once more on my own account. It had been ran-
sacked, I knew, time after time by Robert and his
predecessors. Never mind ; I must look for myself.

So I sprang out of bed, and dragging the box out of
the corner into the middle of the room, I threw open the
lid and began to search, taking out the contents slowly
one by one.

The chest had been left just as it was since the old
man's death. Nothing had been taken away, only it had
been searched a hundred times ; every separate member
of the family had searched it over and over again for
three generations in hopes of finding that lost fortune.
But in vain. And now it was my turn.

The chest certainly contained a collection which
showed travel. It was divided into two unequal compartments, one about two feet six long, and the other
about eighteen inches. Both compartments were provided with a tray about two and a half inches deep.
The things in the chest were not arranged in order, but
just lay about, one on the other, piled up, just as they
were thrown in by the last who examined the contents.
The things were not such as we should now call rare ;
they consisted of curios brought from voyages in the Far

East and sea-going things of the time. Thus, an ancient rusty flint and steel pistol belonged to the sailor. An Oriental dagger must have been picked up in some native shop of Calicut or Bombay. The mariner's compass, the roll of charts, the telescope, the sextant, the large silver watch, belonged to the sailor ; so, I suppose, did a mummified flying-fish, which still preserved something of its ancient salt-sea smell ; a carved sandal-wood box ; one or two Oriental pipes ; a large figure of Buddha, or somebody else, looking supremely wise and philosophic—or perhaps theosophic ; certain silk handkerchiefs, mostly eaten by moths ; slippers in gilt leather ; a book of Hindoo pictures, ugly and fleshly ; one or two things in mother-of-pearl ; half a dozen gold rings ; twenty or thirty silver bangles tied together. All these things spoke of the Eastern traveller, and, a hundred years ago, would be thought curious.

The first thing that made me jump was a leathern belt lying at the bottom of the box. A leathern belt ! Why, it confirmed, I thought, that strange story concerning the fever-stricken passenger. He had his leathern belt. Well, but anybody may have a leathern belt. And this was quite a common thing—a broad strap with a buckle, black with wear or with age. I took it out and examined it. Now, which was a very

remarkable coincidence, the leather was double; it could
be pulled open along the upper line, and there was
room within for just such a long slim bag as was
described by my imaginary Nabob. I passed my
fingers along the whole length of this curious double
belt—the secret-holding belt. No, there were no
jewels left.

Nothing more was in the box of the least importance.
All the things lay on the floor beside the box; the thing
itself, with its lid wide open, stood below the window,
the full light falling into its two compartments. As
you know, I am a fairly good hand at a lathe, and I am
by trade a practical boat-builder—a craftsman; my eye
is therefore trained. Now, as I looked into the empty
chest, thinking about that belt, I perceived that, at the
back of the chest in the larger compartment, the longer
side was not quite at right angles with the bottom of
the chest. The difference was very slight—an inclination of a very few degrees from the right angle; still, it
was there, and to a practised eye quite visible. But in
the smaller compartment the right angle left nothing to
be desired; it was a true right angle. Was this
accidental? I lifted the chest, and changed its position.
Yes; there could be no doubt about the inclination of
the lower two inches all along the back of the larger
compartment. I turned the box over; the back was

perfectly rectangular. But here, again, I observed a curious point. The chest was solidly built: the wood was thick all over; but the wood of the back was two inches thick. Why had they taken such extraordinary precautions to strengthen the chest? And then a strange sense of excitement fell upon me, because I was now quite certain that all these signs meant something which I was going to discover.

The chest was lined with paper of a pattern which contained, at intervals of four or five inches, a black thick line; one of these lines occurred just above the beginning of the angle. The effect of the line was, of course, to darken the part just above and just below. Now, when I looked narrowly into the place, I fancied that I saw below the line another, which looked as if it was a solution of the continuity. Two inches below, at the very bottom of the chest, there was a mark of some kind, but not that of a solution of the continuity.

A practical man in the boat-building trade never goes about, even in his bedroom, without a good strong jack-knife—one that will serve many purposes, if necessary. I found mine, and I tested this apparent juncture. Yes; the blade penetrated easily. I passed it along the box, backwards and forwards; the wood creaked, being old and dry. What was the meaning of this slit? I turned the knife round. The wood slowly gave way, and this part of the box grindingly and grudgingly opened. It turned on creaking hinges, being kept in place by two rusty springs. I dragged it quite open with my fingers. It was a long, narrow, slightly-curved shutter, fitting tightly to the side of the box at a small angle almost imperceptible. Behind, the thick wood of the box had been hollowed out ; and thus a secret cupboard was found, the existence of which would never be suspected.

In that narrow recess lay the thing for which everybody had been searching for nearly a hundred years—the cause of the cousins' quarrel and separation : the long narrow bag of brown canvas stuff, like one of the old-fashioned purses, only open at the end instead of the middle.

With a beating heart I took it out. The narrow brown canvas bag, just as the ruined Nabob had told me ! Did he appear just then in order to tell me ? I laid it on the bed. It was tied very tightly with string at one end. There were things in it. What things ?

I threw the bag on the bed and leaned out of the window. The morning air was fresh ; the sun was bright ; the river—I could see it over the boat-shed—danced in the sunlight and the breeze. I sat there for some time—I know not how long—my brain running away with me, filled with confused murmurs as of people all talking together: the original Robert and George clamouring for a division; old John himself telling us how the great Eastern King bade him fill his pockets and fear not; the poor old ragged Nabob sitting on Wapping Old Stairs in order to bewail his loss; and Isabel whispering that I should be better without these diamonds. A curious jumble of voices and of thoughts.

Perhaps it was not, after all, the bag of diamonds.

I left the window. I dared to put the thing to the proof; I cut the string with my knife, and I poured out the contents upon the sheet of the open bed.

Heavens! what a shower was that which descended! Danaë herself never saw so fine a sight. They fell in a small cascade of splendid light and colour—diamond, pearl, emerald, ruby, sapphire, jasper, topaz, beryl, opal, hyacinth, turquoise, agate, every conceivable gem poured out of the long sack—two feet six long and three inches broad—and there they lay before me in a heap, glittering in the morning light. There were thousands of stones, large and small; not rough stones, but all cut and polished.

I had found the old man's precious hoard. What they were worth I could not imagine, nor have I ever learned. Only to amass such an immense sum in the service of an Eastern Prince in twenty years must, I

should imagine, as the Nabob hinted, be extremely
dangerous to the welfare of the soul.

I ran my fingers through the pile. I played with the
pretty things. I threw them up to watch the light
playing on them as they fell. I rolled them over and
over. Then began various temptations. I am not
ashamed to confess to very elementary suggestions that
I should 'sneak' those jewels. Said the voice of the
Tempter: 'Nobody knows what you have found. Take
the stones and go back to Piccadilly. There will be
heaps and heaps for you to live upon in that bag as
long as you are likely to live, and afterwards. Piccadilly is much more pleasant than Wapping. Boat-
building is a mean, mechanical craft. Remember that
you belong to that end of town. This is a Providential
occasion ; it is sent to you on purpose to restore you
to your old position.'

To this Tempter—I don't know why he took the
trouble to come at all—one could easily find a reply.
'Sir,' I said, with dignity, 'you do not know to whom
you are speaking. Go away, sir. Go to the Devil,
sir !'

The second Tempter said, 'Why, just as this treasure
would have belonged to the original Robert and George
had they found it, so it belongs to the new Robert and
George, now that they have found it. Call him in

quickly, and share it with him. Halves. That will give you both plenty to live upon.'

To which I made answer on reflection : 'My grand-father had brothers and sisters. They went down in the world while he went up. I have cousins somewhere who have as much right to the inheritance as I myself. And Robert has brothers and sisters—no doubt, cousins as well. The inheritance belongs to them as well as to Robert. If every one of us has his share, there will not be much left.'

Then said the Tempter : 'Why tell the far-off unknown cousins anything about it ? Probably they are much better without their share ; much best for most men to keep poor : they are out of temptation. Besides, there is not too much to be divided between you and Robert. You will be able to go back to the West End ; it's a much more pleasant life. Here you will vegetate and grow stupid ; your manners will fall from you ; your ideas will grow sordid, like your business. Better go West again, and stay there. You will never again get such a chance. Boat-building is a mean, mechanical craft.'

'You, too,' I said, with a struggle, 'may go to your own place, wherever that may be.'

I put back the stones in their bag. I closed the shutter ; I filled the chest with its contents. I closed the lid, and pushed the chest back into the corner. Then I lay down on the bed and fell fast asleep.

When I awoke it was past six, and the life on the river had long since begun. Had I dreamed? At first I thought so. The dream of the unfortunate Nabob and his narrative was just as vivid as the dream of finding the diamonds. Fired with this thought, I sprang out of bed and tore open the box; yes, along the bottom ran that thin line which I had opened with my knife. I doubted no longer.

I had found the diamonds.

I dressed quickly and hurried down to the river, where I went out for a pull in one of our own boats—'Burnikel and Burnikel.' The exercise and the fresh air set my brain right. I was able to see the thing in its true light: namely, the find did not affect me at all. For nearly ninety years that sea-chest had been in the possession of the tenant of the house. Robert received it as part of his inheritance; to him, as to the eldest, the family house and the family business; to the others, a small sum of money each and the wide, wide world. The chest was Robert's, with all its contents; just as the old man's bed was Robert's, and all the furniture of the house was his.

After breakfast the Captain retired to his own room. Isabel and I were left alone. She proceeded, according to her wont, to wash up the teacups; it is an ancient, homely custom among old-fashioned housewives, and belongs to a time when china was dear and very precious.

'You look serious, George,' she said. 'Has anything important happened?'

'Something very important.'

'Is it anything that will take you away from this place?'

Then I looked around and considered this maiden, how sweet and good she was, and how much simpler and sweeter than the girls of society; and how lovely she was, especially when the colour, like the dainty delicate bloom of the peach, rose to her cheek. And how she loved me—that I knew; and how I was bent upon taking her away from her cold, unloving *fiancé*; and how she would never find any place in society where she would be happy; and how I could not live without her.

Of course, the chest belonged absolutely to Robert— the chest and all that it contained.

'No, Isabel, nothing will ever happen that will take me from your presence unless you command me to go.'

Despite my promise, some such words would fly out from time to time. My excuse is that I was thinking continually how to effect Isabel's release.

She made no reply, but went on washing up the cups and saucers.

'Isabel,' I said, remembering the tearful Nabob, 'do you remember telling me about a certain member of your family who came home from India and always raved about a lost fortune? Where did your people come from?'

'They lived at Canterbury once.' That was where the Nabob went. 'I do not know how long they lived there.'

'And about that man coming from India? Do you know anything about the fortune that he lost?'

'There was a man once—I have heard my great-grandfather, who lived to a very old age, speak of his uncle, who was a very strange man. He had been abroad, and he was wandering in his wits, and used to sit down and cry over a lost fortune, which he said was in a belt. That is all I know about him. My great-grandfather always said that he believed in the loss of the fortune. But why do you ask?'

'Only because I dreamed about him last night. Odd, wasn't it? Dreamed that he sat on the steps, and wept over his lost fortune.'

'You dreamed about him? About my great-great-uncle, of whom you have heard that strange thing!'

'Yes. It's a strange world. I dreamed about him.

I will tell you some day—soon—what I dreamed. It's a very strange world indeed, Isabel. And the most wonderful things get found out, years and years and years after they have been done and forgotten.'

Then, for reasons of my own, I resolved to tell no one about the diamonds for the present. One or two things had to be done before Robert should learn of his recovered inheritance.

CHAPTER XXIII.

A MAN OF SOCIETY.

NEVER before, I am quite sure, was transformation more rapid than that which changed the Hon. Member for Shadwell in less than six months from a man out of the world to a man of the world. In April he came to my chambers and introduced himself. Before the end of the season he was in the House, in a West End Club, in Society. He was a rising young man of the Party; the leaders were civil to him; he knew a good many people; he was listened to in the House; he wrote a paper in the Vacation about some branches of the Labour Question to the *Contemporary Review*; he also read a paper on some statistics before a learned society; he attended in August a Congress of working men and told them truths. I believe he distributed prizes at a Sunday-school in his Borough. In one way or another the papers were continually talking about him. Now, the first step in the noble art of getting on is to keep

your name well before the public; everybody understands that. You must make people talk about you.
And since people's memories are most miserably short,
you must do something else very soon to make them
talk about you again. The effect of this forced famili-
arity is that when the promotion comes nobody is in
the least astonished. I think, for my own part, that he
was artfully and secretly managed all this time; I have
my suspicions as to the person who pulled the strings.
As for myself, he was incapable of *réclame!* The people
who pulled the strings and made him dance and made
the world talk about him sat in the background or in
the underground. Nobody knows what an enormous
political cellarage there is!

This was his life. It changed him completely in six
months. He was always a man of presence. He was
now in appearance a gentleman of sixteen quarterings
at least; the aristocracy of Castile could produce no
scion of nobler figure. Anyone, however, may have
the appearance of a gentleman. Robert had acquired,
in addition, the manner and the speech of one who has
always lived with gentlefolk, so that their manners
have become his own by a kind of instinct. I suppose
he acquired these manners easily because he had so little
to unlearn. A man who has lived alone among books
can hardly have incurable habits. I do not say that he

talked as a man of his age belonging to public school life, college life, or the army, would talk. No outsider can possibly acquire that manner of speech.

'Your cousin, George,' said Frances, 'reminds me of a certain courteous gentleman of Virginia whom I met some years ago. There was an old-world courtesy about him; he was a gentleman, but not of our stamp; he was conscious of his rank and manners, he thought of both very much, and I should say that he lived among people very much unlike him. Robert reminds me of him. Nobody would deny that he is a man of fine, of rather studied, manners; nobody would deny that he is a gentleman, yet not one of us. He is to spend a fortnight with me at Beau Séjour '—this was her country-house—'in September. He grows apace, George.'

'He is a lucky man, Frances. You have taken him up and advanced him.'

'He is more than lucky. Anybody may be lucky. He is strong.'

When the House rose, about the third week of August, and all the world went out of town, he came home to the house and the dockyard. I looked to see him fall back upon the old life: work in the yard all day, and sit in his study all the evening. He did nothing of the kind. He moved about restlessly, he came to the yard and looked at the work in progress, but without interest. He received the ordinary business communications without interest. He had still a share in the house, yet he behaved as if he no longer cared even to hear what was done. I suppose he had grown out of the work. Strange! And it was just as I was growing into it, feeling the sense of struggle and competition, which gives its living interest to all forms of trade.

One day he was sitting in the yard, looking out upon the river. The men had gone; it was past five o'clock. The day was cloudy, and a driving rain fell upon the river, which looked gray, and stormy, and threatening.

'This is a horrible place to live in!' he said abruptly. 'It is more horrible than it used to be!'

'Come, you lived in it yourself for a long time.'

'But I always knew that it was a horrible place; one couldn't help knowing that. I always intended to get away. Man, if I had known only a tenth part of the pleasures of that other life, I should have been devoured with the rage and fierceness of discontent. I say it is a horrible place—cribbed, cabined, and confined! With whom can you talk? With the Captain and Isabel. George, how can you do it? How could you bring yourself to do it—you who know the other life? I don't understand it. You who know that incomparable woman! Why, now that I do know it, rather than leave it I would go out and rob upon the highway!'

'You like that other life so much? Strange!'

'Why is it strange? It is the only life worth lead-ing. You taught me to like it when you taught me what it meant. I should otherwise have been outside everything all my life.'

'I am not the only one who taught you, Robert.'

'No; there is Lady Frances. Well, I owe it to you that I have learned what a woman may be. I owe it to you. How could I know before to what heights a woman could rise? Good heavens! how could I know?'

'Very little, truly. You remember, however, that you never gave yourself the trouble to inquire into the subject.'

'I had no chance. There is a woman—clever, ac-complished, full of resource, of gracious manners. Good heavens, George! And you could go away, leave her, and come down here!'

'Beautiful too, if you ever think about beauty,' I added calmly.

'I never do when I am in her society.' He meant well, though the compliment was doubtful. He in-tended to explain that the charm of her conversation was so great that he could think of nothing else.

'Some men think her extremely beautiful—I do myself. You may remember, also, that she is well born and rich.'

'I would rather not remember those points,' he said shortly. 'I would rather not remember that there are any barriers between us.'

'Are good birth and fortune barriers? Not always. However, there is one barrier of your own making, Robert. She is sitting in the house over the way at this minute.'

He took up a handful of chips and began to throw them into the river one by one, with gloomy countenance. 'A barrier of your own making, Robert. I suppose you can unmake it if you like?'

'My word is passed.'

'You belong to society now, you much-promoted person. When you marry, your wife must belong to society as well, or you will have to go out of it. Do you think that Isabel is ready to take her place in the world of society as well as, say, Lady Frances?'

Robert, to those who knew him, betrayed any strong emotion by the quick change in his face. It was disgust, plain disgust, which crossed his face when I put this question.

'Isabel,' I went on relentlessly, 'is a girl with many graces.'

'I have never seen any,' he said.

'Of great beauty, of great delicacy of mind, sweet and gentle.'

'So is a doll.'

'You have never even tried to discover the soul of the girl whom you have promised to marry. I know her a great deal better than you.' That, at least, was quite true, yet not exactly as he thought. 'The point is whether she has the training and the knowledge required by a great lady in society; and I am quite certain, Robert, that she has not.'

'My word is passed; but'—he threw all the rest of the chips into the stream and got up—'I am not going to marry yet awhile—not for a very long while yet.'

'Well, but consider—is it right?'

'Does she want to marry somebody else, then? Let her speak to me if she does. And how can I talk of marrying yet?' he added irritably. 'Nobody knows better than you what my resources are; and I haven't got my foot upon the lowest round of the ladder yet.'

'Let Isabel go, then.'

'I have passed my word.'

I said no more. It is always a pity to say too much. We went over the way and had tea.

The day after this conversation he addressed his constituents, not defending or excusing his conduct in ceasing to be an Independent Member, but giving them

his reasons in a lordly and condescending manner, which
I believe pleased these honest fellows much better than
if he had fawned upon them. Who would not wish to
be represented by a man who had opinions of his own,
rather than by one who pretended to accept the imaginary
opinions of the mob? 'You fellows haven't got any
opinions,' said Robert, standing on the platform. 'I
have. You send me to represent my own opinions,
which you know, and not yours, which you don't know.
Opinion! How can fifty men be said to have an
opinion? Well, you all hold certain opinions that
belong to simple law and order. You know that
politicians are necessary. You think that rich men get
too rich. You sometimes think that there ought to be
work and wages for everybody. Some of you allow
yourselves to think what is foolishness: that wages ought
to be always going up. What is the good of such an
opinion as that?' And so on, telling them very plainly
that he thought nothing at all of their intellects. And
they liked it.

After a week, during which we saw very little indeed
of him, he went away again, with scant leave-taking.
He carried away with him all his possessions—his books,
his papers, and all; so that it was manifest that he
meant to return no more. In fact, he came again once
and only once, as you shall hear.

'Has he said anything, Isabel?' I asked anxiously.

'Not a single word. I was horribly afraid that he would. Not one word.'

'It is wonderful,' I said, looking upon this sweet and lovely maiden. 'Well, Isabel, the day of redemption draweth nigh. Yet but a little while, and I shall knock the fetters from your feet, and you shall be free to fly —to soar—to scale the very heavens in the joy of your freedom.'

So we were left alone again, having the quiet house, so quiet when all the workmen had gone home, all to ourselves, with the Captain to take care of us. It was not an unhappy time, despite that betrothal which I fain would snap asunder; partly because we were together, and partly because I was certain that the promise must be broken as soon as Robert understood himself a little better. The evenings grew too short for more than a sail on the river; then too short for that. We spent them at home, by ourselves. Isabel discovered that I could sing; or she played to me with a soft and sympathetic touch, which made me dream things unutterable. On Saturday afternoons we went to picture galleries and to theatres and concerts—always somewhere. On Sunday morning, if it was fine, we went to St. Paul's, or Westminster, or the Temple, where the voices are sweet and pure and the singing is regulated.

When it was wet, we went to St. John's, our own parish church, and sat under the tablets of the Burnikels. I never really enjoyed family pride at the West End; here, on the spot, one felt every inch a Burnikel. We were like Paul and Virginia, and Paul was a most enviable person. I had brought my lathe from Piccadilly and set it up in the study, and Isabel would sit reading while I made the splinters fly; or we read together. I read aloud while she worked, or she read aloud while I took a pipe; or, best of all, she sat opposite me while I had that pipe and talked—talked of things pure, and sweet, and heavenly, insomuch that the hearts of those who heard flowed within them. At such time I loved to turn the lamp low, so that the sweet face of my mistress might be lit and coloured by the red fire in the grate or the lamp in the street. And all this time, during August and September, not a word from Robert.

It was for his sake, in order to advise him, that Frances continued in town till the end of August, and when she went down to her country-house he went, too, as one of her party.

'Your cousin,' she wrote, 'is staying here. He does not go out with the men shooting. I suppose that he cannot shoot. He works in the library; he has brought some books of his own here. He is writing a little

series of three letters for the *Times* on one of his own
subjects. He has read them to me first. I find them
admirably expressed and models of good sense. He
grows every day, George; his head will one day touch
the skies. He still lacks the one grace that will complete his oratory if he arrives at it—the grace of lightness. He can be light and humorous on occasion, but
his general tone is serious. It is a seriousness which sits
well upon a young man, because in this age of badinage
and cynicism no one is serious, except Robert himself,
who looks as serious as a Dean. There is also something on his mind. I do not suppose it is the want of
money, because you told me something about his affairs,
and I believe that he has a few hundreds. It is not
disappointment, because no young man has ever got on
so well in so short a time since the days of Pitt. I think
he will be Pitt the Third. In that case you will see
him in the Cabinet in four or five years at the outside.
It is not that he feels himself out of his element in this
country-house, which is, I suppose, rather a finer house
than the one you have at Wapping. Nothing dazzles
him—neither wealth, nor troops of servants, nor titles,
nor women in grand frocks, nor diamonds. What, then,
is the matter with him? If he were another kind of
man, he would long since have got himself sent away by
making love to me. As you know, George, I am always

sending them away for this very sufficient cause. But this man does not make love. What is on his mind? You who know him may be able to advise upon this subject. The symptoms are a tendency to the gathering of a sudden cloud upon the face; a disposition of the mind to wander away, out of sight, so to speak; a sudden looking forth of the eyes into space. He is thinking of something disagreeable. It cannot be his past, because he is no more ashamed of having been a boat-builder than you are of becoming one; though what is honest self-respect in one case is disgraceful abandonment of caste in the other. What can it be? I suspect—nay, I am sure—that there is some woman in the case. Has he early in youth made a fool of himself with an unworthy woman? Has he trammelled himself? Is he, perchance, a married man, and married to Awfulness and Terribleness? Oh, the having to marry such women! I am very much concerned upon this point, George. Let me know about it, if you can. Don't try to screen him if he wants any screening. I think so much of him, I tell you beforehand, that I would forgive him if I could. Only there are some things which must not be forgiven.

'I am not going to stay here after October, when I shall return to town and to dear, delightful politics, and to you, my dear George, if you can tear yourself from

your abominable chips and come to see me.   Have you
developed more callosities on your hands ?—F.'

What was on Robert's mind ?   Well, I think I could
tell her.   But should I ?   Would it be best to tell
her ?

CHAPTER XXIV.

AN EXPLANATION.

It was about the middle of October that Frances came up from the country. Considering that her uniform practice was to remain there until the middle of January every year, it was reasonable to suppose that there was some urgent cause why she returned so soon.

Perhaps she would tell me. It was her general custom to tell me everything. For instance, when her marriage, at the age of eighteen, with an elderly Secretary of State, was under consideration, we talked it over together, weighing the arguments for and against it, dispassionately, which we could very well do, because Frances was not in love with the elderly statesman, though she greatly admired him, and we were not in love with each other.

I called upon her on Sunday morning, a time when I should be certain to find her quite alone. She received me in her breakfast-room. I observed that her face showed certain signs of trouble, or, at least, uneasiness of some kind. It was in her eyes chiefly, eyes remarkable for their serenity, that the trouble was shown. There was a dark line under them, and her forehead, the forehead remarkable for its sunshine, looked clouded.

'You are not well, Frances?'

'I am always well, George. Sit down and tell me all about yourself.'

'I have got nothing to tell you about myself; but I will tell you, if you please, about Isabel.'

I proceeded to tell her, at length, a great deal about Isabel. Of course, Frances would not believe that a girl could be refined, and graceful, and well mannered, who was living at Wapping, the daughter of a skipper.

'You tell me to believe all this of such a girl, George. It is absurd. Where would the girl find these graces? Believe me, a refined and well-bred girl is a most artificial product. It takes the greatest watchfulness and the most careful companionship to create refinement in a girl—a refined and well-bred girl is not in the least a creature of Nature, nor, I should suppose, of Wapping.'

'I cannot tell you where she found her refinement, Frances. I suppose, where she found her sweet face and her soft voice and her tender eyes.'

'George, you are a lover. Oh! it must be beautiful

to be a man, if only for the man's power of imagination.
I fear your angel would be to me a Common Object.'

'No, Frances.   Have I not known you all my life?
This privilege is an education.   Do you think that, after
going through such a school of manners, I could be
capable of falling in love with a Common Object?'

'It is prettily said, George.   I half believe you on
the strength of that pretty little speech.   Since she
appears to you all these things, I can only hope that
she is really all these things.   You must take me to see
her.   Only, you know, men who fall in love do sometimes permit themselves the most crazy fancies.   It
makes them happy, poor dears, and I suppose it does
no harm to the woman.   I dare say she doesn't even
understand what the man thinks about her.   Well, and
you are engaged, and you are going to be married.
When?'

'Here comes the trouble.   We are not engaged.   And
we cannot become engaged.'

'Why not?'

'On account of Robert.'

'Oh!' She blushed quickly. 'Then, there is a woman,
after all.   What about Robert?'

'Four or five years ago, when she came with her
father to live with him and to keep his accounts, he
told her that some time or other he should want a

wife, and that he should marry her. There was to be no wooing, he said, and there has been no love-making ever since. He has never addressed a word of love-making to her.'

'Well? And why can't the girl let him go? She must feel that she is a clog upon him.'

Frances spoke more harshly than was customary with her.

'Robert says that he has passed his word. Isabel says that she owes everything to Robert, and that she is bound by common gratitude to wait for him until he releases her. She will obey him in all things. If he says "Marry me," she will marry him. If he says "Wait," she will wait. If he says "Go," she will go.'

'Gratitude of this kind, George, is touching, but it may be embarrassing. What does Robert say?'

'Robert says that he has passed his word. But he also says that it will be long years before he can think of marrying her. I have tried to make him understand that it is cruel to keep a girl on like this.'

'Does he love her? Oh, I cannot think he does. I have watched him while he was thinking of her. I knew it was a woman, and I knew he had got into some kind of scrape with a woman. Men who are in love do not glare and glower when they think of the object of their affections.'

'Does he love her?' I repeated, rising, and looking out of the window. 'Nobody can answer that question, Frances, better than you.'

It was a bold thing to say; but one must sometimes say bold things. I remained at the window, looking out upon the Park, but I saw nothing.

Frances made no reply.

I came back and resumed my seat.

'What do you want to do, George?'

'I want Robert to release her.'

'Tell him so, then.'

'I know what he would say. I have told him so already. He says that his word is given. Isabel has assured him that she will wait for him. Isabel has always been so gentle, even meek, with him, that he would understand with difficulty that she would, in fact, rather not.'

'Well, what do you propose, then?'

'I would try to work upon his ambitions. There is no doubt that poor Isabel, who has no social ambitions, would be a clog upon him. Seeing what kind of man he is, and the future that lies before him, would it be provident for him to hamper himself with a wife who can never belong to your world?'

'It would be madness.'

'Well, Frances, you have taken a very kind interest in him from the first.'

'For your sake, George; you know that.'

'It was for my sake at the outset; now, I hope and believe, you continue your interest in him for his own sake.'

She coloured. Thus doth guilt betray itself. Had she taken no such personal interest in the man, there would have been no cause for the mantling soft suffusion. It really was very pretty. Whatever softened Frances's regal beauty improved the attraction of it.

'After all,' she said, 'the girl must be an incomparable nymph to have conquered two such men. However, Robert must not marry a girl of humble rank—at least, for a very long time to come. When he stands quite firmly, and has secured his position—but even then it would be madness.'

'If he were to marry the right kind of woman it would be different. He should have in a wife, first good connections, then social position, then some measure of wealth.'

Frances inclined her head. 'Those are all things that would help a rising man.'

'Since he is a young man, and has eyes in his head, beauty would be a great additional advantage.'

'I suppose it would.'

'Well, Frances, do you know that woman?'

She answered one question with another: 'Where should one look to find such a woman?'

'To be sure, Robert is a man without family; he can't get over that. One may give him the manners of a gentleman, but nothing can make him a gentleman by birth.'

'If,' said Lady Frances, 'your cousin is a gentleman by manners and by instinct, what matters his birth? People may say behind his back that he has been in some kind of trade; that won't hurt him a bit. The fact that he has been a boat-builder of Wapping will never prevent his rising in the House. He is bound to rise. He will probably become in a very few years a Cabinet Minister. I suppose there is hardly any woman in the country who would not think herself fortunate in marrying a man sure to become in a few years a Cabinet Minister.'

'Meantime he is only a candidate for this distinction, and nobody, except yourself, Frances, and one or two others, knows that he is likely to get what he wants. Therefore again I ask, Do you know of any woman—such as we desire for him—who would take him?'

'How am I to know?' she replied sharply. 'I do not look about the town in search of wives for my friends.'

'But you know everybody. Do you know of any woman who possesses all these acquirements?'

'You are very strange to-day, George. Your love affairs make you importunate.'

'You shall be as haughty as you please in five
minutes, Frances.' I took her hand. 'My dear
Frances, you have always been so sisterly with me ;
and now I am in this terrible trouble, and in order to
get out of it, I must speak plainly—very plainly.'

' Well, George '—she threw herself back in her chair
and folded her arms—' you may speak as plainly—yes,
as plainly—as you desire.'

'Thank you. Well, then, do you remember a certain
memorable day—a most disastrous day—when I came
to tell you that my misguided parent had played ducks
and drakes with the whole of my respectable fortune ?
I was very low in spirits that day.'

' Yes, I remember it well.'

' We had a good deal of talk about ways and means.
I disgusted you by the absence of any healthy ambition.'

' You always have disgusted me that way,' she said.
' What has all this to do with your cousin ?'

'I am working round to him. You will see the con-
nection in a moment. Well, you fired up then, and
became indignant, and looked splendid. I like to see
you when you are indignant. You then uttered words
—burning words. You said that all the time you had
been watching another George Burnikel growing up
besides me. You said that he was ever so much taller,
handsomer, more ambitious, more industrious, more

resolute, more everything. You said also that you had
always hoped that, in the fulness of time, the smaller
figure would be absorbed in the greater figure, and
there would then be a George Burnikel worth looking
at. Do you remember saying this?'

'Yes, I remember, at least, thinking in that way.'

'And I have often thought, Frances, that, if I could
have become that bigger animal—the ambitious and
the resolute—perhaps—I don't know, but perhaps—
you might have consented. Well, I must not ask,
because I quite understand that the thing was impossible. You have always been too great for me,
Frances. I must be contented with Isabel, who has no
ambition, poor child! and asks for nothing but love,
which is pretty well all I have to give her.'

'I do not know what might have happened if things
had been different.'

'I was even tempted, being so very small a creature,
to assume that ambition, and to go about tricked with
the feathers that pleased you. Being a humble barn-
door fowl, I thought of pretending to be an eagle.'

'I am very glad you did not, George, because I might
have believed you.'

'Oh! You would have found me out very soon.
However, that nobler creature, that superior George,
that imaginary person whom you figured, he does exist;

he is, in fact, my cousin. Look at him, Frances; he is exactly like me, only bigger all over, body and brain. He is as ambitious as Lucifer, which is exactly what you want; also he is nearly as proud as my Lord Lucifer, which ought to please you; he is masterful through and through, which pleases you; he makes everything and everybody subservient to his ambition; he has learned an immense quantity of things, to serve his own ambition; he is eloquent; he is handsome; he has manners, though he will never acquire the conventional manner—why, that is in itself a distinction.'

'George, you were never so eloquent about yourself.'

'One cannot be. And then, which is something, he is a true man; when he says a thing he means it; he has no past to cover up, like so many men. He will never have anything to conceal in the future. And he will command the whole world, except one person—that person, Frances, is yourself. You are the only person who can rule him; for he worships you, as yet afar off, with no thought of worshipping nearer.'

' What do you mean, George? What authority or grounds have you for saying this? What has Rob—your cousin—said to you?'

'I mean exactly what I say. He has said nothing; but I have eyes in my head.'

'The man has never spoken one word that I could interpret in such a sense.'

'He never will, unless you bid him speak, and until he is released from his word; then you will find him eloquent enough.'

'Well, but even supposing so much, George, it is not in my power to release him. Why cannot he release himself?'

'No; but if a word of hope is authorized—in case.'

She bent her head. Then she looked up and laughed.

'George,' she said, 'you must indeed be desperately in love to undertake the *rôle* of match-maker.'

'That word of hope.' I took her hand, as if I had been her lover indeed, instead of only a go-between. 'What will you say that I may repeat to him? How shall I let him understand that your interest in him is personal?'

'George, you shame me! How can I send a message of hope to a man who is engaged to another woman? The thing is ridiculous. Go away and make him release that girl.'

'Yet I may say—what may I say?' I insisted.

'Say whatever you please, George. Go; you are a meddlesome creature. I hope your Isabel will prove inconstant.   There are Stairs at Wapping—Old Stairs, I believe—and sailors convenient for inconstant maids.'

'You are interested in him.   Confess, Frances,' I persisted.

She covered her face with her hands.   'Oh, George,' she murmured, 'I have always been interested in him from the very first.'   She sprang to her feet.   'Tell him, George, if you wish, that I like a man to be strong and brave.   Yes, I like a man to be capable of sweeping the curs out of his way, as that cousin of yours cleared the stage of those curs at Shadwell.'

'And this great gulf of family.   How can it be bridged over?'

'He must build the bridge if he wishes to cross over.'

'My Lady Greatheart,' I said, and kissed her fingers, 'there is the poem, you know; the lines run like this:

> '" In robe and crown the Queen stooped down
>   To meet and greet him on his way."

The metre is a little dickey in the next lines, but the sense quite makes up for that defect.   The sense is entirely beautiful:

> '" It is no wonder," said the House of Commons;
>   " He is so very much stronger than the whole of the
>   Rest of the House of Commons put together." '

CHAPTER XXV.

THE PROUD LOVER.

THENCE I proceeded straight to Robert. Man, I discovered, is in these matters more difficult than woman. Pride, to begin with—you shall see how horrid an obstacle was pride. Never before had I understood the ecclesiastical hatred of pride. I went about my business in the grand or diplomatic style. That is, I concealed the real object, and worked round to it. I believe that it is always easy to deceive a strong mind. That is to say, it is a part of strength to proclaim a purpose and to march straight towards it. It is your weak, knock-kneed persons who, having always to crawl and wriggle for themselves, see through the wrigglings of some and divine the intentions of others.

Robert was at work, of course. Nobody ever found him doing nothing. He looked up, welcomed his visitor, and carefully covered his papers. He never liked any-one to know what he was forging and contriving.

' Now,' I said, ' let us talk for half an hour. Then
we will go and get some dinner ; after that we will stroll
about. What are you going to do this evening ?'

' I thought of going to Lady Frances's.'

' Good. You see her pretty often, don't you ?'

' Very often. It is quite impossible to see her too
often.'

' Quite impossible,' I replied mechanically, watching
his face. He was nervous when he spoke ; he took up
things and put them down. I had never seen him
nervous before.

' I wonder if there are many other women like her,'
he said slowly.

' There is no other woman like her in the whole world,
my cousin.'

' She understands—that is the extraordinary thing—
she understands everything ; an argument ; a position ;
a combination : one hasn't to explain or to talk about
it—she understands. If she were in the House, she
would lead it. She suggests a policy ; she confers with
Ministers ; she catches the drift of the public mind ; she
knows how far they can go, and what they should attempt.
George, I declare that I never before imagined it possible
that such a woman could be found !'

All these things he had said before. Robert was not
accustomed so to repeat himself.

'And now you have found her, Robert, and she is your fast friend. Of course, I've known her all my life; she has become a kind of sister, you know, by long habit; but my admiration of her is quite equal to yours. And have you nothing to say about her beauty?'

'She is the most perfect woman I have ever seen,' said Robert, his voice dropping, because when a man feels strongly on such a subject he doesn't like to talk loudly about it. 'Tall and queenly: she looks born to command'—the quality which he most desired for himself he must needs admire in a woman.

'But her beauty, Robert? Her eyes—her face—her features.'

'Yes. I think less of them—that is, of course, they belong to her—they make up the greatness and the splendour of her. If it were not for her beauty, she would not be half so queenly.'

'She advises you in your public work; does she talk to you ever of your more private affairs?'

'She knows my history, such as it is, of course. I was not going to her under false pretences. Besides, there is nothing to be ashamed of. I told her at the outset that I am but a Craftsman—a Master Craftsman.'

'Have you told her that you once—a good long time ago—promised to marry Isabel?'

Robert changed colour. 'No,' he said shortly.
' There was no need to tell her that.'

'I think, if I were you, Robert, I should tell her.'

'Why? What is the use of telling her such an insignificant fact?'

'Insignificant? Your marriage an insignificant fact
to your best friend? Why, Robert, it is the most significant fact in the world. All your future depends
upon your marriage.'

'It will not come off for years; I must make my
position first. You must know I cannot take upon me
for ever so long the burden of a wife—and a wife who
would only pull me down instead of helping me up.'

'I know that very well. You want a wife who would
help you up.'

'What does Isabel understand about these things?
Nothing. What does she care? Nothing.' His voice
showed the bitterness within him. ' Has she shown the
least interest in my ambitions? Why, from the very
first she has been content to be my clerk when she might
have been my companion.'

' Come—come—you have never given her any encouragement. You never suffered her to think of being
a companion. She has always been afraid of you. She
is afraid of you still. Robert, I shouldn't like to marry
a woman who was afraid of me.'

So it began all over again; but this time with results.

'There is no question of like or dislike, unfortunately.'

'I would let her go before the wedding-bells began to ring.'

'You forget, George. I have promised to marry her. I will keep my promise—some day.'

'All very well. But there is her side of the question. Is it fair or right to keep this girl waiting for you year after year—living almost alone in that corner of the earth, wasting her youth, wasting her beauty, longing for love, every year widening the distance between you, while you chafe at the chain you drag and she droops and languishes in bondage?'

'I must keep my word,' he repeated obstinately. 'And, besides, Isabel promised to wait for me as long as I choose. She knows she has got to wait. As for my marrying now, she knows, and you know, that it is impossible. What have I got to live upon? The money which you paid for your share, and about two hundred pounds a year for my share. Do you suppose that I can marry and live among my new friends on two or three hundred pounds a year?'

'Then let Isabel go,' I repeated, as obstinate as my cousin for once.

'If I do, who is to protect the child? Am I to turn her, penniless, into the street? No, George, I am bound to her; and I must make the best of it. Otherwise——' His head fell.

I became more hopeful. When a man—any man, the most obstinate of men—talks about making the best of it, he would certainly like to get rid of it.

'A man like you, Robert,' I went on after a bit, saying the thing which was in his mind at the time (there's a diplomatic move for you; always, if you can, make use of the other man's own mind), 'wants above all things a wife who will stand by him, and think for him, and advance him by her influence and her personality. The wife or you, or for any man with such ambitions as yours, should supplement your qualities; she should be well born, well mannered, influential; well considered, beautiful, and rich.'

'Should be—yes, should be. But there is only one such woman that I know of——'

'Yes. There is only one that I know of. Her name is Lady Frances.'

He sprang to his feet and began to walk about.

'What do you mean?' he asked. 'I believe you've got something or other up your sleeve. Out with it, man. Don't let us have any fencing here.'

'I mean that with such a wife as Lady Frances to

back you up, and with your own abilities to help you
on, you would be quite certain to step into your place
in the front before very long—far sooner, Robert, than
you can hope to do by your unaided efforts. That is
all I mean.'

'It is impossible. There is, first—Isabel in the way.
You are a good fellow to think about me—I don't
believe any other man in the world would do so much
for me. But no——'

'Never mind Isabel for the moment. Let us talk
only about yourself. Do you—do you——' I remembered the stipulation in the other engagement about
the foolishness of kisses : did the man, when he made
that stipulation, understand, the least in the world, the
meaning of love ? Had he ever felt any kind of love at
all for poor Isabel ? and I put a leading question : ' Have
you the—the kind of regard for Lady Frances which
you ought to have for the woman you would marry ?
I don't mean the kind of regard which you have for
Isabel, because she is not the woman you would
marry.'

'Man !' he cried passionately ; 'you don't know—I
haven't told you. Nobody would think it possible that
I should have the presumption.'

One has seen the passion of love represented on the
stage, with exaggeration, as we think everything on the

stage must be exaggerated.   One has read of the passion of love in the older poets, with their hot flames, and darts, and swoons, and fierce consuming fires, and ecstatics, and raptures — exaggeration, we say.   One reads of love in modern novels, and sometimes we ask how these writers can set down the exaggeration of passion with which they do sometimes regale their readers.   Henceforth I declare that I shall never witness a love scene on the stage, never read an Elizabethan love poem, never read a burning page in a novel, and be able to call it exaggeration.   Because the confession, the scene, the monologue, the unfolding of a heart, which now I witnessed, proved to me that there can be no exaggeration in poet and dramatist.   Imagination cannot cross the bounds of possibility in love.   They spoke of flames and fires, because there are no words with which to speak of the strength of the passion which may sometimes seize and hold the heart.

Yet only in the nobler natures, in the strongest men, and in the men who have never known before the smarting of love, nor wasted the passion that is in them on objects unworthy.

This man, hitherto so cold to love, so contemptuous of women, now raged about the room like a caged wild beast.   It seems a breach of confidence only to hint at his broken voice, his distorted face, his features aflame,

half shamed, while he confessed the passion which possessed him.

'George!' he cried, 'I worship her. Yes, for every
quality that she possesses—for her quickness, for her
sympathy, for her insight, for her beauty, for all, for
all, I worship her.'

'You do well,' I said weakly.

But he regarded not what I said.

'Good heavens!' he went on; 'I count the hours
between my visits. I make a thousand excuses to go
there. When I reach the door, I remember that I was
there only yesterday, and I creep away again. I lie
awake at nights thinking of her. The only time when
I am not thinking of her is when I am at work, for
then I am doing what I know she would approve.'

I murmured something, I know not what.

'I confess to you, George, I want no other music
than her voice. I think I could gaze upon her face
and in her eyes for ever, and never grow tired. Only
to pass other women in the street makes me angry to
think that they look so small and common.'

'They are small and common, perhaps, because they
are meant for small and common lovers.'

'If you come to think about her beauty, why, I
hardly ever think of it except that it is a part of her,
always a part of her; and she is always in my mind.'

'Poor Robert! Yet perhaps there may be hope; no woman is so far above you as to be impossible.'

'Hope? How can there be hope? Don't talk nonsense!'

'I should think—but, then, I am not a woman—that love like this, so real, so full of worship, does not come often in the way of a woman. I can tell you, if the fact afford you any hope, that Frances has refused men by scores. She will never marry any man—I am quite sure; she has told me as much—unless he is a strong and able man. Why should such a woman give herself away to a man of the lower nature?'

'What hope can that bring me? George——' And here he broke out into a torrent of passionate cries and ejaculations. For my own part, I kept myself in hand. I let him bring it all out. Every ejaculation, every word of the confession, strengthened my position.

'Always in my mind,' he concluded, throwing himself into a chair, 'always in my mind, day and night. There! now you know!'

'Yes, now I know. I have guessed as much a long time. Of course it was inevitable. You were bound to fall in love with her, from the beginning. That was certain.'

'I might ask why you took me, then, if it was certain. But I don't ask. For I would rather go on hopelessly all my life, than never meet and speak with her at all.

Yes, I have had to thank you for many things, George, but for nothing so much as this.'

'Thank you, Robert,' I said. 'Well, you are in love at last. That is the cardinal fact. Poor Isabel! You never thought of her like this.'

'Never. Poor child! Don't imagine that I ever thought of Isabel in this way at all. I was only sorry for her. I thought that her father was dying—and she was a very good clerk—so I said I would marry her, partly to keep her on as a clerk, and partly to protect her from poverty. It didn't seem to me that it would make any difference to my future. But as for love! How could one love a girl and despise her for her intellect?'

'You have no cause to despise Isabel,' I replied, with some wrath. 'Let me tell you that. You never took the trouble to consider her intellect at all. Well, the long and the short of it is that, whatever else happens, you must let her go.'

'No, she must release herself. I will never go back from my word.'

'Well then, Robert, here is a bargain. If I bring you her release—by her own wish, written in her own hand; if I show you that she will not suffer but rather gain in the long-run for her release; if I can assure you that she will be happier for the present by being released—will you accept that letter of hers and let her go ?'

Anybody else would have understood at once what I meant. Robert did not. He had not yet acquired the habit of thinking about other people and their motives and minds. That would come by contact with a sympathetic woman. He told me afterwards that it seemed to him the very last thing possible, for me to fall in love with Isabel—whom he himself could not love—and to desire to marry a girl without any knowledge of society. Perhaps, being new to the thing, he thought at this moment too much about society. Perhaps I knew a great deal more about society, and therefore thought too little of its advantages. Besides, I was now a boat-builder, quite disconnected from society, and I really never asked whether Isabel was a woman who might be relied upon to shine at her own receptions, and to receive at her dinner-table the most distinguished people in political circles.

'You make three conditions,' he said. 'Every one of these seems to me impossible. Yet you have a way of your own. I do not believe that Isabel will send me a release; after these five years she has grown accustomed to consider me as her future husband. She moves in a groove; she considers me as her guardian, and her father as my dependent. No; Isabel will never release me—she cannot.'

'But,' I insisted, 'supposing these conditions to be fulfilled?'

'Oh, if they are fulfilled, of course I am the last man in the world to keep a woman against her wish. If she would rather marry a foreman of works——'

There was the least touch of coldness; perhaps no man, not even my cousin Robert, likes to be dismissed by any woman.

'That is settled, then. And now to return to Lady Frances.'

He shook his head. 'Oh, that is hopeless.'

'I am not so sure. Consider the thing from a political point of view. You offer yourself, with your career; she brings herself, with all that it means—an immense contribution. Perhaps she may think in her modesty that your side of the balance lifts up her side.'

Robert shook his head again, but with less firmness. The shaking of a man's head is a most expressive gesture, because there are so many shades in it.

'Next, we will consider the situation from a personal point of view. Frances is in every way admirable and delightful, it is true.'

'Yes,' he sighed—'admirable and delightful.'

'But you, my cousin, are not a bad specimen of a man—well set up, and well looking, and well mannered. And you are a masterful kind of creature, and women

admire masterfulness in a man. And you have already
shown cleverness, and women admire cleverness.'

'Yes. It is all very well, but——'

'And then the lady is a young widow, her own
mistress; free to please herself, and she has shown herself difficult to please. She is wealthy, and——'

Here he jumped up again. He was very jumpy this
afternoon. 'Yes,' he cried; 'she is wealthy, and there—
there you have the whole difficulty. We will suppose
that she might possibly get over the differences of birth
and rank, and all that, because they mean nothing.'
You perceive that Robert was as yet imperfectly ac-
quainted with the true inwardness of things—birth and
rank to mean nothing? Dear me! And to hear these
words from my own pupil! 'They mean nothing,' he
repeated. 'She is the daughter of an Earl, and I am
a boat-builder. What do I care about that, eh?' He
turned upon me quite fiercely. 'As if that could be
any real obstacle! I am a man, I say'—he snorted in
his wrath—'I say, a man in whom a woman may take
pride. I know that very well. I believe that even
Lady Frances—though she is all that she is—might
take a pride in me. Lesser women,' he added, with his
usual arrogance, 'would. Of course they would.'

'Well, what bee have you got in your bonnet now?'

'Can't you understand? You say she is rich. I

know she is rich. And that's the real obstacle. As for the rest, I have thought over all that you said by myself. Only I liked to hear it from you as well. It's the money, George.'

'What about the money? Now, don't go raising foolish ghosts about Frances's money. What if she is rich? What does that matter?'

'I have tried to get over it, and I can't. One must keep some self-respect. George, how would you like to live in your wife's palace—your wife's, not your own?'

'Her country house isn't a palace.' But it is, as Robert knew.

'How would you like to be every day sitting at your wife's table, not your own; drinking your wife's wine, not your own; waited on by your wife's servants, not your own; spending the money that your wife—your wife—chose to give you? No, I could not—I could not—say no more about it. I would rather remain as I am, and go on thinking about her without hope all my life, than marry her for her money—for her money! Pah!'

'If you come to that, you might just as well say to another woman, "How would you like, all your life, going about enjoying honour—not your own, but your husband's; a name not your own, but your husband's?"'

'Nonsense!' said Robert; 'the things are not parallel.

Of course a woman may take all that a man has to give.'

'And a man all that a woman has to give.'

What was it my solicitor had told me? 'Marry money—marry money.' And I despised that advice, and now I was trying to make Robert do just exactly that very same thing. Well, it was quite certain that this proud, independent person would never become a dependent on his wife. Fortunately I had a card up my sleeve.

'You are perhaps right,' I said, with assumed thoughtfulness. 'You could never become that unhappy creature—the man who lives upon his wife's money. You have got some hundreds a year, however.'

'And she has how many thousands a year? My whole income would not pay my share of the servants.'

'Then, again, a man and wife are not obliged to have equal fortunes. If one is a little richer than the other——'

'A little—oh, he says a little!'

'Go on; you will give me a chance presently.'

'Let her give away all but two hundred pounds a year; then we should start on equal terms.'

'No, because you would have still before you your ambition, with its solid side, and she would have nothing left. In ten years' time you might be drawing five thousand pounds a year official salary, and she have nothing more than her three hundred. No, Robert; the equitable way would be to reckon your future prospects and your future position as an asset worth ten thousand pounds a year, or anything you please a year.'

Robert shook his head. 'An asset is something that can be realized. No one would advance a farthing on the security of my prospects. As a business man, George, you really ought to know by this time what an asset means.'

'You are not going to a pawnbroker or a bank. You have an asset, I say, that in a certain lady's eyes would outweigh all her own advantages.'

'All the same, George,' he replied doggedly, 'I shall not stoop to live upon my wife.'

'You are nothing but a perverse, obstinate, and pig-headed *bourgeois*. You had better come back to Wapping. Come, then ; I will meet you on your own ground. You admit that a few thousands more or less matter nothing.'

'I'm sure I don't know. All I do know is, that I've got about two hundred pounds a year, and that Lady Frances has got twenty thousand pounds a year, and that the thing is impossible on that ground alone.'

'It isn't impossible on that ground, if you could rise to the situation. You have done very well, Robert, so far; but you ought to throw off the last vestige of the shop.'

'What the devil has the shop got to do with Lady Frances and her money?'

'Why, you are not going into partnership! Her money would be simply a means of keeping you in a set of people and style of life necessary for your ambitions. It is a detail. You feel that you belong to that kind of life. You don't want to use her money for gambling, or for horse-racing, or anything at all. The roof, which would perhaps be hers, and the food, and the wine, and the rest of it, would be nothing—nothing at all—in comparison with the solid advantages of society and influence. You ought to rise above such considerations, really. I am ashamed that you are tied down by such unworthy considerations. They belong to Wapping-in-the-Ouse, believe me, not to Piccadilly.'

He laughed and shook his head. 'I cannot live upon my wife,' he said doggedly. 'Wapping or Piccadilly, I care not where I live, so that I do not live upon my wife.'

'Well, then——'

'Say no more about it, George; she is as far from me now as if I were at Wapping. I am sorry I told you. Yet, I don't know; it's a relief to tell somebody, and you are the only man to whom I ever told anything. Meantime, there's an end. She doesn't suspect, at any rate.'

I was for the moment diplomatically doubtful. I might tell him at once of the wonderful find that would clear away one obstacle at least. But, then, I knew so well beforehand the lofty scorn with which Frances would sweep away such an obstacle; how she would make him understand the paltry nature of her own wealth compared with the riches and abundance of his own abilities; how she would make him ashamed of his own weakness in not perceiving this fact for himself, and how he could become converted and resigned and submissive, this strong, proud man. Knowing all this, I would not tell him—yet.

'There are,' I summed up, 'three obstacles in the way. There is Isabel. Very good; you shall be released. Oh, I am not guessing. I tell you plainly that she does not care for you, except as a generous benefactor. You can't marry a girl who is only grateful. You have never made love to her.'

'Of course not; I had no time.'

'And therefore you cannot expect her to be in love with you. Moreover, my dear cousin, I have reason to believe that, if she were free to-day, she would be engaged to-morrow.'

'Oh! To some little clerk in the docks, I suppose. Isabel has no greater ambition than that.'

'Perhaps.' He had no suspicion at all, yet he knew that I had been wandering about with this girl all the summer evenings. 'Girls,' I said, 'are sometimes singularly free from ambition. Some of them want nothing but love and a tranquil home; they are easily contented.'

'I suppose that is so,' he said with pity. 'And so Isabel really wants to be released. That is the meaning of your mysterious offer, is it?'

'At least, she has always been afraid of you, as well as grateful. She would never want to be released unless she knew that you wished it. I shall fill her heart with happiness to-night when I tell her what you really want.'

'Then let her be happy—with her dock clerk.' His face cleared immediately, and he laughed. 'Poor child!' he said. 'She was a good clerk and a good accountant. How should her mind soar any higher?'

'As for the other obstacle, Robert, that objection, I tell you again, on the score of wealth—it is unworthy of you; it is also unpractical. You ought to be quite above such considerations.'

'All the same, George,' he repeated, 'to live upon my wife would choke me.'

'You shall not be choked, my dear Robert. This obstacle, too, shall be removed. Trust me—believe me —when I tell you, on my word of honour, that it shall be removed.'

I had, I say, the greatest confidence in Lady Frances and in the arguments which I knew she would employ to break down this heart of stone; but there was also the additional comfort of feeling that the bag of precious jewels was in that seaman's chest. How beautiful is the working out of the Doctrine of Chances! When one takes up a hand at cards there are millions to one against the particular hand that turns up; yet it does turn up—it always turns up—in the face of those overwhelming odds. So with that bag of diamonds. Everybody in the Wapping branch of the Burnikel family had examined that chest—turned it upside down, taken everything out—yet had never found that hiding-place. If it had been found at any time it would have changed the fortune and altered the future of the whole family. Robert would have been impossible. Had Robert been born, brought up and trained otherwise, he would have been quite another Robert. He would have understood, for instance— which he has never yet perfectly succeeded in under-standing—the audacity of his ambition, and, as it would seem to those who know the world—but not to himself—

its impossibility. Why do young men of obscure birth and poverty succeed so often and so greatly ? Because they do not understand the audacity of their own ambition. 'I will win scholarships ; I will go to Cambridge ; I will be Senior Wrangler ; I will be Master of my college ; I will be Vice-Chancellor of the University,' says the lad of parts, low down in the world. The lad of parts higher up understands that the very flower of the English-speaking youth are his rivals ; that he must beat the best ; that he must actually be the best ; and he is discouraged. For climb-ing—for nerve and hand and eye—the poor boy has a far better chance than the rich. All our boys, before they are born, ought to pray for poverty—with brains and courage.

All these fine reflections passed through my head between my last speech and Robert's reply. He held out his hand. 'Trust you, George ?' he said. 'Isn't it rather late in the day to ask that question ? But how —how can that obstacle be removed ?'

'I shall not tell you. Now go on without any mis-giving, and conquer—if you can. Only, Robert, pray remember, this is not quite the same thing as the other venture, you know. Then you had to do with a school-girl—a child ; now you have an equal. You cannot un-derstand ; you must stoop to woo, even you, O Samson.'

'Only an equal? An equal? Don't speak like a fool, George—you who know her!'

'You think that way at last. You have found someone to whom you are not equal. So much the better. But—I say, how about the foolishness of fondling and kisses?'

'Oh!' There rose upon his cheek the roseate hues of early dawn, yet he was six-and-twenty. 'Of course this is different—quite different. Isabel was only a school-girl, as you say. That kind of thing would only unsettle her at that age. This is quite different.'

CHAPTER XXVI.

RELEASE.

I FOUND my mistress—it was nearly nine o'clock in the evening—in the parlour playing her thoughts to herself. The room had no light except that of the street-lamp, which showed her in her light gray dress, something like a ghost. She turned her head as I opened the door. In the lamplight I saw her sweet, serious face and her limpid eyes. I was dragged by ropes to fall at her feet. But I refrained. There was something to be said first.

' George,' she said, ' you are worried about something. What has happened ?'

There must have been something in my eyes—yet the room was so dark. Perhaps she could feel in some magnetic way—the way of love—the presence of emotion. This kind of thought-reading is a branch of the science which has been too much neglected. It is, unfortunately, incapable of being put upon any stage, or even illustrated in any drawing-room. Which is, of course, the reason of this neglect.

'Isabel,' I said, 'you are a witch. Come into the study, and I will tell you why I am moved.'

The study was also in twilight, the light of the same lamp in the street falling upon the polished wainscot, and reflected about the room. My hand touched Isabel's, and again that temptation fell upon me to take the girl in my arms and to kiss her, and never to be weary of that kissing.

'You promised, George,' she said, reading my mind a second time. 'Not yet—not yet.'

'I promised, Isabel, only until there was no longer need to keep that promise.'

'There is still the need, and greater need than ever. Quiet yourself, George—I can hear your heart beating. Tell me, or let me go.'

I lit the candles. 'I am quiet, Isabel.'

'Now tell me what has happened.'

'That need, Isabel, exists no longer.'

'Exists no longer? Is Robert dead?'

'No, he is living still; but that need exists no longer.'

'What has happened, then?'

'Sit down, Isabel. Take a pen and paper. So! Now, write at my dictation. It is the only act of obedience that I shall ever ask of you. All the future I shall be your slave. This evening alone I ask you to obey me.'

She hesitated. Then she sat down.

'Write: "My dear Robert."'

'I am to write to Robert?'

'You shall hear, if you will be obedient for this one and only occasion. "My dear Robert"—have you got that?'

'It looks very odd on paper. This is the first letter I have ever written to him.'

'Write: "I learn that you yourself are anxious that our engagement should be broken off." Have you got that?'

'But, George, anxious? Robert anxious? What does this mean?'

'Finish the letter. "To me it has always been a meaningless engagement, and really impossible. When you made that promise to me I was only a schoolgirl, and I was frightened. My only comfort was in thinking that it was to be a long engagement. I release you from your promise very willingly. You made a mistake, and you have been too proud to acknowledge it, though I have never ceased from the beginning to understand that it was a mistake.—Yours." What will you be — "yours sincerely"? That will do. "Isabel." Have you written it?'

'Yes, I have written it. But I do not understand it.
Does he really and truly desire his release? Why?'

'He does, really and truly. But he will never ask
you himself. The release must come from you.'

'You have not told me why. Is Robert going to be
engaged to someone else?'

'Perhaps. You are not jealous? But of course not.
How could you be jealous? I think it is very likely
that he will be engaged before long.'

'No,' she smiled. 'I have no right to be jealous.
He never loved me. I never cared enough about him
to be jealous. His engagement was just a part of his
kindness. It gave him the right to maintain us without the appearance of almsgiving. No, George, I am
not jealous.'

'At present he could not afford to marry, unless it
was some woman with money. He understands, however, that he has no right to bind you any longer to a
loveless engagement. He says he has had no time to
make love. If he marries, it should be to some woman
of political influence, and with political friends, who
would advance him.'

'He never thinks of anything at all but his own
advancement. I wonder if he has a heart somewhere
hidden away?'

'He has plenty of heart, Isabel, if you can get at it.

The misfortune in your case was that while he was here
the business of his own advancement did occupy all his
soul, and all his strength, and all his mind, and all his
heart. The ground is cleared now, and he has begun
his march. The rest is easy, and now is the time
for the flowers of passion to show themselves and to
expand. We may look to see strange things before
long.' With such shallow humbug did I attempt to
veil the truth. But in vain. Women's minds are swift
and far-shooting.

'There must be another woman,' she said thoughtfully, and not in the least jealously; 'otherwise he would
not have considered the question of his engagement at
all. Why should he? I am hidden away down here:
he was not going to marry me for years—any number
of years. He never writes to me; he takes no notice of
me; his engagement did not make the least difference to
him. Yet he suddenly expresses his wish to be released.
Well, George, he shall be released. About that other
woman you will tell me what you please.'

Therefore I told her all.

'Robert in love!' she laughed gently. 'I cannot
understand it. Will he tell her, as he told me, that
there is to be no foolishness of fondling?'

'I don't think he will, Isabel.'

She heaved a deep sigh. 'I have worked for him,'

she said, 'for five long years—you will never understand
how long those years have been.   He is a hard master;
he expects the best work always; no one must be tired
or sick or weak who works for him.'

'A hard master indeed.'

'And never a word of praise or approbation.   Oh,
George! I have longed for a word of kindness.   It was
dreadful to be engaged to a man who was only a master
all the time.   Never a word of kindness would he give
me.'

'He was absorbed, Isabel; he thought of nothing
but the work—never anything of the people who helped
in the work.'

'What was the work?   What did he intend?   He
never told me.   I was like a man blindfolded dragging
a heavy cart along a road that led whither he knew
not.   Well, he wants his release; he shall have it,' she
repeated.

'Since he wants that, Isabel, forgive him all the
rest.'

'I have forgiven him, George.   I have forgiven him
since you came—and—and—and since my heart was
softened.'   The tears rose to her eyes.

'Isabel!'

'Are   you   sure, George,   that   he   desires   his
release?'

'Quite sure. Robert knows that I have come this evening with the intention of asking you for it.'

'Then I will write him a longer letter than this.' She tore up the little note that I had dictated, and wrote another and a much longer letter. 'I shall not suffer my loveless lover, my patient bridegroom, to depart without a little explanation. I am glad—oh, so glad!—to be released. But, still, no one likes to be told to go without a little understanding of things.'

It was certainly a much finer letter than mine. But then, you see, I was thinking of nothing but the release, and Isabel was thinking of what the man had done for her.

'DEAR ROBERT' (she wrote),

'George tells me that the time has come when you desire the termination of our engagement, entered upon by you out of pity. You wanted an excuse for maintaining two penniless people—one of them helpless, and the second too young and ignorant to be of much use. I understand now exactly why you forced this engagement upon yourself without any thought of love. That was four years ago. I was then seventeen, and am now one-and-twenty. During this long time I have looked for any word of interest, for any look of affection from you. No such word or look have I ever received from you. It has been quite plain to me, all along, that you had no kind of love for me. I could not tell you this—partly because we owe you so much that we must always do whatever you desire ; partly because it is hard for a woman to say such things ; and partly because I was afraid. That you should release me, therefore, is a great relief to me. It must be un-happiness enough for a woman to marry a man whom she does not love : it must be far worse if that man does not even pretend to love her.

'You are quite free, Robert. You have lifted a great weight from my heart. You will be far happier your-self without the fetters of an engagement which had proved impossible. You must marry a woman who will help you in your ambitions. This I could never do, and when you become a great and famous man you will be pleased to remember that you released one who would feel no pride in your success, and could take no part in your ambition. And so I am always, and just as much as ever, your grateful and obedient servant, clerk, and housekeeper, but never your bride,

'ISABEL.'

I took the letter and placed it in an envelope. It was done. Robert had got his release, and Isabel was free.

' Oh, my love !' I cried, and held out my arms.

'Oh ! No—George !' She shrank back. 'Not so soon. Oh ! I am like a newly-made widow, but I am full of joy. Is it right ? Oh ! George—so soon !'

' Isabel ! At last ! At last !'

CHAPTER XXVII.

I should very much like to tell you exactly what Robert said, and what Frances said, and how he played the wooer, and how she accepted the wooing. I cannot, however, for the very sufficient reason that I have not been told by either what passed between them. It is enough that Frances accepted as her husband this man of the people, who will remain a man of the people, though he has joined a party, and now fights under the banner of his party, and is almost the party chief. He will remain a man of the people, working for them in legislation so far as laws can help, which is not much : by teaching, by addresses, by writing. He can never cast off the early conditions of his life, nor get rid of the early impulses, nor forget the nobler ambitions. What was it that Frances said ? The lesser nature puts the reward first and the work second ; the nobler nature puts the work first and the reward second. There lies

before him, unless accident prevents, a long and perhaps
a successful career; the labours of the future may wear
him out, though this kind of work seems to prolong
life and strength; he will have beside him a woman as
strong as himself in her way, full of sympathy with his
work, full of admiration for his strength; a woman
who loves him all the more, perhaps, because he needs
not so much as some men do, the support and encouragement of love. I think of them, not as those
who cling together like the columns of a cathedral aisle,
but as those who stand together side by side; but the
man looks out upon the world, and the woman looks
up towards the man.

And now there only remains to tell you about the
diamonds.

Robert brought her down to Wapping. She came
to tea with us—the homely *bourgeois* five o'clock meal
which Isabel prepared, just as she had prepared the
little banquet for my first visit. I laughed when I saw
once more this noble spread: the plate of ham in slices,
the plate of shrimps, the cakes—half a dozen kinds of
cake—the biscuits, the muffins, the buttered toast, the
thin bread-and-butter. Isabel saw nothing to laugh
at; nor, indeed, was there. Tea, considered as a meal,
is most properly graced by these delightful accompani-
ments. And it is the principal meal, the most social

meal of the greater part of our people, and the greater part of the American people.

To this feast, then, came the Lady Frances. She came dressed like a queen, with wonderful lace and embroidery. She looked like a queen, gracious and kindly. Isabel had put on a plain white dress. She had never looked better—my dainty mistress—than when she stood, so simple and so sweet, beside that reginal woman.

'George has told me about you,' said Frances, taking Isabel's hand. 'I have been wanting to make your acquaintance. My dear, we shall be cousins; we must be great friends.' So she stooped and kissed her, and I could see that she was pleased with my simple maid of Wapping Old Stairs.

Then the Captain was presented, and behaved as an honest old sailor should : full of admiration of so much beauty and grandeur, and not afraid.

Frances took off her hat, and we all sat down to tea, and were cheerful. The talking was conducted chiefly by Frances and myself. Robert sat silent, preoccupied. Only from time to time he lifted his eyes and rested them for a moment on Frances with a softer light in them than I had ever seen before. Love doth tame speedily the most masterful of men.

Tea despatched, I took Frances over the way to see

the Yard. I thought that Robert would perhaps like to say something to Isabel. What he did say was very simple and straightforward. He said, quite meekly, in the presence of the Captain : ' Isabel, I thank you for the release. You have forgiven me, I am sure, for what was meant for the best—a great mistake, a great cruelty to you, as now I understand.'

' Oh yes,' she said ; ' it was impossible. Why did you not let me know before ? But there is nothing to forgive. The gratitude remains, Robert, and the obligation ; and you will be very happy, I am sure.'

' Believe me, Isabel,' he replied humbly, ' I could not be happy unless I was sure you were happy too, in the same way.'

As for me, Frances spoke very gracious words. ' George,' she said, not pretending in the least to be interested in the ribs of a barge which we were building —yet a beautiful barge—' you have brought me to this place of chips and shavings for no other purpose than merely to ask me what I think of her. Well, she seems a sweet and lovely girl ; and she loves you, George. I saw it in her eyes and in her voice. What do you chiefly desire of life, George ? Love and tranquillity, is it not ?'

' Indeed, Frances, there seems nothing better to desire.'

'Then you will have the desire of your heart. But, George, if you have sons, remember that you have a hereditary title. Rank has its uses, and yours may be useful to them. Perhaps your sons may aspire. I can perfectly understand how Robert came to make so great a mistake—who could bear to think of that delicate creature turned out upon the world ?—and I understand why Robert desired his release; and I understand as well, my dear George, that your Isabel will make you perfectly happy.'

Looking at this little speech as it is written down in cold language, I perceive that it has a suspicion of con-descension in it, as if Isabel was good enough for me, and not good enough for Robert. But one cannot convey the manner of the words, which was wholly sweet and sisterly.

So she glanced round the shed, and stepped to the edge of the quay, and looked up and down the river.

'It is all impossible, George,' she said. 'I cannot understand how Robert came out of such a place, or how you could go into it. Why, it is nothing more than a kind of carpenter's shop.'

'By your leave, Frances, a boat-builder's yard. Chips and chunks and shavings belong to the craft of carpenter, it is true, but to that of boat-builder as well.'

'Well, I am glad that Robert is out of it. I confess, my dear George, that I could not live down here, nor can I promise to come here often—perhaps never again. All this side of life, with the warehouses, the ships, the wharves, the waggons, seems to me to belong to the Service. The place is kitchen, scullery, pantry, cellars. You and I were born in the class that is served, not in the Service. I do not want so much as to see the kitchen. Yet you—well, I say no more. Curiosity brought you here, an interesting couple made you stay here, love has chained you here. Let us go back to the others.'

The moment had arrived for my surprise, which I had arranged with the greatest care, so as to produce a fine dramatic effect. I took the party into the study. On the rug before the fireplace stood old John Burnikel's sea-chest, hidden by a table-cover. No one in the house, not even Isabel, knew what I was doing. And even Isabel did not know why I did it.

'This, Frances,' I said, 'is Robert's study. In this room he learned all he knows.'

'It is a beautiful old room. I had no idea that there could be among these warehouses so lovely a house. This wainscoting is worthy of any house, however fine. So this was your room, Robert, was it?'

'This was my room. What have you got on the floor, George?'

'You shall see directly, as soon as Frances has done admiring the walls. Sit down, Frances; sit down, Isabel. I am going to show you something of interest. Now, Robert, remember the last talk we had. We spoke of obstacles—did we not?—in the way of a certain event of some importance to you.'

'Yes, we did.'

'I told you that the first obstacle was waiting for your wish to be expressed. Is that obstacle removed?'

'It is.'

'The second obstacle was a difference in birth and social position which cannot be removed, but may be trampled upon.'

'We have trampled upon it,' said Frances, for her lover looked at her. 'Robert has forgotten that there ever existed this apparent, not real, obstacle.'

'There remains the third obstacle. Shall I remind you of what you said?'

'I said that it would choke me to live upon my wife's money.'

'And now you say?'

'Let me say it for him.' Frances rose and placed her hand upon his shoulder. Yes, I am quite right: she will not cling to her husband, she will stand beside him—the Queen Consort. 'Robert forgot that wealth is nothing. It can give me no more than a house, and servants, and carriages. It is of no other use to me. But it may be of use to Robert, and he takes it—with me. It is a part of me; he takes me altogether, just as I am. The woman herself, with her heart, and her soul, and her thoughts, and her abilities, if she has any, and with the woman her rank, and her family, and her wealth. Is that so, Robert?'

'It is so, Frances,' he replied humbly.

'Wealth may be useful to such a man as Robert. It is good for such a man to have a well-appointed house. Freedom from money anxieties with some men is almost a necessity. Do you not agree, Robert?'

'You have made me understand,' he said. 'I thought I was asserting my independence when I was only betraying narrow prejudice. That you—you should give me money shames me no more now than that you should give me yourself, and that will shame me always.' Oh, the change in Robert, that he should say this!

'You know, you two,' Frances went on, 'I want Robert to become a great man. It is his ambition, and it is mine as well. I want him to become greater—far greater—than he allows himself to dream. I want him

to be such a leader of men as has not been seen for
many a century in this country. He must never be
accused of mean or sordid motives; never be led aside
by temptations which ruin smaller men. Oh! be certain
that he will become what I think he may become. I
would give not only all my heart and all my soul and
all my strength and all my wealth—which is nothing—
but I would give my very life—my heart's blood—at
this moment to make him great.' She laid her hand
upon his shoulder; he stooped and kissed her forehead,
and in his softened eye I saw—oh, the wonder of it!—
actually a tear! In Robert's eyes, a tear! This foolish
love makes schoolgirls of us all. And Frances was
splendid—she was splendid.

'Well,' I said, after a moment, 'things being as they
are, I am inclined to stop. However, we must carry
this thing through to the end. I understand, Robert,
that you no longer desire that kind of equality of which
we spoke the other day.'

'No longer,' he replied. 'I would rather owe everything to—Frances.' It was quite pretty to notice how
he dropped his voice at the very mention of her name.
'Everything,' he repeated.

'I am truly sorry, Robert, I continued, 'to disturb
an arrangement which is so beautiful. But when I told
you that the obstacle of comparative income was re-

moved, I meant more than its removal by Frances, though of that I was certain. I meant, my cousin, that I was able to place in your hands a fortune which would go far at least to equalize things.'

'What do you mean?' asked Robert.

'I am now going to show you. In fact, Robert, I am about to restore to you, as the sole and rightful heir, the family fortune.'

'The family fortune? What is that?'

'Oh, basest of Burnikels! He has forgotten the lost bag of jewels.'

With these words I removed the tablecloth and exposed the sea-chest.

'The jewels? Is it possible that you have found them?'

'It is more than possible. Isabel, dear child, help me to take out the contents of the chest.'

We took out everything—the sextant, the Indian things, the mummified flying fish, the odds and ends, and laid them on the floor.

'I have done that a hundred times,' said Robert.

'What is the bag of jewels?' asked Frances.

'It is a bag full of the most lovely precious stones,' I told her. 'Our great-great uncle, John Burnikel, master mariner, possessed this treasure. How he got it I do not know. That is, a knowledge of the truth

came to me in a dream, and I do know. Some day I
will tell you. He used to say himself that an Indian
Rajah, presumably the Great Mogul of Delhi, took him
into his treasury and bade him fill his pockets with
jewels in return for some signal services rendered to the
Mogullian Dynasty. Well, he died, and his nephews
could not find that bag anywhere, and nobody has ever
been able to find it—until now. It was reserved for
me to make this discovery. Is the box quite empty,
Isabel? One moment. The nephews quarrelled over
the loss, Frances ; they fought, I believe ; they dissolved
partnership. One was my great-grandfather, and the
other was Robert's. That's all the history. Now, you
will observe that the box and all that it contains belongs
to Robert. His great-grandfather bought or took over
the old mariner's furniture. His own father bequeathed
it to him. The box with all its contents, therefore,
without any possible doubt, or dispute, is his own.
Now, then, you've got nothing to say to that, I suppose, Robert ?'

'I suppose not. But why so fierce ?'

'Very good. I thought you might begin advancing
absurd objections about other people's imaginary rights.
It's all yours. And now look at the box. Do you see
any possible hiding-place in it, Frances ? See. It is
empty ; the sides are papered. I hold it up and turn

it over. There are two compartments, both of the same depth. Is there any possibility of a hiding-place?'

'I can see none,' said Frances; 'but, of course, there must be. You are like a conjurer before he shows his trick. Why don't you turn up your sleeves, and assure us that there is no deception?'

'What do you think, Robert?'

'I have thought of a false bottom, and I have measured. I used to think that there is no possibility of a hiding-place. But I am now convinced that there must be, otherwise you would not talk in this way.'

'Well, look along the lower line of the pattern at the back—the thick dark line. Can you discern nothing?'

'No, no. Yet there seems to be a line not in the paper. What is that?'

'You shall see.' So I knelt down, opened my knife, and slowly passed it along the almost invisible junction of the shutter or lid of which you have heard. This widened the opening.

'There is a secret pocket, after all!' cried Robert.

'There is. This is a lid with a spring which keeps it tightly pressed. You do not look for hinges at the bottom of the box, and you do not observe the line of juncture. I think it is one of the most admirable hiding-places I ever saw, and I have seen a good many. Now, Robert, I pull open this lid. You see this side of the chest is made of wood much thicker than the other side; also, if you look at the outside, you will observe that it widens at the bottom. The widening is designed by the cabinet-maker who made this excellent box, for in it he has cut out a narrow little cupboard in which anything could be hidden, and where nothing could be suspected. In this cupboard '—I pulled open the lid—' look, Robert—lies the bag.'

I took out the bag. It was, as I have told you, more like one of those long round things which they lay on the windows in order to keep out the draught. I gave it to Robert. 'There is your fortune, Robert. You are the heir to the family fortune. It is yours, and yours only.'

He received the bag with the awkwardness of one who has the most unexpected thing in the world sprung upon him.

' Pour out the contents, man,' I said. ' Let us see your treasure.'

He poured out the glittering contents on the table. There they were—diamond, ruby, emerald, turquoise, pearl, opal, chalcedony, and the rest; of all sizes from a seed pearl to a ruby as big as a pigeon's egg; diamonds worth thousands; pearls worth the ransom of an earl.

' Oh, heavens!' cried Frances. ' What are we to do with all these things?'

'They are yours,' said Robert. 'Let me give them all to you.'

'No; they are your fortune. They are yours. Stay, I will take them, Robert, in case at any time you may want something—I know not what. Oh! after all these years that you should find them, George! Oh! but you should have some of them.'

'Take half of them, George.'

'No,' I said. 'Your house is the best place for them, Frances. We will have none of them. Put all back in the bag—so.' I tied the mouth. 'Take it home with you, Frances. In the High Street of Wapping-on-the-Wall we want no diamonds—do we, Isabel?'

So she consented and took the jewels, greatly marvelling. And, lo! it was time for them to go. So we said farewell.

'We shall see each other seldom, Frances,' I said. 'We are setting off along roads that never meet. Perhaps in the years to come we may try to meet, if only to ask each other whether the tranquil life is better than the fight and struggle.'

So the two women kissed with tears, and Robert gave me his hand, and they left me down at Wapping-on-the-Wall—a Master Craftsman—with Isabel.

THE END.

BILLING AND SONS, PRINTERS, GUILDFORD.

LIST OF BOOKS PUBLISHED BY

CHATTO & WINDUS

214 PICCADILLY, LONDON, W.

About (Edmond).—The Fellah: An Egyptian Novel. Translated by
Sir RANDAL R----T. Post 8vo, illustrated boards, 2s.

Adams (W. Davenport), Works by.
A **Dictionary of the Drama:** being a comprehensive Guide to the Plays, Playwrights, Players,
and Playhouses of the United Kingdom and America, from the Earliest Times to the Present
Day. Crown 8vo, half-bound, 12s. 6d. [Preparing.
Quips and Quiddities. Selected by W. DAVENPORT ADAMS. Post 8vo, cloth limp, 2s. 6d.

Agony Column (The) of 'The Times,' from 1800 to 1870. Edited,
with an Introduction, by ALICE CLAY. Post 8vo, cloth limp, 2s. 6d.

Aidé (Hamilton), Novels by. Post 8vo, illustrated boards, 2s. each.
Carr of Carrlyon. | **Confidences.**

Albert (Mary).—Brooke Finchley's Daughter. Post 8vo, picture
boards, 2s. ; cloth limp. 2s. 6d.

Alden (W. L.).—A Lost Soul: Being the Confession and Defence of
Charles Lindsay. Fcap. 8vo, cloth boards, 1s. 6d.

Alexander (Mrs.), Novels by. Post 8vo, illustrated boards, 2s. each.
Maid, Wife. or Widow? | **Valerie's Fate.**

Allen (F. M.).—Green as Grass. With a Frontispiece. Crown 8vo,
cloth, 3s. 6d.

Allen (Grant), Works by.
The **Evolutionist at Large.** Crown 8vo, cloth extra, 6s.
Post-Prandial Philosophy. Crown 8vo, art linen, 3s. 6d.
Moorland Idylls. Crown 8vo, cloth decorated,

Crown 8vo, cloth extra, 3s. 6d. each ; post 8vo, illustrated boards, 2s. each.

Philistia.	**In all Shades.**	**Dumaresq's Daughter.**
Babylon.	**The Devil's Die.**	**The Duchess of Powysland**
Strange Stories.	**This Mortal Coil.**	**Blood Royal.**
The Beckoning Hand.	**The Tents of Shem.**	**Ivan Greet's Masterpiece.**
For Maimie's Sake.	**The Great Taboo.**	**The Scallywag.**

Crown 8vo, cloth extra, 3s. 6d. ea.

At Market Value. **Under Sealed Orders.**

Dr. Palliser's Patient. Fcap. 8vo, cloth boards, 1s. 6d.

Anderson (Mary). Othello's Occupation: A Novel. Crown 8vo,
cloth, 3s. 6d.

Arnold (Edwin Lester), Stories by.
The **Wonderful Adventures of Phra the Phœnician.** Crown 8vo, cloth extra, with
Illustrations by H. M. PAGET, 3s. 6d. ; post 8vo, illustrated boards, 2s.
The **Constable of St. Nicholas.** With Frontispiece, Crown 8vo, cloth, 3s. 6d.

Artemus Ward's Works. With Portrait and Facsimile. Crown 8vo,
cloth extra, 3s. 6d.—Also a POPULAR EDITION, post 8vo, picture boards, 2s.
The **Genial Showman:** The Life and Adventures of ARTEMUS WARD. By EDWARD P.
HINGSTON. With a Frontispiece. Crown 8vo, cloth extra, 3s. 6d.

Ashton (John), Works by. Crown 8vo, cloth extra, 7s. 6d. each.
History of the Chap-Books of the 18th Century. With 334 Illustrations.
Social Life in the Reign of Queen Anne. With 85 Illustrations.
Humour, Wit, and Satire of the Seventeenth Century. With 82 Illustrations.
English Caricature and Satire on Napoleon the First. With 115 Illustrations.
Modern Street Ballads. With 57 Illustrations.

Bacteria, Yeast Fungi, and Allied Species, A Synopsis of. By
W. B. GROVE, B.A. With 87 Illustrations. Crown 8vo, cloth extra, 3s. 6d.

Bardsley (Rev. C. Wareing, M.A.), Works by.
English Surnames: Their Sources and Significations. Crown 8vo, cloth, 7s. 6d.
Curiosities of Puritan Nomenclature. Crown 8vo, cloth extra, 6s.

Baring Gould (Sabine, Author of 'John Herring,' &c.), Novels by.
Crown 8vo, cloth extra, 3s. 6d. each; post 8vo, Illustrated boards, 2s. each.
Red Spider. | Eve.

Barr (Robert: Luke Sharp), Stories by. Cr. 8vo, cl., 3s. 6d. each.
In a Steamer Chair. With Frontispiece and Vignette by DEMAIN HAMMOND.
From Whose Bourne, &c. With 47 Illustrations by HAL HURST and others.
A Woman Intervenes. With 8 Illustrations by HAL HURST. Crown 8vo, cloth extra, 6s.
Revenge! With numerous Illustrations. Crown 8vo, cloth extra, 6s.   [Shortly.

Barrett (Frank), Novels by.
Post 8vo, illustrated boards, 2s. each; cloth, 2s. 6d. each.
Fettered for Life. | A Prodigal's Progress.
The Sin of Olga Zassoulich. | John Ford; and His Helpmate.
Between Life and Death. | A Recoiling Vengeance.
Folly Morrison. | Honest Davie. | Lieut. Barnabas. | Found Guilty.
Little Lady Linton. | For Love and Honour.
The Woman of the Iron Bracelets. Cr. 8vo, cloth, 3s. 6d.; post 8vo, boards, 2s.; cl. limp, 2s. 6d.
The Harding Scandal. 2 vols., 10s. net.   [Shortly.

Barrett (Joan).—Monte Carlo Stories. Fcap. 8vo, cloth, 1s. 6d.

Beaconsfield, Lord. By T. P. O'CONNOR, M.P. Cr. 8vo, cloth, 5s.

Beauchamp (Shelsley).—Grantley Grange. Post 8vo, boards, 2s.

Beautiful Pictures by British Artists: A Gathering of Favourites
from the Picture Galleries, engraved on Steel. Imperial 4to, cloth extra, gilt edges, 21s.

Besant (Sir Walter) and James Rice, Novels by.
Crown 8vo, cloth extra, 3s. 6d. each; post 8vo, Illustrated boards, 2s. each; cloth limp, 2s. 6d. each.
Ready-Money Mortiboy. | By Celia's Arbour.
My Little Girl. | The Chaplain of the Fleet.
With Harp and Crown. | The Seamy Side.
This Son of Vulcan. | The Case of Mr. Lucraft, &c.
The Golden Butterfly. | 'Twas in Trafalgar's Bay, &c.
The Monks of Thelema. | The Ten Years' Tenant, &c.
. There is also a LIBRARY EDITION of the above Twelve Volumes, handsomely set in new type on a
large crown 8vo page, and bound in cloth extra, 6s. each; and a POPULAR EDITION of The Golden
Butterfly, medium 8vo, 6d.; cloth, 1s.—NEW EDITIONS, printed in large type on crown 8vo laid paper,
bound in figured cloth, 3s. 6d. each, are also in course of publication.

Besant (Sir Walter), Novels by.
Crown 8vo, cloth extra, 3s. 6d. each; post 8vo, illustrated boards, 2s. each; cloth limp, 2s. 6d. each.
All Sorts and Conditions of Men. With 12 Illustrations by FRED. BARNARD
The Captains' Room, &c. With Frontispiece by E. J. WHEELER.
All in a Garden Fair. With 6 Illustrations by HARRY FURNISS.
Dorothy Forster. With Frontispiece by CHARLES GREEN.
Uncle Jack, and other Stories. | Children of Gibeon.
The World Went Very Well Then. With 12 Illustrations by A. FORESTIER.
Herr Paulus: His Rise, his Greatness, and his Fall. | The Bell of St. Paul's.
For Faith and Freedom. With Illustrations by A. FORESTIER and F. WADDY.
To Call Her Mine, &c. With 9 Illustrations by A. FORESTIER.
The Holy Rose, &c. With Frontispiece by F. BARNARD.
Armorel of Lyonesse: A Romance of To-day. With 12 Illustrations by F. BARNARD.
St. Katherine's by the Tower. With 12 Illustrations by C. GREEN.
Verbena Camellia Stephanotis, &c. With a Frontispiece by GORDON BROWNE.
The Ivory Gate. | The Rebel Queen.
Beyond the Dreams of Avarice. With 12 Illusts. by W. H. HYDE. Crown 8vo, cloth extra, 3s. 6d.
In Deacon's Orders, &c. With Frontispiece by A. FORESTIER. Crown 8vo, cloth, 6s.
The Master Craftsman. 2 vols., crown 8vo, 10s. net.   [May
Fifty Years Ago. With 144 Plates and Woodcuts. Crown 8vo, cloth extra, 5s.
The Eulogy of Richard Jefferies. With Portrait. Crown 8vo, cloth extra, 6s.
London. With 125 Illustrations. Demy 8vo, cloth extra, 7s. 6d.
Westminster. With Etched Frontispiece by F. S. WALKER, R.P.E., and 130 Illustrations by
WILLIAM PATTEN and others. Demy 8vo, cloth, 18s.
Sir Richard Whittington. With Frontispiece. Crown 8vo, art linen, 3s. 6d.
Gaspard de Coligny. With a Portrait. Crown 8vo, art linen, 3s. 6d.
As we Are: As we May Be: Social Essays. Crown 8vo, linen, 6s.   [Shortly.

Bechstein (Ludwig).—As Pretty as Seven, and other German
Stories. With Additional Tales by the Brothers GRIMM, and 98 Illustrations by RICHTER. Square
8vo, cloth extra, 6s. 6d.; gilt edges, 7s. 6d.

Beerbohm (Julius).—Wanderings in Patagonia; or, Life among
the Ostrich-Hunters. With Illustrations. Crown 8vo, cloth extra, 3s. 6d.

Bellew (Frank).—The Art of Amusing: A Collection of Graceful
Arts, Games, Tricks, Puzzles, and Charades. With 300 Illustrations. Crown 8vo, cloth extra, 4s. 6d.

Bennett (W. C., LL.D.).—Songs for Sailors. Post 8vo, cl. limp, 2s.

Bewick (Thomas) and his Pupils. By AUSTIN DOBSON. With 95
Illustrations. Square 8vo, cloth extra, 6s.

Bierce (Ambrose).—In the Midst of Life: Tales of Soldiers and
Civilians. Crown 8vo, cloth extra, 6s.; post 8vo, illustrated boards, 2s.

Bill Nye's History of the United States. With 146 Illustrations
by F. OPPER. Crown 8vo, cloth extra, 3s. 6d.

**Bire (Edmond). — Diary of a Citizen of Paris during 'The
Terror.'** Translated and Edited by JOHN DE VILLIERS. With 2 Photogravures. Two Vols., 8vo, cloth,
21s. [Shortly.

Blackburn's (Henry) Art Handbooks.

**Academy Notes, 1875, 1877-86, 1889,
1890, 1892-1895.** Illustrated, each 1s.
Academy Notes, 1896. 1s. [May.
Academy Notes, 1875-79. Complete in
One Vol., with 600 Illustrations. Cloth, 6s.
Academy Notes, 1880-84. Complete in
One Vol., with 700 Illustrations. Cloth, 6s.
Academy Notes, 1890-94. Complete in
One Vol., with 800 Illustrations. Cloth, 7s. 6d.
Grosvenor Notes, 1877. 6d.
Grosvenor Notes, separate years from
1878-1890, each 1s.
Grosvenor Notes, Vol. I., 1877-82. With
300 Illustrations. Demy 8vo, cloth, 6s.
The Paris Salon, 1895. With 300 Facsimile Sketches. 3s.

Grosvenor Notes, Vol. II., 1883-87. With
300 Illustrations. Demy 8vo, cloth, 6s.
Grosvenor Notes, Vol. III., 1888-90. With
230 Illustrations. Demy 8vo, cloth, 3s. 6d.
The New Gallery, 1888-1895. With nu-
merous Illustrations, each 1s.
The New Gallery, 1896. [May.
The New Gallery, Vol. I., 1888-1892. With
250 Illustrations. Demy 8vo, cloth, 6s.
English Pictures at the National Gallery.
With 114 Illustrations. 1s.
Old Masters at the National Gallery.
With 128 Illustrations. 1s. 6d.
**Illustrated Catalogue to the National
Gallery.** With 242 Illusts. Demy 8vo, cloth, 3s.

Blind (Mathilde), Poems by.

The Ascent of Man. Crown 8vo, cloth, 5s.
Dramas in Miniature. With a Frontispiece by F. MADOX BROWN. Crown 8vo, cloth, 5s.
Songs and Sonnets. Fcap. 8vo, vellum and gold, 5s.
Birds of Passage: Songs of the Orient and Occident. Second Edition. Crown 8vo, linen, 6s. net.

Bourget (Paul).—A Living Lie. Translated by JOHN DE VILLIERS.
With special Preface for the English Edition. Crown 8vo, cloth, 3s. 6d.

Bourne (H. R. Fox), Books by.

English Merchants: Memoirs in Illustration of the Progress of British Commerce. With numerous
Illustrations. Crown 8vo, cloth extra, 7s. 6d.
English Newspapers: Chapters in the History of Journalism. Two Vols., demy 8vo, cloth, 25s.
The Other Side of the Emin Pasha Relief Expedition. Crown 8vo, cloth, 6s.

Bowers (George).—Leaves from a Hunting Journal. Coloured
Plates. Oblong folio, half-bound, 21s.

Boyle (Frederick), Works by. Post 8vo, illustrated bds., 2s. each.
Chronicles of No-Man's Land. | **Camp Notes.** | **Savage Life.**

Brand (John).— Observations on Popular Antiquities; chiefly
illustrating the Origin of our Vulgar Customs, Ceremonies, and Superstitions. With the Additions of Sir
HENRY ELLIS, and numerous Illustrations. Crown 8vo, cloth extra, 7s. 6d.

Brewer (Rev. Dr.), Works by.

The Reader's Handbook of Allusions, References, Plots, and Stories. Seventeenth
Thousand. Crown 8vo, cloth extra, 7s. 6d.
Authors and their Works, with the Dates: Being the Appendices to 'The Reader's Hand-
book,' separately printed. Crown 8vo, cloth limp, 2s.
A Dictionary of Miracles. Crown 8vo, cloth extra, 7s. 6d.

Brewster (Sir David), Works by. Post 8vo, cloth, 4s. 6d. each.
More Worlds than One: Creed of the Philosopher and Hope of the Christian. With Plates.
The Martyrs of Science: GALILEO, TYCHO BRAHE, and KEPLER. With Portraits.
Letters on Natural Magic. With numerous Illustrations.

Brillat-Savarin.— Gastronomy as a Fine Art. Translated by
R. E. ANDERSON, M.A. Post 8vo, half-bound, 2s.

Brydges (Harold).—Uncle Sam at Home. With 91 Illustrations.
Post 8vo, illustrated boards, 2s.; cloth limp, 2s. 6d.

Buchanan (Robert), Novels, &c., by.
Crown 8vo, cloth extra, 3s. 6d. each; post 8vo, illustrated boards, 2s. each.

The Shadow of the Sword.
A Child of Nature. With Frontispiece.
God and the Man. With 11 Illustrations by FRED BARNARD.
The Martyrdom of Madeline. With Frontispiece by A. W. COOPER.

Love Me for Ever. With Frontispiece.
Annan Water. | Foxglove Manor.
The New Abelard.
Matt: A Story of a Caravan. With Frontispiece.
The Master of the Mine. With Frontispiece.
The Heir of Linne. | Woman and the Man.

Crown 8vo, cloth extra, 3s. 6d. each.
Red and White Heather. | Rachel Dene.

Lady Kilpatrick. Crown 8vo, cloth extra, 6s.
The Wandering Jew: a Christmas Carol. Crown 8vo, cloth, 6s.

The Charlatan. By ROBERT BUCHANAN and HENRY MURRAY. With a Frontispiece by T. H. ROBINSON. Crown 8vo, cloth, 3s. 6d.

Burton (Richard F.).—The Book of the Sword. With over 400 Illustrations. Demy 4to, cloth extra, 32s.

Burton (Robert).—The Anatomy of Melancholy. With Translations of the Quotations. Demy 8vo, cloth extra, 7s. 6d.
Melancholy Anatomised: An Abridgment of BURTON'S ANATOMY. Post 8vo, half-bd., 2s. 6d.

Caine (T. Hall), Novels by. Crown 8vo, cloth extra, 3s. 6d. each; post 8vo, illustrated boards, 2s. each; cloth limp, 2s. 6d. each.
The Shadow of a Crime. | A Son of Hagar. | The Deemster.
A LIBRARY EDITION of The Deemster is now ready; and one of The Shadow of a Crime is in preparation, set in new type, crown 8vo, cloth decorated, 6s. each.

Cameron (Commander V. Lovett).—The Cruise of the 'Black Prince' Privateer. Post 8vo, picture boards, 2s.

Cameron (Mrs. H. Lovett), Novels by. Post 8vo, illust. bds. 2s. ea.
Juliet's Guardian. | Deceivers Ever.

Carlyle (Jane Welsh), Life of. By Mrs. ALEXANDER IRELAND. With Portrait and Facsimile Letter. Small demy 8vo, cloth extra, 7s. 6d.

Carlyle (Thomas).—On the Choice of Books. Post 8vo, cl., 1s. 6d.
Correspondence of Thomas Carlyle and R. W. Emerson, 1834-1872. Edited by C. E. NORTON. With Portraits. Two Vols., crown 8vo, cloth, 24s.

Carruth (Hayden).—The Adventures of Jones. With 17 Illustrations. Fcap. 8vo, cloth, 2s.

Chambers (Robert W.), Stories of Paris Life by. Long fcap. 8vo, cloth, 2s. 6d. each.
The King in Yellow. | In the Quarter.

Chapman's (George), Works. Vol. I., Plays Complete, including the Doubtful Ones.—Vol. II., Poems and Minor Translations, with Essay by A. C. SWINBURNE.—Vol. III., Translations of the Iliad and Odyssey. Three Vols., crown 8vo, cloth, 6s. each.

Chapple (J. Mitchell).—The Minor Chord: The Story of a Prima Donna. Crown 8vo, cloth, 3s. 6d.

Chatto (W. A.) and J. Jackson.—A Treatise on Wood Engraving, Historical and Practical. With Chapter by H. G. BOHN, and 450 fine Illusts. Large 4to, half-leather, 28s.

Chaucer for Children: A Golden Key. By Mrs. H. R. HAWEIS. With 8 Coloured Plates and 30 Wood cuts. Crown 4to, cloth extra, 3s. 6d.
Chaucer for Schools. By Mrs. H. R. HAWEIS. Demy 8vo, cloth limp, 2s. 6d.

Chess, The Laws and Practice of. With an Analysis of the Openings. By HOWARD STAUNTON. Edited by R. B. WORMALD. Crown 8vo, cloth, 5s.
The Minor Tactics of Chess: A Treatise on the Deployment of the Forces in obedience to Strategic Principle. By F. K. YOUNG and E. C. HOWELL. Long fcap. 8vo, cloth, 2s. 6d.
The Hastings Chess Tournament Book (Aug.-Sept. 1895). Containing the Official Report of the 231 Games played in the Tournament, with Notes by the Players, and Diagrams of Interesting Positions; Portraits and Biographical Sketches of the Chess Masters; and an Account of the Congress and its surroundings. Crown 8vo, cloth extra, 7s. 6d. net. [Shortly.

Clare (Austin).—For the Love of a Lass. Post 8vo, 2s.; cl., 2s. 6d.

Clive (Mrs. Archer), Novels by. Post 8vo, illust. boards, 2s. each.
Paul Ferroll. | Why Paul Ferroll Killed his Wife.

Clodd (Edward, F.R.A.S.).—Myths and Dreams. Cr. 8vo, 3s. 6d.

Cobban (J. Maclaren), Novels by.
The Cure of Souls. Post 8vo, Illustrated boards, 2s.
The Red Sultan. Crown 8vo, cloth extra, 3s. 6d. ; post 8vo, Illustrated boards, 2s.
The Burden of Isabel. Crown 8vo, cloth extra, 3s. 6d.

Coleman (John).—Players and Playwrights I have Known. Two
Vols., demy 8vo, cloth, 24s.

Coleridge (M. E.).—The Seven Sleepers of Ephesus. Cloth, 1s. 6d.

Collins (C. Allston). The Bar Sinister. Post 8vo, boards, 2s.

Collins (John Churton, M.A.), Books by.
Illustrations of Tennyson. Crown 8vo, cloth extra, 6s.
Jonathan Swift: A Biographical and Critical Study. Crown 8vo, cloth extra, 8s.

Collins (Mortimer and Frances), Novels by.
Crown 8vo, cloth extra, 3s. 6d. each ; post 8vo, Illustrated boards, 2s. each.
From Midnight to Midnight. | Blacksmith and Scholar.
Transmigration. | You Play me False. | A Village Comedy.
Post 8vo, Illustrated boards, 2s. each.
Sweet Anne Page. | A Fight with Fortune. | Sweet and Twenty. | Frances.

Collins (Wilkie), Novels by.
Crown 8vo, cloth extra, 3s. 6d. each ; post 8vo, Illustrated boards, 2s. each ; cloth limp, 2s. 6d. each.
Antonina. With a Frontispiece by Sir JOHN GILBERT, R.A.
Basil. Illustrated by Sir JOHN GILBERT, R.A., and J. MAHONEY
Hide and Seek. Illustrated by Sir JOHN GILBERT, R.A., and J. MAHONEY.
After Dark. With Illustrations by A. B. HOUGHTON. | The Two Destinies.
The Dead Secret. With a Frontispiece by Sir JOHN GILBERT, R.A
Queen of Hearts. With a Frontispiece by Sir JOHN GILBERT, R.A.
The Woman In White. With Illustrations by Sir JOHN GILBERT, R.A., and F. A. FRASER.
No Name. With Illustrations by Sir J. E. MILLAIS, R.A., and A. W. COOPER.
My Miscellanies. With a Steel-plate Portrait of WILKIE COLLINS.
Armadale. With Illustrations by G. H. THOMAS.
The Moonstone. With Illustrations by G. DU MAURIER and F. A. FRASER.
Man and Wife. With Illustrations by WILLIAM SMALL.
Poor Miss Finch. Illustrated by G. DU MAURIER and EDWARD HUGHES.
Miss or Mrs.? With Illustrations by S. L. FILDES, R.A., and HENRY WOODS, A.R.A.
The New Magdalen. Illustrated by G. DU MAURIER and C. S. REINHARDT.
The Frozen Deep. Illustrated by G. DU MAURIER and J. MAHONEY
The Law and the Lady. With Illustrations by S. L. FILDES, R.A., and SYDNEY HALL.
The Haunted Hotel. With Illustrations by ARTHUR HOPKINS.
The Fallen Leaves. | Heart and Science. | The Evil Genius.
Jezebel's Daughter. | 'I Say No.' | Little Novels. From s.
The Black Robe. | A Rogue's Life. | The Legacy of Cain.
Blind Love. With a Preface by Sir WALTER BESANT, and Illustrations by A. FORESTIER.

POPULAR EDITIONS, Medium 8vo, 6d. each, cloth, 1s. each.
The Woman In White. | The Moonstone.

The Woman In White and The Moonstone In One Volume, medium 8vo, cloth, 2s.

Colman's (George) Humorous Works: 'Broad Grins,' 'My Night-
gown and Slippers,' &c. With Life and Frontispiece. Crown 8vo, cloth extra, 7s. 6d.

Colquhoun (M. J.).—Every Inch a Soldier. Post 8vo, boards, 2s.

Colt-breaking, Hints on. By W. M. HUTCHISON. Cr. 8vo, cl., 3s. 6d.

Convalescent Cookery. By CATHERINE RYAN. Cr. 8vo, 1s., cl., 1s. 6d.

Conway (Moncure D.), Works by.
Demonology and Devil-Lore. With 65 Illustrations. Two Vols., demy 8vo, cloth, 28s.
George Washington's Rules of Civility. Fcap. 8vo, Japanese vellum, 2s. 6d.

Cook (Dutton), Novels by.
Paul Foster's Daughter. Crown 8vo, cloth extra, 3s. 6d. ; post 8vo, Illustrated boards, 2s.
Leo. Post 8vo, Illustrated boards, 2s.

Cooper (Edward H.).—Geoffory Hamilton. Cr. 8vo, cloth, 3s. 6d.

Cornwall.—Popular Romances of the West of England; or, The
Trolls, Traditions, and Superstitions of Old Cornwall. Collected by ROBERT HUNT, F.R.S. With
two Steel Plates by GEORGE CRUIKSHANK. Crown 8vo, cloth, 7s. 6d.

Cotes (V. Cecil).—Two Girls on a Barge. With 44 Illustrations by
F. H. TOWNSEND. Post 8vo, cloth, 2s. 6d.

Craddock (C. Egbert), Stories by.
The Prophet of the Great Smoky Mountains. Post 8vo, illustrated boards, 2s.
His Vanished Star. Crown 8vo, cloth extra, 3s. 6d.

Cram (Ralph Adams).—Black Spirits and White. Fcap. 8vo, cloth 1s. 6d.

Crellin (H. N.) Books by.
Romances of the Old Seraglio. With 28 Illustrations by S. L. WOOD. Crown 8vo, cloth, 3s. 6d.
Tales of the Caliph. Crown 8vo, cloth, 2s.
The Nazarenes: A Drama. Crown 8vo, 1s.

Crim (Matt.).—Adventures of a Fair Rebel. Crown 8vo, cloth extra, with a Frontispiece by DAN. BEARD, 3s. 6d.; post 8vo, illustrated boards, 2s.

Crockett (S. R.) and others.—Tales of Our Coast. By S. R. CROCKETT, GILBERT PARKER, HAROLD FREDERIC, 'Q.,' and W. CLARK RUSSELL. With 12 Illustrations by FRANK BRANGWYN. Crown 8vo, cloth, 3s. 6d. [Shortly.

Croker (Mrs. B. M.), Novels by. Crown 8vo, cloth extra, 3s. 6d. each; post 8vo, illustrated boards, 2s. each; cloth limp, 2s. 6d. each.
Pretty Miss Neville. | Diana Barrington. | A Family Likeness.
A Bird of Passage. | Proper Pride. | 'To Let.'
Village Tales and Jungle Tragedies.
Crown 8vo, cloth extra, 3s. 6d. each.
Mr. Jervis. | The Real Lady Hilda.
Married or Single? Three Vols., crown 8vo, 15s. net.

Cruikshank's Comic Almanack. Complete in TWO SERIES: The FIRST, from 1835 to 1843; the SECOND, from 1844 to 1853. A Gathering of the Best Humour of THACKERAY, HOOD, MAYHEW, ALBERT SMITH, A'BECKETT, ROBERT BROUGH, &c. With numerous Steel Engravings and Woodcuts by GEORGE CRUIKSHANK, HINE, LANDELLS, &c. Two Vols., crown 8vo, cloth gilt, 7s. 6d. each.
The Life of George Cruikshank. By BLANCHARD JERROLD. With 84 Illustrations and a Bibliography. Crown 8vo, cloth extra, 6s.

Cumming (C. F. Gordon), Works by. Demy 8vo, cl. ex., 8s. 6d. ea.
In the Hebrides. With an Autotype Frontispiece and 23 Illustrations.
In the Himalayas and on the Indian Plains. With 42 Illustrations.
Two Happy Years in Ceylon. With 29 Illustrations.
Via Cornwall to Egypt. With a Photogravure Frontispiece. Demy 8vo, cloth, 7s. 6d.

Cussans (John E.).—A Handbook of Heraldry; with Instructions for Tracing Pedigrees and Deciphering Ancient MSS., &c. Fourth Edition, revised, with 408 Woodcuts and 2 Coloured Plates. Crown 8vo, cloth extra, 6s.

Cyples (W.).—Hearts of Gold. Cr. 8vo, cl., 3s. 6d.; post 8vo, bds., 2s.

Daniel (George).—Merrie England in the Olden Time. With Illustrations by ROBERT CRUIKSHANK. Crown 8vo, cloth extra, 3s. 6d.

Daudet (Alphonse).—The Evangelist; or, Port Salvation. Crown 8vo, cloth extra, 3s. 6d.; post 8vo, illustrated boards, 2s.

Davenant (Francis, M.A.).—Hints for Parents on the Choice of a Profession for their Sons when Starting in Life. Crown 8vo, 1s. cloth, 1s. 6d.

Davidson (Hugh Coleman).—Mr. Sadler's Daughters. With a Frontispiece by STANLEY WOOD. Crown 8vo, cloth extra, 3s. 6d.

Davies (Dr. N. E. Yorke-), Works by. Cr. 8vo, 1s. ea.; cl., 1s. 6d. ea.
One Thousand Medical Maxims and Surgical Hints.
Nursery Hints: A Mother's Guide in Health and Disease.
Foods for the Fat: A Treatise on Corpulency, and a Dietary for its Cure.
Aids to Long Life. Crown 8vo, 2s.; cloth limp, 2s. 6d.

Davies' (Sir John) Complete Poetical Works. Collected and Edited, with Introduction and Notes, by Rev. A. B. GROSART, D.D. Two Vols., crown 8vo, cloth, 12s.

Dawson (Erasmus, M.B.).—The Fountain of Youth. Crown 8vo, cloth extra, with Two Illustrations by HUME NISBET, 3s. 6d.; post 8vo, illustrated boards, 2s.

De Guerin (Maurice), The Journal of. Edited by G. S. TREBUTIEN. With a Memoir by SAINTE-BEUVE. Translated from the 20th French Edition by JESSIE P. FROTHINGHAM. Fcap. 8vo, half-bound, 2s. 6d.

De Maistre (Xavier).—A Journey Round my Room. Translated by Sir HENRY ATTWELL. Post 8vo, cloth limp, 2s. 6d.

De Mille (James).—A Castle in Spain. Crown 8vo, cloth extra, with a Frontispiece 3s. 6d.; post 8vo, illustrated boards, 2s.

Derby (The): The Blue Ribbon of the Turf. With Brief Accounts of THE OAKS. By LOUIS HENRY CURZON. Crown 8vo, cloth limp, 2s. 6d.

Derwent (Leith), Novels by. Cr. 8vo, cl., 3s. 6d. ea.; post 8vo, 2s. ea.
Our Lady of Tears. | Circe's Lovers.

Dewar (T. R.).—A Ramble Round the Globe. With 220 Illustrations. Crown 8vo, cloth extra, 7s. 6d.

Dickens (Charles), Novels by. Post 8vo, illustrated boards, 2s. each.
Sketches by Boz. | Nicholas Nickleby. | Oliver Twist.
About England with Dickens. By ALFRED RIMMER. With 57 Illustrations by C. A. VANDER-
HOOF, ALFRED RIMMER, and others. Square 8vo, cloth extra, 7s. 6d.

Dictionaries.
A Dictionary of Miracles: Imitative, Realistic, and Dogmatic. By the Rev. E. C. BREWER,
LL.D. Crown 8vo, cloth extra, 7s. 6d.
The Reader's Handbook of Allusions, References, Plots, and Stories. By the Rev.
E. C. BREWER, LL.D. With an ENGLISH BIBLIOGRAPHY. Crown 8vo, cloth extra, 7s. 6d.
Authors and their Works, with the Dates. Crown 8vo, cloth limp, 2s.
Familiar Short Sayings of Great Men. With Historical and Explanatory Notes by SAMUEL
A. BENT, A.M. Crown 8vo, cloth extra, 7s. 6d.
The Slang Dictionary: Etymological, Historical, and Anecdotal. Crown 8vo, cloth, 6s. 6d.
Words, Facts, and Phrases: A Dictionary of Curious, Quaint, and Out-of-the-Way Matters. By
ELIEZER EDWARDS. Crown 8vo, cloth extra, 7s. 6d.

Diderot.—The Paradox of Acting. Translated, with Notes, by
WALTER HERRIES POLLOCK. With Preface by Sir HENRY IRVING. Crown 8vo, parchment, 4s. 6d.

Dobson (Austin), Works by.
Thomas Bewick and his Pupils. With 95 Illustrations. Square 8vo, cloth, 6s.
Four Frenchwomen. With Four Portraits. Crown 8vo, buckram, gilt top, 6s.
Eighteenth Century Vignettes. TWO SERIES Crown 8vo, buckram, 6s. each.—A THIRD
SERIES is in preparation.

Dobson (W. T.).—Poetical Ingenuities and Eccentricities. Post
8vo, cloth limp, 2s. 6d.

Donovan (Dick), Detective Stories by.
Post 8vo, illustrated boards, 2s. each; cloth limp, 2s. 6d. each.

The Man-Hunter. | Wanted.   A Detective's Triumphs.
Caught at Last.   In the Grip of the Law.
Tracked and Taken.   From Information Received.
Who Poisoned Hetty Duncan?   Link by Link. | Dark Deeds.
Suspicion Aroused.   Riddles Read.

Crown 8vo, cloth extra, 3s. 6d. each; post 8vo, illustrated boards, 2s. each; cloth, 2s. 6d. each.
The Man from Manchester. With 23 Illustrations.
Tracked to Doom. With Six full-page Illustrations by GORDON BROWNE.

The Mystery of Jamaica Terrace. Crown 8vo, cloth, 3s. 6d.

Doyle (A. Conan).—The Firm of Girdlestone. Cr. 8vo, cl., 3s. 6d.

Dramatists, The Old. Crown 8vo, cl. ex., with Portraits, 6s. per Vol.
Ben Jonson's Works. With Notes, Critical and Explanatory, and a Biographical Memoir by
WILLIAM GIFFORD. Edited by Colonel CUNNINGHAM. Three Vols.
Chapman's Works. Three Vols. Vol. I. contains the Plays complete; Vol. II., Poems and Minor
Translations, with an Essay by A. C. SWINBURNE; Vol. III., Translations of the Iliad and Odyssey.
Marlowe's Works. Edited, with Notes, by Colonel CUNNINGHAM. One Vol.
Massinger's Plays. From GIFFORD'S Text. Edited by Colonel CUNNINGHAM. One Vol.

Duncan (Sara Jeannette: Mrs. EVERARD COTES), Works by.
Crown 8vo, cloth extra, 7s. 6d. each.
A Social Departure. With 111 Illustrations by F. H. TOWNSEND.
An American Girl in London. With 80 Illustrations by F. H. TOWNSEND.
The Simple Adventures of a Memsahib. With 37 Illustrations by F. H. TOWNSEND.

Crown 8vo, cloth extra, 3s. 6d. each.
A Daughter of To-Day. | Vernon's Aunt. With 47 Illustrations by HAL HURST.

Dyer (T. F. Thiselton).—The Folk-Lore of Plants. Cr. 8vo, cl., 6s.

Early English Poets. Edited, with Introductions and Annotations,
by Rev. A. B. GROSART, D.D. Crown 8vo, cloth boards, 6s. per Volume.
Fletcher's (Giles) Complete Poems. One Vol.
Davies' (Sir John) Complete Poetical Works. Two Vols.
Herrick's (Robert) Complete Collected Poems. Three Vols.
Sidney's (Sir Philip) Complete Poetical Works. Three Vols.

Edgcumbe (Sir E. R. Pearce).—Zephyrus: A Holiday in Brazil
and on the River Plate. With 41 Illustrations. Crown 8vo, cloth extra, 5s.

Edison, The Life and Inventions of Thomas A. By W. K. L. and
ANTONIA DICKSON. With 200 Illustrations by R. F. OUTCALT, &c. Demy 4to, cloth gilt.

Edwardes (Mrs. Annie), Novels by.
Post 8vo, illustrated boards, 2s. each.
Archie Lovell. | A Point of Honour.

Edwards (Ellezer).—Words, Facts, and Phrases: A Dictionary
of Curious Quaint, and Out-of-the-Way Matters. Crown 8vo, cloth, 7s. 6d.

Edwards (M. Betham-), Novels by.
Kitty. Post 8vo, boards, 2s.; cloth, 2s. 6d. | Felicia. Post 8vo, illustrated boards, 2s.

Egerton (Rev. J. C., M.A.).—Sussex Folk and Sussex Ways.
With Introduction by Rev. Dr. H. WACE, and Four Illustrations. Crown 8vo, cloth extra, 5s.

Eggleston (Edward).—Roxy: A Novel. Post 8vo, illust. boards, 2s.

Englishman's House, The: A Practical Guide for Selecting or Build-
ing a House. By C. J. RICHARDSON. Coloured Frontispiece and 534 Illusts. Cr. 8vo, cloth, 7s. 6d.

Ewald (Alex. Charles, F.S.A.), Works by.
The Life and Times of Prince Charles Stuart, Count of Albany (THE YOUNG PRETEN-
DER). With a Portrait. Crown 8vo, cloth extra, 7s. 6d.
Stories from the State Papers. With Autotype Frontispiece. Crown 8vo, cloth, 6s.

Eyes, Our: How to Preserve Them. By JOHN BROWNING. Cr. 8vo, 1s.

Familiar Short Sayings of Great Men. By SAMUEL ARTHUR BENT,
A.M. Fifth Edition, Revised and Enlarged. Crown 8vo, cloth extra, 7s. 6d.

Faraday (Michael), Works by. Post 8vo, cloth extra, 4s. 6d. each.
The Chemical History of a Candle: Lectures delivered before a Juvenile Audience. Edited
by WILLIAM CROOKES, F.C.S. With numerous Illustrations.
On the Various Forces of Nature, and their Relations to each other. Edited by
WILLIAM CROOKES, F.C.S. With Illustrations.

Farrer (J. Anson), Works by.
Military Manners and Customs. Crown 8vo, cloth extra, 6s.
War: Three Essays, reprinted from 'Military Manners and Customs.' Crown 8vo, 1s.; cloth, 1s. 6d.

Fenn (G. Manville), Novels by.
Crown 8vo, cloth extra, 3s. 6d. each; post 8vo, illustrated boards, 2s. each.
The New Mistress. | Witness to the Deed.
The Tiger Lily: A Tale of Two Passions.
The White Virgin. Crown 8vo, cloth extra, 3s. 6d.

Fin-Bec.—The Cupboard Papers: Observations on the Art of Living
and Dining. Post 8vo, cloth limp, 2s. 6d.

Fireworks, The Complete Art of Making; or, The Pyrotechnist's
Treasury. By THOMAS KENTISH. With 267 Illustrations. Crown 8vo, cloth, 5s.

First Book, My. By WALTER BESANT, JAMES PAYN, W. CLARK RUS-
SELL, GRANT ALLEN, HALL CAINE, GEORGE R. SIMS, RUDYARD KIPLING, A. CONAN DOYLE,
M. E. BRADDON, F. W. ROBINSON, H. RIDER HAGGARD, R. M. BALLANTYNE, I. ZANGWILL,
MORLEY ROBERTS, D. CHRISTIE MURRAY, MARY CORELLI, J. K. JEROME, JOHN STRANGE
WINTER, BRET HARTE, 'Q.,' ROBERT BUCHANAN, and R. L. STEVENSON. With a Prefatory Story
by JEROME K. JEROME, and 185 Illustrations. Small demy 8vo, cloth extra, 7s. 6d.

Fitzgerald (Percy), Works by.
The World Behind the Scenes. Crown 8vo, cloth extra, 3s. 6d.
Little Essays: Passages from the Letters of CHARLES LAMB. Post 8vo, cloth, 2s. 6d.
A Day's Tour: A Journey through France and Belgium. With Sketches. Crown 4to, 1s.
Fatal Zero. Crown 8vo, cloth extra, 3s. 6d.; post 8vo, illustrated boards, 2s.

Post 8vo, illustrated boards, 2s. each.
Bella Donna. | The Lady of Brantome. | The Second Mrs. Tillotson.
Polly. | Never Forgotten. | Seventy-five Brooke Street.

The Life of James Boswell (of Auchinleck). With Illusts. Two Vols., demy 8vo, cloth, 24s.
The Savoy Opera. With 60 Illustrations and Portraits. Crown 8vo, cloth, 3s. 6d.
Sir Henry Irving: Twenty Years at the Lyceum. With Portrait. Crown 8vo, 1s.; cloth, 1s. 6d.

Flammarion (Camille), Works by.
Popular Astronomy: A General Description of the Heavens. Translated by J. ELLARD GORE,
F.R.A.S. With Three Plates and 288 Illustrations. Medium 8vo, cloth, 16s.
Urania: A Romance. With 87 Illustrations. Crown 8vo, cloth extra, 5s.

Fletcher's (Giles, B.D.) Complete Poems: Christ's Victorie in
Heaven, Christ's Victorie on Earth, Christ's Triumph over Death, and Minor Poems. With Notes by
Rev. A. B. GROSART, D.D. Crown 8vo, cloth boards, 6s.

Fonblanque (Albany).—Filthy Lucre. Post 8vo, illust. boards, 2s.

Francillon (R. E.), Novels by.
Crown 8vo, cloth extra, 3s. 6d. each; post 8vo, illustrated boards, 2s. each.
One by One.	**A Real Queen.**	**A Dog and his Shadow.**
Ropes of Sand. Illustrated.		

Post 8vo, illustrated boards, 2s. each.
Queen Cophetua.	**Olympia.**	**Romances of the Law.**	**King or Knave?**

Jack Doyle's Daughter. Crown 8vo, cloth, 3s. 6d.
Esther's Glove. Fcap. 8vo, picture cover, 1s.

Frederic (Harold), Novels by. Post 8vo, illust. boards, 2s. each.
Seth's Brother's Wife. | **The Lawton Girl.**

French Literature, A History of. By HENRY VAN LAUN. Three
Vols., demy 8vo, cloth boards, 7s. 6d. each.

Friswell (Hain).—One of Two: A Novel. Post 8vo, illust. bds., 2s.

Frost (Thomas), Works by. Crown 8vo, cloth extra, 3s. 6d. each.
Circus Life and Circus Celebrities. | **Lives of the Conjurers.**
The Old Showmen and the Old London Fairs.

Fry's (Herbert) Royal Guide to the London Charities. Edited
by JOHN LANE. Published Annually. Crown 8vo, cloth, 1s. 6d.

Gardening Books. Post 8vo, 1s. each; cloth limp. 1s. 6d. each.
A Year's Work in Garden and Greenhouse. By GEORGE GLENNY.
Household Horticulture. By TOM and JANE JERROLD. Illustrated.
The Garden that Paid the Rent. By TOM JERROLD.

My Garden Wild. By FRANCIS G. HEATH. Crown 8vo, cloth extra, 6s.

Gardner (Mrs. Alan).—Rifle and Spear with the Rajpoots: Being
the Narrative of a Winter's Travel and Sport in Northern India. With numerous Illustrations by the
Author and F. H. TOWNSEND. Demy 4to, half-bound, 21s.

Garrett (Edward).—The Capel Girls: A Novel. Crown 8vo, cloth
extra, with two Illustrations, 3s. 6d.; post 8vo, illustrated boards, 2s.

Gaulot (Paul).—The Red Shirts: A Story of the Revolution. Translated by JOHN DE VILLIERS. With a Frontispiece by STANLEY WOOD. Crown 8vo, cloth, 3s. 6d.

Gentleman's Magazine, The. 1s. Monthly. Contains Stories,
Articles upon Literature, Science, Biography, and Art, and 'Table Talk' by SYLVANUS URBAN.
. Bound Volumes for recent years kept in stock, 8s. 6d. each. Cases for binding, 2s.

Gentleman's Annual, The. Published Annually in November. 1s.

German Popular Stories. Collected by the Brothers GRIMM and
Translated by EDGAR TAYLOR. With Introduction by JOHN RUSKIN, and 22 Steel Plates after
GEORGE CRUIKSHANK. Square 8vo, cloth, 6s. 6d.; gilt edges, 7s. 6d.

Gibbon (Charles), Novels by.
Crown 8vo, cloth extra, 3s. 6d. each; post 8vo, illustrated boards, 2s. each.
Robin Gray. Frontispiece. | **The Golden Shaft.** Frontispiece. | **Loving a Dream.**

Post 8vo, illustrated boards, 2s. each.
The Flower of the Forest.	**In Love and War.**
The Dead Heart.	**A Heart's Problem.**
For Lack of Gold.	**By Mead and Stream.**
What Will the World Say?	**The Braes of Yarrow.**
For the King.	**A Hard Knot.**	**Fancy Free.**	**Of High Degree.**
Queen of the Meadow.	**In Honour Bound.**
In Pastures Green.	**Heart's Delight.**	**Blood-Money.**

Gibney (Somerville).—Sentenced! Crown 8vo, 1s.; cloth, 1s. 6d.

Gilbert (W. S.), Original Plays by. In Three Series, 2s. 6d. each.
The FIRST SERIES contains: The Wicked World—Pygmalion and Galatea—Charity—The Princess—
The Palace of Truth—Trial by Jury.
The SECOND SERIES: Broken Hearts—Engaged—Sweethearts—Gretchen—Dan'l Druce—Tom Cobb
—H.M.S. 'Pinafore'—The Sorcerer—The Pirates of Penzance.
The THIRD SERIES: Comedy and Tragedy—Foggerty's Fairy—Rosencrantz and Guildenstern—
Patience—Princess Ida—The Mikado—Ruddigore—The Yeomen of the Guard—The Gondoliers—
The Mountebanks—Utopia.

Eight Original Comic Operas written by W. S. GILBERT. Containing: The Sorcerer—H.M.S.
'Pinafore'—The Pirates of Penzance—Iolanthe—Patience—Princess Ida—The Mikado—Trial by
Jury. Demy 8vo, cloth limp, 2s. 6d.

The Gilbert and Sullivan Birthday Book: Quotations for Every Day in the Year, selected
from Plays by W. S. GILBERT set to Music by Sir A. SULLIVAN. Compiled by ALEX. WATSON.
Royal 16mo, Japanese leather, 2s. 6d.

Gilbert (William), Novels by. Post 8vo, illustrated bds., 2s. each.
Dr. Austin's Guests. | James Duke, Costermonger.
The Wizard of the Mountain.

Glanville (Ernest), Novels by.
Crown 8vo, cloth extra, 3s. 6d. each; post 8vo, illustrated boards, 2s. each.
The Lost Heiress: A Tale of Love, Battle, and Adventure. With Two Illustrations by H. NISBET.
The Fossicker: A Romance of Mashonaland. With Two Illustrations by HUME NISBET.
A Fair Colonist. With a Frontispiece by STANLEY WOOD.

The Golden Rock. With a Frontispiece by STANLEY WOOD. Crown 8vo, cloth extra, 3s. 6d.
Kloof Yarns. Crown 8vo, picture cover, 1s.; cloth, 1s. 6d. [Shortly.

Glenny (George).—A Year's Work In Garden and Greenhouse :
Practical Advice as to the Management of the Flower, Fruit, and Frame Garden. Post 8vo, 1s.; cloth, 1s. 6d.

Godwin (William).—Lives of the Necromancers. Post 8vo, cl., 2s.

Golden Treasury of Thought, The : An Encyclopædia of QUOTA-
TIONS. Edited by THEODORE TAYLOR. Crown 8vo, cloth gilt, 7s. 6d.

Gontaut, Memoirs of the Duchesse de (Gouvernante to the Chil-
dren of France), 1773-1836. With Two Photogravures. Two Vols., demy 8vo, cloth extra, 21s.

Goodman (E. J.).—The Fate of Herbert Wayne. Cr. 8vo, 3s. 6d.

Graham (Leonard).—The Professor's Wife : A Story. Fcp. 8vo, 1s.

Greeks and Romans, The Life of the, described from Antique
Monuments. By ERNST GUHL and W. KONER. Edited by Dr. F. HUEFFER. With 545 Illustrations. Large crown 8vo, cloth extra, 7s. 6d.

Greenwood (James), Works by. Crown 8vo, cloth extra, 3s. 6d. each.
The Wilds of London. | Low-Life Deeps.

Greville (Henry), Novels by.
Nikanor. Translated by ELIZA E. CHASE. Post 8vo, illustrated boards, 2s.
A Noble Woman. Crown 8vo, cloth extra, 5s.; post 8vo, illustrated boards, 2s.

Griffith (Cecil).—Corinthia Marazion : A Novel. Crown 8vo, cloth
extra, 3s. 6d.; post 8vo, illustrated boards, 2s.

Grundy (Sydney).—The Days of his Vanity : A Passage in the
Life of a Young Man. Crown 8vo, cloth extra, 3s. 6d.; post 8vo, illustrated boards, 2s.

Habberton (John, Author of ' Helen's Babies '), **Novels by.**
Post 8vo, illustrated boards, 2s. each; cloth limp, 2s. 6d. each.
Brueton's Bayou. | Country Luck.

Hair, The : Its Treatment in Health, Weakness, and Disease. Translated from the German of Dr. J. PINCUS. Crown 8vo, 1s.; cloth, 1s. 6d.

Hake (Dr. Thomas Gordon), Poems by. Cr. 8vo, cl. ex., 6s. each.
New Symbols. | Legends of the Morrow. | The Serpent Play.
Maiden Ecstasy. Small 4to, cloth extra, 8s.

Hall (Owen).—The Track of a Storm. Crown 8vo, cloth, 6s.

Hall (Mrs. S. C.).—Sketches of Irish Character. With numerous
Illustrations on Steel and Wood by MACLISE, GILBERT, HARVEY, and GEORGE CRUIKSHANK.
Small demy 8vo, cloth extra, 7s. 6d.

Halliday (Andrew).—Every-day Papers. Post 8vo, boards, 2s.

Handwriting, The Philosophy of. With over 100 Facsimiles and
Explanatory Text. By DON FELIX DE SALAMANCA. Post 8vo, cloth limp, 2s. 6d.

Hanky-Panky : Easy and Difficult Tricks, White Magic, Sleight of
Hand, &c. Edited by W. H. CREMER. With 200 Illustrations. Crown 8vo, cloth extra, 4s. 6d.

Hardy (Lady Duffus).—Paul Wynter's Sacrifice. Post 8vo, bds., 2s.

Hardy (Thomas).—Under the Greenwood Tree. Crown 8vo, cloth
extra, with Portrait and 15 Illustrations, 3s. 6d.; post 8vo, illustrated boards, 2s.; cloth limp, 2s. 6d.

Harper (Charles G.), Works by. Demy 8vo, cloth extra, 16s. each.
The Brighton Road. With Photogravure Frontispiece and 90 Illustrations.
From Paddington to Penzance : The Record of a Summer Tramp. With 10 Illustrations.

Harwood (J. Berwick).—The Tenth Earl. Post 8vo, boards, 2s.

Harte's (Bret) Collected Works. Revised by the Author. LIBRARY
EDITION, in Eight Volumes, crown 8vo, cloth extra, 6s. each.
Vol. I. COMPLETE POETICAL AND DRAMATIC WORKS. With Steel-plate Portrait.
" II. THE LUCK OF ROARING CAMP—BOHEMIAN PAPERS—AMERICAN LEGENDS.
" III. TALES OF THE ARGONAUTS—EASTERN SKETCHES.
" IV. GABRIEL CONROY. | Vol. V. STORIES—CONDENSED NOVELS, &c.
" VI. TALES OF THE PACIFIC SLOPE.
" VII. TALES OF THE PACIFIC SLOPE—II. With Portrait by JOHN PETTIE, R.A.
" VIII. TALES OF THE PINE AND THE CYPRESS.

The Select Works of Bret Harte, in Prose and Poetry. With Introductory Essay by J. M.
BELLEW, Portrait of the Author, and 50 Illustrations. Crown 8vo, cloth extra, 7s. 6d.
Bret Harte's Poetical Works. Printed on hand-made paper. Crown 8vo, buckram, 4s. 6d.
The Queen of the Pirate Isle. With 28 Original Drawings by KATE GREENAWAY, reproduced
in Colours by EDMUND EVANS. Small 4to, cloth, 5s.

Crown 8vo, cloth extra, 3s. 6d. each ; post 8vo, picture boards, 2s. each.
A Waif of the Plains. With 60 Illustrations by STANLEY L. WOOD.
A Ward of the Golden Gate. With 59 Illustrations by STANLEY L. WOOD.

Crown 8vo, cloth extra, 3s. 6d. each.
A Sappho of Green Springs, &c. With Two Illustrations by HUME NISBET.
Colonel Starbottle's Client, and Some Other People. With a Frontispiece.
Susy: A Novel. With Frontispiece and Vignette by J. A. CHRISTIE.
Sally Dows, &c. With 47 Illustrations by W. D. ALMOND and others.
A Protégee of Jack Hamlin's. With 26 Illustrations by W. SMALL and others.
The Bell-Ringer of Angel's, &c. With 39 Illustrations by DUDLEY HARDY and others.
Clarence: A Story of the American War. With Eight Illustrations by A. JULE GOODMAN.

Post 8vo, illustrated boards, 2s. each.
Gabriel Conroy. | **The Luck of Roaring Camp, &c.**
An Heiress of Red Dog, &c. | **Californian Stories.**

Post 8vo, illustrated boards, 2s. each ; cloth, 2s. 6d. each.
Flip. | **Maruja.** | **A Phyllis of the Sierras.**

Fcap. 8vo, picture cover, 1s. each.
Snow-Bound at Eagle's. | **Jeff Briggs's Love Story.**

Hawels (Mrs. H. R.), Books by.
The Art of Beauty. With Coloured Frontispiece and 91 Illustrations. Square 8vo, cloth bds., 6s.
The Art of Decoration. With Coloured Frontispiece and 74 Illustrations. Sq. 8vo, cloth bds., 6s.
The Art of Dress. With 32 Illustrations. Post 8vo, 1s. ; cloth, 1s. 6d.
Chaucer for Schools. Demy 8vo, cloth limp, 2s. 6d.
Chaucer for Children. With 38 Illustrations (8 Coloured). Crown 4to, cloth extra, 3s. 6d.

Hawels (Rev. H. R., M.A.), Books by.
American Humorists: WASHINGTON IRVING, OLIVER WENDELL HOLMES, JAMES RUSSELL
LOWELL, ARTEMUS WARD, MARK TWAIN, and BRET HARTE. Third Edition. Crown 8vo,
cloth extra, 6s.
Travel and Talk, 1885, 1893, 1895: America—New Zealand—Tasmania—Ceylon. With Pho-
togravure Frontispieces. Two Vols., crown 8vo, cloth, 21s. [Shortly.

Hawthorne (Julian), Novels by.
Crown 8vo, cloth extra, 3s. 6d. each ; post 8vo, illustrated boards, 2s. each.
Garth. | **Ellice Quentin.** | **Beatrix Randolph.** With Four Illusts.
Sebastian Strome. | | **David Poindexter's Disappearance.**
Fortune's Fool. | **Dust.** Four Illusts. | **The Spectre of the Camera.**

Post 8vo, illustrated boards, 2s. each.
Miss Cadogna. | **Love — or a Name.**
Mrs. Gainsborough's Diamonds. Fcap. 8vo, illustrated cover, 1s.

Hawthorne (Nathaniel).—Our Old Home. Annotated with Pas-
sages from the Author's Note-books, and Illustrated with 31 Photogravures. Two Vols., cr. 8vo, 15s.

Heath (Francis George).—My Garden Wild, and What I Grew
There. Crown 8vo, cloth extra, gilt edges, 6s.

Helps (Sir Arthur), Works by. Post 8vo, cloth limp, 2s. 6d. each.
Animals and their Masters. | **Social Pressure.**
Ivan de Biron: A Novel. Crown 8vo, cloth extra, 3s. 6d. ; post 8vo, illustrated boards, 2s.

Henderson (Isaac). — Agatha Page: A Novel. Cr. 8vo, cl., 3s. 6d.

Henty (G. A.), Novels by.
Rujub the Juggler. With Eight Illustrations by STANLEY L. WOOD. Crown 8vo, cloth, 3s. 6d. ;
post 8vo, illustrated boards, 2s.
Dorothy's Double. Crown 8vo, cloth, 3s. 6d.

Herman (Henry).—A Leading Lady. Post 8vo, bds., 2s. ; cl., 2s. 6d.

Herrick's (Robert) Hesperides, Noble Numbers, and Complete
Collected Poems. With Memorial-Introduction and Notes by the Rev. A. B. GROSART, D.D.,
Steel Portrait, &c. Three Vols., crown 8vo, cloth boards, 18s.

Hertzka (Dr. Theodor).—Freeland: A Social Anticipation. Trans-
lated by ARTHUR RANSOM. Crown 8vo, cloth extra, 6s.

Hesse-Wartegg (Chevalier Ernst von).— Tunis: The Land and
the People. With 22 Illustrations. Crown 8vo, cloth extra, 3s. 6d.

Hill (Headon).—Zambra the Detective. Post 8vo, bds., 2s.; cl., 2s. 6d

Hill (John), Works by.
Treason-Felony. Post 8vo, boards, 2s. | The Common Ancestor. Cr. 8vo, cloth, 3s 6d.

Hindley (Charles), Works by.
Tavern Anecdotes and Sayings: Including Reminiscences connected with Coffee Houses,
Clubs, &c. With Illustrations. Crown 8vo, cloth extra, 3s. 6d.
The Life and Adventures of a Cheap Jack. Crown 8vo, cloth extra, 3s. 6d.

Hodges (Sydney).—When Leaves were Green. 3 vols., 15s. net.

Hoey (Mrs. Cashel).—The Lover's Creed. Post 8vo, boards, 2s.

Hollingshead (John).—Niagara Spray. Crown 8vo, 1s.

Holmes (Gordon, M.D.)—The Science of Voice Production and
Voice Preservation. Crown 8vo, 1s.; cloth, 1s. 6d.

Holmes (Oliver Wendell), Works by.
The Autocrat of the Breakfast-Table. Illustrated by J. GORDON THOMSON. Post 8vo, cloth
limp, 2s. 6d.—Another Edition, post 8vo, cloth, 2s.
The Autocrat of the Breakfast-Table and The Professor at the Breakfast-Table.
In One Vol. Post 8vo, half-bound, 2s.

Hood's (Thomas) Choice Works in Prose and Verse. With Life of
the Author, Portrait, and 200 Illustrations. Crown 8vo, cloth extra, 7s. 6d.
Hood's Whims and Oddities. With 85 Illustrations. Post 8vo, half-bound, 2s.

Hood (Tom).—From Nowhere to the North Pole: A Noah's
Arkæological Narrative. With 25 Illustrations by W. BRUNTON and E. C. BARNES. Cr. 8vo, cloth, 6s.

Hook's (Theodore) Choice Humorous Works; including his Ludi-
crous Adventures, Bons Mots, Puns, and Hoaxes. With Life of the Author, Portraits, Facsimiles, and
Illustrations. Crown 8vo, cloth extra, 7s. 6d.

Hooper (Mrs. Geo.).—The House of Raby. Post 8vo, boards, 2s.

Hopkins (Tighe). "Twixt Love and Duty.' Post 8vo, boards, 2s.

Horne (R. Hengist). — Orion: An Epic Poem. With Photograph
Portrait by SUMMERS. Tenth Edition. Crown 8vo, cloth extra, 7s.

Hungerford (Mrs., Author of 'Molly Bawn'), Novels by.
Post 8vo, Illustrated boards, 2s. each; cloth limp, 2s. 6d. each.

A Maiden All Forlorn.	In Durance Vile.	A Mental Struggle.
Marvel.	A Modern Circe.	

Crown 8vo, cloth extra, 3s. 6d. each; post 8vo, illustrated boards, 2s. each; cloth limp, 2s. 6d. each.

Lady Verner's Flight.	The Red-House Mystery.

The Three Graces. With 6 Illustrations. Crown 8vo, cloth extra, 3s. 6d.   [Shortly.
The Professor's Experiment. Three Vols., crown 8vo, 15s. net.
A Point of Conscience. Three Vols., crown 8vo, 15s. net.

Hunt's (Leigh) Essays: A Tale for a Chimney Corner, &c. Edited
by EDMUND OLLIER. Post 8vo, half-bound, 2s.

Hunt (Mrs. Alfred), Novels by.
Crown 8vo, cloth extra, 3s. 6d. each; post 8vo, illustrated boards, 2s. each.

The Leaden Casket.	Self-Condemned.	That Other Person.

Thornicroft's Model. Post 8vo, boards, 2s. | Mrs. Juliet. Crown 8vo, cloth extra, 3s. 6d.

Hutchison (W. M.). Hints on Colt-breaking. With 25 Illustrations. Crown 8vo, cloth extra, 3s. 6d.

Hydrophobia: An Account of M. PASTEUR's System; The Technique of
his Method, and Statistics. By RENAUD SUZOR, M.B. Crown 8vo, cloth extra, 6s.

Hyne (C. J. Cutcliffe).— Honour of Thieves. Cr. 8vo, cloth, 3s. 6d.

Idler (The): An Illustrated Magazine. Edited by J. K. JEROME. 1s.
Monthly. The First EIGHT VOLS. are now ready, cloth extra, 5s. each; Cases for Binding, 1s. 6d. each.

Impressions (The) of Aureole. Crown 8vo, printed on blush-rose paper and handsomely bound, 6s.

Indoor Paupers. By ONE OF THEM. Crown 8vo, 1s. ; cloth, 1s. 6d.

Ingelow (Jean).—Fated to be Free. Post 8vo, illustrated bds., 2s.

Innkeeper's Handbook (The) and Licensed Victualler's Manual. By J. TREVOR-DAVIES. Crown 8vo, 1s. : cloth, 1s. 6d.

Irish Wit and Humour, Songs of. Collected and Edited by A. PERCEVAL GRAVES. Post 8vo, cloth limp, 2s. 6d.

Irving (Sir Henry) : A Record of over Twenty Years at the Lyceum. By PERCY FITZGERALD. With Portrait. Crown 8vo, 1s. ; cloth, 1s. 6d.

James (C. T. C.). — A Romance of the Queen's Hounds. Post 8vo, picture cover, 1s. ; cloth limp, 1s. 6d.

Jameson (William).—My Dead Self. Post 8vo, bds., 2s. ; cl., 2s. 6d

Japp (Alex. H., LL.D.).—Dramatic Pictures, &c. Cr. 8vo, cloth, 5s.

Jay (Harriett), Novels by. Post 8vo, illustrated boards, 2s. each.
The Dark Colleen. | The Queen of Connaught.

Jefferies (Richard), Works by. Post 8vo, cloth limp, 2s. 6d. each.
Nature near London. | The Life of the Fields. | The Open Air.
, Also the HAND-MADE PAPER EDITION, crown 8vo, buckram, gilt top, 6s. each.

The Eulogy of Richard Jefferies. By Sir WALTER BESANT. With a Photograph Portrait. Crown 8vo, cloth extra, 6s.

Jennings (Henry J.), Works by.
Curiosities of Criticism. Post 8vo, cloth limp, 2s. 6d.
Lord Tennyson: A Biographical Sketch. With Portrait. Post 8vo, 1s. ; cloth, 1s. 6d.

Jerome (Jerome K.), Books by.
Stageland. With 64 Illustrations by J. BERNARD PARTRIDGE. Fcap. 4to, picture cover, 1s.
John Ingerfield, &c. With 9 Illusts. by A. S. BOYD and JOHN GULICH. Fcap. 8vo, pic. cov. 1s. 6d.
The Prude's Progress: A Comedy by J. K. JEROME and EDEN PHILLPOTTS. Cr. 8vo, 1s. 6d.

Jerrold (Douglas).—The Barber's Chair; and The Hedgehog Letters. Post 8vo, printed on laid paper and half-bound, 2s.

Jerrold (Tom), Works by. Post 8vo, 1s. ea. ; cloth limp, 1s. 6d. each.
The Garden that Paid the Rent.
Household Horticulture : A Gossip about Flowers. Illustrated.

Jesse (Edward).—Scenes and Occupations of a Country Life. Post 8vo, cloth limp, 2s.

Jones (William, F.S.A.), Works by. Cr. 8vo, cl. extra, 7s. 6d. each
Finger-Ring Lore : Historical, Legendary, and Anecdotal. With nearly 300 Illustrations. Second Edition, Revised and Enlarged.
Credulities, Past and Present. Including the Sea and Seamen, Miners, Talismans, Word and Letter Divination, Exorcising and Blessing of Animals, Birds, Eggs, Luck, &c. With Frontispiece.
Crowns and Coronations : A History of Regalia. With 100 Illustrations.

Jonson's (Ben) Works. With Notes Critical and Explanatory and a Biographical Memoir by WILLIAM GIFFORD. Edited by Colonel CUNNINGHAM. Three Vols. crown 8vo, cloth extra, 6s. each.

Josephus, The Complete Works of. Translated by WHISTON. Containing 'The Antiquities of the Jews' and 'The Wars of the Jews.' With 52 Illustrations and Maps. Two Vols., demy 8vo, half-bound, 12s. 6d.

Kempt (Robert).—Pencil and Palette : Chapters on Art and Artists. Post 8vo, cloth limp, 2s. 6d.

Kershaw (Mark). — Colonial Facts and Fictions : Humorous Sketches. Post 8vo, illustrated boards, 2s. ; cloth, 2s. 6d.

Keyser (Arthur).—Cut by the Mess. Crown 8vo, 1s. ; cloth, 1s. 6d.

King (R. Ashe), Novels by. Cr. 8vo, cl., 3s. 6d. ea ; post 8vo, bds., 2s. ea.
A Drawn Game. | 'The Wearing of the Green.'

Post 8vo, illustrated boards, 2s. each.
Passion's Slave. | Bell Barry.

Knight (William, M.R.C.S., and Edward, L.R.C.P.). — The Patient's Vade Mecum: How to Get Most Benefit from Medical Advice. Cr. 8vo, 1s.; cl., 1s. 6d.

Knights (The) of the Lion: A Romance of the Thirteenth Century. Edited, with an Introduction, by the MARQUESS OF LORNE, K.T. Crown 8vo, cloth extra, 6s.

Lamb's (Charles) Complete Works in Prose and Verse, including 'Poetry for Children' and 'Prince Dorus.' Edited, with Notes and Introduction, by R. H. SHEP-HERD. With Two Portraits and Facsimile of the 'Essay on Roast Pig.' Crown 8vo, half-bd., 7s. 6d.
   The Essays of Elia. Post 8vo, printed on laid paper and half-bound, 2s.
   Little Essays: Sketches and Characters by CHARLES LAMB, selected from his Letters by PERCY FITZGERALD. Post 8vo, cloth limp, 2s. 6d.
   The Dramatic Essays of Charles Lamb. With Introduction and Notes by BRANDER MAT-THEWS, and Steel-plate Portrait. Fcap. 8vo, half-bound, 2s. 6d.

Landor (Walter Savage). — Citation and Examination of William Shakspeare, &c., before Sir Thomas Lucy, touching Deer-stealing, 19th September, 1582. To which is added, **A Conference of Master Edmund Spenser** with the Earl of Essex, touching the State of Ireland, 1595. Fcap. 8vo, half-Roxburghe, 2s. 6d.

Lane (Edward William). — The Thousand and One Nights, com-monly called in England **The Arabian Nights' Entertainments.** Translated from the Arabic, with Notes. Illustrated with many hundred Engravings from Designs by HARVEY. Edited by EDWARD STANLEY POOLE. With Preface by STANLEY LANE POOLE. Three Vols., demy 8vo, cloth, 7s. 6d. ea.

Larwood (Jacob), Works by.
   The Story of the London Parks. With Illustrations. Crown 8vo, cloth extra, 3s. 6d.
   Anecdotes of the Clergy. Post 8vo, laid paper, half bound, 2s.

Post 8vo, cloth limp, 2s. 6d. each.

Forensic Anecdotes.	**Theatrical Anecdotes.**

Lehmann (R. C.), Works by. Post 8vo, 1s. each; cloth, 1s. 6d. each.
   Harry Fludyer at Cambridge.
   Conversational Hints for Young Shooters: A Guide to Polite Talk.

Leigh (Henry S.), Works by.
   Carols of Cockayne. Printed on hand-made paper, bound in buckram, 5s.
   Jeux d'Esprit. Edited by HENRY S. LEIGH. Post 8vo, cloth limp, 2s. 6d.

Leland (C. Godfrey). — A Manual of Mending and Repairing. With Diagrams. Crown 8vo, cloth, 5s.   [Shortly.

Lepelletier (Edmond). — Madame Sans-Gène. Translated from the French by JOHN DE VILLIERS. Crown 8vo, cloth extra, 3s. 6d.

Leys (John). — The Lindsays: A Romance. Post 8vo, illust. bds., 2s.

Lindsay (Harry). — Rhoda Roberts: A Welsh Mining Story. Crown 8vo, cloth, 3s. 6d.

Linton (E. Lynn), Works by.
   Crown 8vo, cloth extra, 3s. 6d. each; post 8vo, illustrated boards, 2s. each.

Patricia Kemball. | **Ione.**	**Under which Lord?** With 12 Illustrations.
The Atonement of Leam Dundas.	**'My Love!'** | **Sowing the Wind.**
The World Well Lost. With 12 Illusts.	**Paston Carew,** Millionaire and Miser.

The One Too Many.

Post 8vo, illustrated boards, 2s. each.

The Rebel of the Family.	**With a Silken Thread.**

Post 8vo, cloth limp, 2s. 6d. each.

Witch Stories.	**Ourselves:** Essays on Women.
Freeshooting: Extracts from the Works of Mrs. LYNN LINTON.	

Lucy (Henry W.). — Gideon Fleyce: A Novel. Crown 8vo, cloth extra, 3s. 6d.; post 8vo, illustrated boards, 2s.

Macalpine (Avery), Novels by.
   Teresa Itasca. Crown 8vo, cloth extra, 1s.
   Broken Wings. With Six Illustrations by W. J. HENNESSY. Crown 8vo, cloth extra, 6s.

MacColl (Hugh), Novels by.
   Mr. Stranger's Sealed Packet. Post 8vo, Illustrated boards, 2s.
   Ednor Whitlock. Crown 8vo, cloth extra, 6s.

Macdonell (Agnes). — Quaker Cousins. Post 8vo, boards, 2s.

MacGregor (Robert). — Pastimes and Players: Notes on Popular Games. Post 8vo, cloth limp, 2s. 6d.

Mackay (Charles, LL.D.). — Interludes and Undertones; or, Music at Twilight. Crown 8vo, cloth extra, 6s.

McCarthy (Justin, M.P.), Works by.

A History of Our Own Times, from the Accession of Queen Victoria to the General Election of 1880. Four Vols., demy 8vo, cloth extra, 12s. each.—Also a POPULAR EDITION, in Four Vols., crown 8vo, cloth extra, 6s. each.—And the JUBILEE EDITION, with an Appendix of Events to the end of 1886, in Two Vols., large crown 8vo, cloth extra, 7s. 6d. each.

A Short History of Our Own Times. One Vol., crown 8vo, cloth extra, 6s.—Also a CHEAP POPULAR EDITION, post 8vo, cloth limp, 2s. 6d.

A History of the Four Georges. Four Vols., demy 8vo, cl. ex., 12s. each.   [Vols. I. & II. *ready*

Crown 8vo, cloth extra, 3s. 6d. each; post 8vo, illustrated boards, 2s. each; cloth limp, 2s. 6d. each.

The Waterdale Neighbours.	Donna Quixote. With 12 Illustrations.
My Enemy's Daughter.	The Comet of a Season.
A Fair Saxon.	Maid of Athens. With 12 Illustrations.
Linley Rochford.	Camiola: A Girl with a Fortune.
Dear Lady Disdain.	The Dictator.
Miss Misanthrope. With 12 Illustrations.	Red Diamonds.

'**The Right Honourable.**' By JUSTIN McCARTHY, M.P., and Mrs. CAMPBELL PRAED. Crown 8vo, cloth extra, 6s.

McCarthy (Justin Huntly), Works by.

The French Revolution. (Constituent Assembly, 1789-91). Four Vols., demy 8vo, cloth extra, 12s. each.   Vols. I. & II. *ready;* Vols. III. & IV. *in the press*
An Outline of the History of Ireland. Crown 8vo, 1s.; cloth, 1s. 6d.
Ireland Since the Union: Sketches of Irish History, 1798-1886. Crown 8vo, cloth, 6s.

Hafiz in London: Poems. Small 8vo, gold cloth, 3s. 6d.

Our Sensation Novel. Crown 8vo, picture cover, 1s.; cloth limp, 1s. 6d.
Doom: An Atlantic Episode. Crown 8vo, picture cover, 1s.
Dolly: A Sketch. Crown 8vo, picture cover, 1s.; cloth limp, 1s. 6d.
Lily Lass: A Romance. Crown 8vo, picture cover, 1s.; cloth limp, 1s. 6d.
The Thousand and One Days. With Two Photogravures. Two Vols., crown 8vo, half-bd., 12s.
A London Legend. Crown 8vo, cloth, 3s. 6d.

MacDonald (George, LL.D.), Books by.

Works of Fancy and Imagination. Ten Vols., 16mo, cloth, gilt edges, in cloth case, 21s.; or the Volumes may be had separately, in Grolier cloth, at 2s. 6d. each.
Vol.   I. WITHIN AND WITHOUT.—THE HIDDEN LIFE.
  „   II. THE DISCIPLE.—THE GOSPEL WOMEN.—BOOK OF SONNETS.—ORGAN SONGS.
  „   III. VIOLIN SONGS.—SONGS OF THE DAYS AND NIGHTS.—A BOOK OF DREAMS.—ROADSIDE POEMS.—POEMS FOR CHILDREN.
  „   IV. PARABLES.—BALLADS.—SCOTCH SONGS.
  „ V. & VI. PHANTASTES: A Faerie Romance. | Vol. VII. THE PORTENT.
  „ VIII. THE LIGHT PRINCESS.—THE GIANT'S HEART.—SHADOWS.
  „   IX. CROSS PURPOSES.—THE GOLDEN KEY.—THE CARASOYN.—LITTLE DAYLIGHT.
  „   X. THE CRUEL PAINTER.—THE WOW O' RIVVEN.—THE CASTLE.—THE BROKEN SWORDS.—THE GRAY WOLF.—UNCLE CORNELIUS.

Poetical Works of George MacDonald. Collected and Arranged by the Author. Two Vols. crown 8vo, buckram, 12s.
A Threefold Cord. Edited by GEORGE MACDONALD. Post 8vo, cloth, 5s.

Phantastes: A Faerie Romance. With 25 Illustrations by J. BELL. Crown 8vo, cloth extra, 3s. 6d.
Heather and Snow: A Novel. Crown 8vo, cloth extra, 3s. 6d.; post 8vo, illustrated boards, 2s.
Lilith: A Romance. SECOND EDITION. Crown 8vo, cloth extra, 6s.

Maclise Portrait Gallery (The) of Illustrious Literary Charac-

ters: 85 Portraits by DANIEL MACLISE; with Memoirs—Biographical, Critical, Bibliographical, and Anecdotal—illustrative of the Literature of the former half of the Present Century, by WILLIAM BATES, B.A. Crown 8vo, cloth extra, 7s. 6d.

Macquoid (Mrs.), Works by. Square 8vo, cloth extra, 6s. each.

In the Ardennes. With 50 Illustrations by THOMAS R. MACQUOID.
Pictures and Legends from Normandy and Brittany. 34 Illusts. by T. R. MACQUOID.
Through Normandy. With 92 Illustrations by T. R. MACQUOID, and a Map.
Through Brittany. With 35 Illustrations by T. R. MACQUOID, and a Map.
About Yorkshire. With 67 Illustrations by T. R. MACQUOID.

Post 8vo, illustrated boards, 2s. each.

The Evil Eye, and other Stories.	Lost Rose, and other Stories.

Magician's Own Book, The: Performances with Eggs, Hats, &c.

Edited by W. H. CREMER. With 200 Illustrations. Crown 8vo, cloth extra, 4s. 6d.

Magic Lantern, The, and its Management : Including full Practical

Directions. By T. C. HEPWORTH. With 10 Illustrations. Crown 8vo, 1s.; cloth, 1s. 6d.

Magna Charta: An Exact Facsimile of the Original in the British

Museum, 3 feet by 2 feet, with Arms and Seals emblazoned in Gold and Colours, 5s.

Mallory (Sir Thomas). — Mort d'Arthur: The Stories of King

Arthur and of the Knights of the Round Table. (A Selection.) Edited by B. MONTGOMERIE RANKING. Post 8vo, cloth limp, 2s.

Mallock (W. H.), Works by.
The New Republic. Post 8vo, picture cover, 2s.; cloth limp, 2s. 6d.
The New Paul & Virginia: Positivism on an Island. Post 8vo, cloth, 2s. 6d.
A Romance of the Nineteenth Century. Crown 8vo, cloth 6s.; pos 8vo, illust. boards, 2s,

Poems. Small 4to, parchment, 8s.
Is Life Worth Living? Crown 8vo, cloth extra, 6s.

Mark Twain, Books by. Crown 8vo, cloth extra, 7s. 6d. each.
The Choice Works of Mark Twain. Revised and Corrected throughout by the Author. With Life, Portrait, and numerous Illustrations.
Roughing It; and The Innocents at Home. With 200 Illustrations by F. A. FRASER.
Mark Twain's Library of Humour. With 197 Illustrations.

Crown 8vo, cloth extra (Illustrated), 7s. 6d. each; post 8vo, Illustrated boards, 2s. each.
The Innocents Abroad; or, The New Pilgrim's Progress. With 234 Illustrations. (The Two Shilling Edition is entitled Mark Twain's Pleasure Trip.)
The Gilded Age. By MARK TWAIN and C. D. WARNER. With 212 Illustrations.
The Adventures of Tom Sawyer. With 111 Illustrations.
A Tramp Abroad. With 314 Illustrations.
The Prince and the Pauper. With 190 Illustrations.
Life on the Mississippi. With 300 Illustrations.
The Adventures of Huckleberry Finn. With 174 Illustrations by E. W. KEMBLE.
A Yankee at the Court of King Arthur. With 220 Illustrations by DAN BEARD.

Crown 8vo, cloth extra, 3s. 6d. each.
The American Claimant. With 81 Illustrations by HAL HURST and others.
Tom Sawyer Abroad. With 26 Illustrations by DAN. BEARD.
Pudd'nhead Wilson. With Portrait and Six Illustrations by LOUIS LOEB.
Tom Sawyer, Detective, &c. With numerous Illustrations. [Shortly.

The £1,000,000 Bank-Note. Crown 8vo, cloth, 3s. 6d.; post 8vo, picture boards 2s.

Post 8vo, Illustrated boards, 2s. each.
The Stolen White Elephant. | Mark Twain's Sketches.

Marks (H. S., R.A.), Pen and Pencil Sketches by. With Four Photogravures and 126 Illustrations. Two Vols. demy 8vo, cloth, 32s.

Marlowe's Works. Including his Translations. Edited, with Notes and Introductions, by Colonel CUNNINGHAM. Crown 8vo, cloth extra, 6s.

Marryat (Florence), Novels by. Post 8vo, illust. boards, 2s. each.
A Harvest of Wild Oats. | Fighting the Air.
Open! Sesame! | Written in Fire.

Massinger's Plays. From the Text of WILLIAM GIFFORD. Edited by Col. CUNNINGHAM. Crown 8vo, cloth extra, 6s.

Masterman (J.).—Half-a-Dozen Daughters. Post 8vo, boards, 2s.

Matthews (Brander).—A Secret of the Sea, &c. Post 8vo, illustrated boards, 2s.; cloth limp, 2s. 6d.

Mayhew (Henry).—London Characters, and the Humorous Side of London Life. With numerous Illustrations. Crown 8vo, cloth, 3s. 6d.

Meade (L. T.), Novels by.
A Soldier of Fortune. Crown 8vo, cloth, 3s. 6d.; post 8vo, illustrated board, 2s.
In an Iron Grip. Crown 8vo, cloth, 6s.
The Voice of the Charmer. Three Vols.

Merrick (Leonard).—The Man who was Good. Post 8vo, illustrated boards, 2s.

Mexican Mustang (On a), through Texas to the Rio Grande. By A. E. SWEET and J. ARMOY KNOX. With 265 Illustrations. Crown 8vo, cloth extra, 7s. 6d.

Middlemass (Jean), Novels by. Post 8vo, illust. boards, 2s. each.
Touch and Go. | Mr. Dorillion.

Miller (Mrs. F. Fenwick).—Physiology for the Young; or, The House of Life. With numerous Illustrations. Post 8vo, cloth limp, 2s. 6d.

Milton (J. L.), Works by. Post 8vo, 1s. each; cloth, 1s. 6d. each.
The Hygiene of the Skin. With Directions for Diet, Soaps, Baths, Wines, &c.
The Bath in Diseases of the Skin.
The Laws of Life, and their Relation to Diseases of the Skin.

Minto (Wm.).—Was She Good or Bad? Cr. 8vo, 1s.; cloth. 1s. 6d.

Mitford (Bertram), Novels by. Crown 8vo, cloth extra, 3s. 6d. each.
The Gun-Runner: A Romance of Zululand. With a Frontispiece by STANLEY L. WOOD.
The Luck of Gerard Ridgeley. With a Frontispiece by STANLEY L. WOOD.
The King's Assegal. With Six full-page Illustrations by STANLEY L. WOOD.
Renshaw Fanning's Quest. With a Frontispiece by STANLEY L. WOOD.

Molesworth (Mrs.), Novels by.
Hathercourt Rectory. Post 8vo, Illustrated boards, 2s.
That Girl in Black. Crown 8vo, cloth, 1s. 6d.

Moncrieff (W. D. Scott-).—The Abdication: An Historical Drama.
With Seven Etchings by JOHN PETTIE, W. Q. ORCHARDSON, J. MACWHIRTER, COLIN HUNTER,
R. MACBETH and TOM GRAHAM. Imperial 4to, buckram, 21s.

Moore (Thomas), Works by.
The Epicurean; and Alciphron. Post 8vo, half-bound, 2s.
Prose and Verse; including Suppressed Passages from the MEMOIRS OF LORD BYRON. Edited
by R. H. SHEPHERD. With Portrait. Crown 8vo, cloth extra, 7s. 6d.

Muddock (J. E.) Stories by.
Stories Weird and Wonderful. Post 8vo, illustrated boards, 2s.; cloth, 2s. 6d.
The Dead Man's Secret. With Frontispiece by F. BARNARD. Post 8vo, picture boards, 2s.
From the Bosom of the Deep. Post 8vo, illustrated boards, 2s.
Maid Marian and Robin Hood. With 12 Illusts. by STANLEY WOOD. Cr. 8vo, cloth extra, 3s. 6d.
Basile the Jester. With Frontispiece by STANLEY WOOD. Crown 8vo, cloth, 3s. 6d.

Murray (D. Christie), Novels by.

Crown 8vo, cloth extra, 3s. 6d. each; post 8vo, illustrated boards, 2s. each.

A Life's Atonement.	A Model Father.	First Person Singular.
Joseph's Coat. 12 Illusts.	Old Blazer's Hero.	Bob Martin's Little Girl.
Coals of Fire. 3 Illusts.	Cynic Fortune. Frontisp.	Time's Revenges.
Val Strange.	By the Gate of the Sea.	A Wasted Crime.
Hearts.	A Bit of Human Nature.	In Direst Peril.
The Way of the World.		

Mount Despair, &c. With Frontispiece by GRENVILLE MANTON. Crown 8vo, cloth, 3s. 6d.
The Making of a Novelist: An Experiment in Autobiography. With a Collotype Portrait and
Vignette. Crown 8vo, art linen, 6s.

Murray (D. Christie) and Henry Herman, Novels by.
Crown 8vo, cloth extra, 3s. 6d. each; post 8vo, illustrated boards, 2s. each.
One Traveller Returns. | The Bishops' Bible.
Paul Jones's Alias, &c. With Illustrations by A. FORESTIER and G. NICOLET.

Murray (Henry), Novels by.
Post 8vo, illustrated boards, 2s. each; cloth, 2s. 6d. each.
A Game of Bluff. | A Song of Sixpence.

Newbolt (Henry).—Taken from the Enemy. Fcp. 8vo, cloth, 1s. 6d.

Nisbet (Hume), Books by.
'Bail Up.' Crown 8vo, cloth extra, 3s. 6d.; post 8vo, illustrated boards, 2s.
Dr. Bernard St. Vincent. Post 8vo, illustrated boards, 2s.

Lessons in Art. With 21 Illustrations. Crown 8vo, cloth extra, 2s. 6d.
Where Art Begins. With 27 Illustrations. Square 8vo, cloth extra, 7s. 6d.

Norris (W. E.), Novels by. Crown 8vo, cloth, 3s. 6d. each.
Saint Ann's. | Billy Bellew. With Frontispiece.

O'Hanlon (Alice), Novels by. Post 8vo, illustrated boards, 2s. each.
The Unforeseen. | Chance? or Fate?

Ouida, Novels by. Cr. 8vo, cl, 3s. 6d. ea.; post 8vo, illust. bds., 2s. ea.

Held in Bondage.	Folle-Farine.	Moths.	Pipistrello.
Tricotrin.	A Dog of Flanders.	In Maremma.	Wanda.
Strathmore.	Pascarel.	Signa.	Bimbi.	Syrlin.
Chandos.	Two Wooden Shoes.	Frescoes.	Othmar.
Cecil Castlemaine's Gage	In a Winter City.	Princess Napraxine.
Under Two Flags.	Ariadne.	Friendship.	Guilderoy.	Ruffino.
Puck.	Idalia.	A Village Commune.	Two Offenders.

Square 8vo, cloth extra, 5s. each.
Bimbi. With Nine Illustrations by EDMUND H. GARRETT.
A Dog of Flanders, &c. With Six Illustrations by EDMUND H. GARRETT.

Santa Barbara, &c. Square 8vo, cloth, 6s.; crown 8vo, cloth, 3s. 6d.; post 8vo, illustrated boards, 2s.
Under Two Flags. POPULAR EDITION. Medium 8vo, 6d.; cloth, 1s. [Shortly.

Wisdom, Wit, and Pathos, selected from the Works of OUIDA by F. SYDNEY MORRIS. Post
8vo, cloth extra, 5s.—CHEAP EDITION, Illustrated boards, 2s.

Ohnet (Georges), Novels by. Post 8vo, illustrated boards, 2s. each.
Doctor Rameau. | A Last Love.

A Weird Gift. Crown 8vo, cloth, 3s. 6d.; post 8vo, picture boards, 2s.

Oliphant (Mrs.), Novels by. Post 8vo, illustrated boards, 2s. each.
The Primrose Path. | Whiteladies.
The Greatest Heiress in England.

O'Reilly (Mrs.).—Phœbe's Fortunes. Post 8vo, illust. boards, 2s.

Page (H. A.), Works by.
Thoreau: His Life and Aims. With Portrait. Post 8vo, cloth limp, 2s. 6d.
Animal Anecdotes. Arranged on a New Principle. Crown 8vo, cloth extra, 5s.

Pandurang Hari; or, Memoirs of a Hindoo. With Preface by Sir
BARTLE FRERE. Crown 8vo, cloth, 3s. 6d.; post 8vo, illustrated boards, 2s.

Pascal's Provincial Letters. A New Translation, with Historical
Introduction and Notes by T. M'CRIE, D.D. Post 8vo, cloth limp, 2s.

Paul (Margaret A.).—Gentle and Simple. Crown 8vo, cloth, with
Frontispiece by HELEN PATERSON, 3s. 6d.; post 8vo, illustrated boards, 2s.

Payn (James), Novels by.

Crown 8vo, cloth extra, 3s. 6d. each; post 8vo, illustrated boards, 2s. each.

Lost Sir Massingberd. | Holiday Tasks.
Walter's Word. | The Canon's Ward. With Portrait.
Less Black than We're Painted. | The Talk of the Town. With 12 Illusts.
By Proxy. | For Cash Only. | Glow-Worm Tales.
High Spirits. | The Mystery of Mirbridge.
Under One Roof. | The Word and the Will.
A Confidential Agent. With 12 Illusts. | The Burnt Million.
A Grape from a Thorn. With 12 Illusts. | Sunny Stories. | A Trying Patient.

Post 8vo, illustrated boards, 2s. each.

Humorous Stories. | From Exile. | Found Dead.
The Foster Brothers. | Gwendoline's Harvest.
The Family Scapegrace. | A Marine Residence.
Married Beneath Him. | Mirk Abbey.
Bentinck's Tutor. | Some Private Views.
A Perfect Treasure. | Not Wooed, But Won.
A County Family. | Two Hundred Pounds Reward.
Like Father, Like Son. | The Best of Husbands.
A Woman's Vengeance. | Halves.
Carlyon's Year. | Cecil's Tryst. | Fallen Fortunes.
Murphy's Master. | What He Cost Her.
At Her Mercy. | Kit: A Memory.
The Clyffards of Clyffe. | A Prince of the Blood.

In Peril and Privation. With 17 Illustrations. Crown 8vo, cloth, 3s. 6d.
Notes from the 'News.' Crown 8vo, portrait cover, 1s.; cloth, 1s. 6d.

Pennell (H. Cholmondeley), Works by. Post 8vo, cloth, 2s. 6d. ea.
Puck on Pegasus. With Illustrations.
Pegasus Re-Saddled. With Ten full-page Illustrations by G. DU MAURIER.
The Muses of Mayfair: Vers de Société. Selected by H. C. PENNELL.

Phelps (E. Stuart), Works by. Post 8vo, 1s. ea.; cloth, 1s. 6d. ea.
Beyond the Gates. | An Old Maid's Paradise. | Burglars in Paradise.

Jack the Fisherman. Illustrated by C. W. REED. Crown 8vo, 1s.; cloth, 1s. 6d.

Phil May's Sketch-Book. Containing 50 full-page Drawings. Imp.
4to, art canvas, gilt top, 10s. 6d.

Pirkis (C. L.), Novels by.
Trooping with Crows. Fcap. 8vo, picture cover, 1s.
Lady Lovelace. Post 8vo, illustrated boards, 2s.

Planche (J. R.), Works by.
The Pursuivant of Arms. With Six Plates and 2 Illustrations. Crown 8vo, cloth, 7s. 6d.
Songs and Poems, 1819-1879. With Introduction by Mrs. MACKARNESS. Crown 8vo, cloth, 6s.

Plutarch's Lives of Illustrious Men. With Notes and a Life of
Plutarch by JOHN and WM. LANGHORNE, and Portrait. Two Vols., demy 8vo, half bound, 10s. 6d.

Poe's (Edgar Allan) Choice Works in Prose and Poetry. With Introduction by CHARLES BAUDELAIRE, Portrait and Facsimiles. Crown 8vo, cloth, 7s. 6d.
The Mystery of Marie Roget, &c. Post 8vo, illustrated boards, 2s.

Pope's Poetical Works. Post 8vo, cloth limp, 2s.

Praed (Mrs. Campbell), Novels by. Post 8vo, illust. bds., 2s. each.
The Romance of a Station. | **The Soul of Countess Adrian.**
Crown 8vo, cloth, 3s. 6d. each : post 8vo, boards, 2s. each.
Outlaw and Lawmaker. | **Christina Chard.** With Frontispiece by W. PAGET.
Mrs. Tregaskiss. Three Vols., crown 8vo, 15s. net.

Price (E. C.), Novels by.
Crown 8vo, cloth extra, 3s. 6d. each; post 8vo, illustrated boards, 2s. each.
Valentina. | **The Foreigners.** | **Mrs. Lancaster's Rival.**
Gerald. Post 8vo, illustrated boards, 2s.

Princess Olga.—Radna: A Novel. Crown 8vo, cloth extra, 6s.

Proctor (Richard A., B.A.), Works by.
Flowers of the Sky. With 55 Illustrations. Small crown 8vo, cloth extra, 3s. 6d.
Easy Star Lessons. With Star Maps for every Night in the Year. Crown 8vo, cloth, 6s.
Familiar Science Studies. Crown 8vo, cloth extra, 6s.
Saturn and its System. With 13 Steel Plates. Demy 8vo, cloth extra, 10s. 6d.
Mysteries of Time and Space. With numerous Illustrations. Crown 8vo, cloth extra, 6s.
The Universe of Suns, &c. With numerous Illustrations. Crown 8vo, cloth extra, 6s.
Wages and Wants of Science Workers. Crown 8vo, 1s. 6d.

Pryce (Richard).—Miss Maxwell's Affections. Crown 8vo, cloth,
with Frontispiece by HAL LUDLOW, 3s. 6d.; post 8vo, illustrated boards, 2s.

Rambosson (J.).—Popular Astronomy. Translated by C. B. PIT-
MAN. With Coloured Frontispiece and numerous Illustrations. Crown 8vo, cloth extra, 7s. 6d.

Randolph (Lieut.-Col. George, U.S.A.). — Aunt Abigail Dykes:
A Novel. Crown 8vo, cloth extra, 7s. 6d.

Reade's (Charles) Novels.
Crown 8vo, cloth extra, mostly Illustrated, 3s. 6d. each; post 8vo, illustrated boards, 2s. each.
Peg Woffington. | **Christie Johnstone.** | **Hard Cash.** | **Griffith Gaunt.**
'It is Never Too Late to Mend.' | **Foul Play.** | **Put Yourself in His Place.**
The Course of True Love Never Did Run | **A Terrible Temptation.**
Smooth. | **A Simpleton.** | **The Wandering Heir.**
The Autobiography of a Thief; Jack of | **A Woman-Hater.**
all Trades; and James Lambert. | **Singleheart and Doubleface.**
Love Me Little, Love Me Long. | **Good Stories of Men and other Animals.**
The Double Marriage. | **The Jilt,** and other Stories.
The Cloister and the Hearth. | **A Perilous Secret.** | **Readiana.**

A New Collected LIBRARY EDITION, complete in Seventeen Volumes, set in new long primer type, printed on laid paper, and elegantly bound in cloth, price 3s. 6d. each, is now in course of publication. The volumes will appear in the following order.
1. **Peg Woffington; and Christie John-** 7. **Love Me Little, Love me Long.**
stone. 8. **The Double Marriage.** [April.
2. **Hard Cash.** 9. **Griffith Gaunt.** [May.
3. **The Cloister and the Hearth.** With a 10. **Foul Play.** [June.
Preface by Sir WALTER BESANT. 11. **Put Yourself in His Place.** [July.
4. **'It is Never too Late to Mend.'** 12. **A Terrible Temptation.** [Aug.
5. **The Course of True Love Never Did** 13. **A Simpleton.** [Sept.
Run Smooth; and Singleheart and 14. **A Woman-Hater.** [Oct.
Doubleface. 15. **The Jilt, and other Stories; and Good**
6. **The Autobiography of a Thief; Jack** **Stories of Men & other Animals.** [Nov.
of all Trades; A Hero and a Mar- 16. **A Perilous Secret.** [Dec.
tyr; and The Wandering Heir. 17. **Readiana; & Bible Characters.** [Jan. 97

POPULAR EDITIONS, medium 8vo, 6d. each; cloth, 1s. each.
'It is Never Too Late to Mend.' | **The Cloister and the Hearth.**
Peg Woffington; and Christie Johnstone.

'It is Never Too Late to Mend' and The Cloister and the Hearth in One Volume,
medium 8vo, cloth, 2s.

Christie Johnstone. With Frontispiece. Choicely printed in Elzevir style. Fcap. 8vo, half-Roxb. 2s. 6d.
Peg Woffington. Choicely printed in Elzevir style. Fcap. 8vo, half-Roxburghe, 2s. 6d.
The Cloister and the Hearth. In Four Vols., post 8vo, with an Introduction by Sir WALTER BE-
SANT, and a Frontispiece to each Vol., 14s. the set; and the ILLUSTRATED LIBRARY EDITION,
with Illustrations on every page, Two Vols., crown 8vo, cloth gilt, 4s. net.
Bible Characters. Fcap. 8vo, leatherette, 1s.
Selections from the Works of Charles Reade. With an Introduction by Mrs. ALEX. IRE-
LAND. Crown 8vo, buckram, with Portrait, 6s.; CHEAP EDITION, post 8vo, cloth limp, 2s. 6d.

Riddell (Mrs. J. H.), Novels by.
Weird Stories. Crown 8vo, cloth extra, 3s. 6d.; post 8vo, illustrated boards, 2s.

Post 8vo, illustrated boards, 2s. each.
The Uninhabited House. | **Fairy Water.**
The Prince of Wales's Garden Party. | **Her Mother's Darling.**
The Mystery in Palace Gardens. | **The Nun's Curse.** | **Idle Tales.**

Rimmer (Alfred), Works by. Square 8vo, cloth gilt, 7s. 6d. each.
Our Old Country Towns. With 55 Illustrations by the Author.
Rambles Round Eton and Harrow. With 50 Illustrations by the Author.
About England with Dickens. With 58 Illustrations by C. A. VANDERHOOF and A. RIMMER.

Rives (Amelie).—Barbara Dering. Crown 8vo, cloth extra, 3s. 6d. ;
post 8vo, illustrated boards, 2s.

Robinson Crusoe. By DANIEL DEFOE. With 37 Illustrations by
GEORGE CRUIKSHANK. Post 8vo, half-cloth, 2s. ; cloth extra, gilt edges, 2s. 6d.

Robinson (F. W.), Novels by.
Women are Strange. Post 8vo, Illustrated boards, 2s.
The Hands of Justice. Crown 8vo, cloth extra, 3s. 6d. ; post 8vo, Illustrated boards, 2s.

The Woman in the Dark. Two Vols., 10s. net.

Robinson (Phil), Works by. Crown 8vo, cloth extra, 6s. each.
The Poets' Birds. | The Poets' Beasts.
The Poets and Nature: Reptiles, Fishes, and Insects.

Rochefoucauld's Maxims and Moral Reflections. With Notes
and an Introductory Essay by SAINTE-BEUVE. Post 8vo, cloth limp, 2s.

Roll of Battle Abbey, The: A List of the Principal Warriors who
came from Normandy with William the Conqueror, 1066. Printed in Gold and Colours, 5s.

Rosengarten (A.).—A Handbook of Architectural Styles. Translated by W. COLLETT-SANDARS. With 639 Illustrations. Crown 8vo, cloth extra, 7s. 6d.

Rowley (Hon. Hugh), Works by. Post 8vo, cloth, 2s. 6d. each.
Puniana: Riddles and Jokes. With numerous Illustrations.
More Puniana. Profusely Illustrated.

Runciman (James), Stories by. Post 8vo, bds., 2s. ea ; cl., 2s. 6d. ea.
Skippers and Shellbacks. | Grace Balmaign's Sweetheart.
Schools and Scholars.

Russell (Dora), Novels by. Crown 8vo, cloth, 3s. 6d. each.
A Country Sweetheart. | The Drift of Fate. [Shortly.

Russell (W. Clark), Books and Novels by.
Crown 8vo, cloth extra, 6s. each ; post 8vo, Illustrated boards, 2s. each ; cloth limp, 2s. 6d. each.
Round the Galley-Fire. | A Book for the Hammock.
In the Middle Watch. | The Mystery of the 'Ocean Star.'
A Voyage to the Cape. | The Romance of Jenny Harlowe.

Crown 8vo, cloth extra, 3s. 6d. each ; post 8vo, Illustrated boards, 2s. each ; cloth limp, 2s. 6d. each.
An Ocean Tragedy. | My Shipmate Louise. | Alone on a Wide Wide Sea.

Crown 8vo, cloth, 3s. 6d. each.
Is He the Man? | The Phantom Death, &c. With Frontispiece.
The Good Ship 'Mohock.' | The Convict Ship. [Shortly.
On the Fo'k'sle Head. Post 8vo, Illustrated boards, 2s. ; cloth limp, 2s. 6d.
Heart of Oak. Three Vols., crown 8vo, 15s. net.
The Tale of the Ten. Three Vols., crown 8vo, 15s. net.

Saint Aubyn (Alan), Novels by.
Crown 8vo, cloth extra, 3s. 6d. each ; post 8vo, Illustrated boards, 2s. each.
A Fellow of Trinity. With a Note by OLIVER WENDELL HOLMES and a Frontispiece.
The Junior Dean. | The Master of St. Benedict's. | To His Own Master.
Orchard Damerel.

Fcap. 8vo, cloth boards, 1s. 6d. each.
The Old Maid's Sweetheart. | Modest Little Sara.

Crown 8vo, cloth extra, 3s. 6d. each.
In the Face of the World. | The Tremlett Diamonds. [Shortly.

Sala (George A.).—Gaslight and Daylight. Post 8vo, boards, 2s.

Sanson. — Seven Generations of Executioners: Memoirs of the
Sanson Family (1688 to 1847). Crown 8vo, cloth extra, 3s. 6d.

Saunders (John), Novels by.
Crown 8vo, cloth extra, 3s. 6d. each ; post 8vo, Illustrated boards, 2s. each.
Guy Waterman. | The Lion in the Path. | The Two Dreamers.
Bound to the Wheel. Crown 8vo, cloth extra, 3s. 6d.

Saunders (Katharine), Novels by.
Crown 8vo, cloth extra, 3s. 6d. each; post 8vo, illustrated boards, 2s. each.

Margaret and Elizabeth.
The High Mills.

Heart Salvage.
Sebastian.

Joan Merryweather. Post 8vo, illustrated boards, 2s.
Gideon's Rock. Crown 8vo, cloth extra, 3s. 6d.

Scotland Yard, Past and Present: Experiences of Thirty-seven Years.
By Ex-Chief-Inspector CAVANAGH. Post 8vo, illustrated boards, 2s.; cloth, 2s. 6d.

Secret Out, The: One Thousand Tricks with Cards; with Entertaining Experiments in Drawing-room or 'White' Magic. By W. H. CREMER. With 300 Illustrations. Crown 8vo, cloth extra, 4s. 6d.

Seguin (L. G.), Works by.
The Country of the Passion Play (Oberammergau) and the Highlands of Bavaria. With Map and 37 Illustrations. Crown 8vo, cloth extra, 3s. 6d.
Walks in Algiers. With Two Maps and 16 Illustrations. Crown 8vo, cloth extra, 6s.

Senior (Wm.).—By Stream and Sea. Post 8vo, cloth, 2s. 6d.

Sergeant (Adeline).—Dr. Endicott's Experiment. Crown 8vo, buckram, 3s. 6d.

Shakespeare for Children: Lamb's Tales from Shakespeare.
With Illustrations, coloured and plain, by J. MOYR SMITH. Crown 4to, cloth gilt, 3s. 6d.

Sharp (William).—Children of To-morrow. Crown 8vo, cloth, 6s.

Shelley's (Percy Bysshe) Complete Works in Verse and Prose.
Edited, Prefaced, and Annotated by R. HERNE SHEPHERD. Five Vols., crown 8vo, cloth, 3s. 6d. each.
Poetical Works, in Three Vols.:
Vol. I. Introduction by the Editor; Posthumous Fragments of Margaret Nicholson; Shelley's Correspondence with Stockdale; The Wandering Jew; Queen Mab, with the Notes; Alastor, and other Poems; Rosalind and Helen; Prometheus Unbound; Adonais, &c.
" II. Laon and Cythna; The Cenci; Julian and Maddalo; Swellfoot the Tyrant; The Witch of Atlas; Epipsychidion; Hellas.
" III. Posthumous Poems; The Masque of Anarchy; and other Pieces.
Prose Works, in Two Vols.:
Vol. I. The Two Romances of Zastrozzi and St. Irvyne; the Dublin and Marlow Pamphlets; A Refutation of Deism; Letters to Leigh Hunt, and some Minor Writings and Fragments.
" II. The Essays; Letters from Abroad; Translations and Fragments, edited by Mrs. SHELLEY. With a Biography of Shelley, and an Index of the Prose Works.
. Also a few copies of a LARGE-PAPER EDITION, 5 vols., cloth, £2 12s. 6d.

Sherard (R. H.).—Rogues: A Novel. Crown 8vo, 1s.; cloth, 1s. 6d.

Sheridan (General P. H.), Personal Memoirs of. With Portraits,
Maps, and Facsimiles. Two Vols., demy 8vo, cloth, 24s.

Sheridan's (Richard Brinsley) Complete Works, with Life and
Anecdotes. Including his Dramatic Writings, his Works in Prose and Poetry, Translations, Speeches, and Jokes. With 10 Illustrations. Crown 8vo, half-bound, 7s. 6d.
The Rivals. The School for Scandal, and other Plays. Post 8vo, half-bound, 2s.
Sheridan's Comedies: The Rivals and The School for Scandal. Edited, with an Introduction and Notes to each Play, and a Biographical Sketch, by BRANDER MATTHEWS. With Illustrations. Demy 8vo, half-parchment, 12s. 6d.

Sidney's (Sir Philip) Complete Poetical Works, including all
those in 'Arcadia.' With Portrait, Memorial-Introduction, Notes, &c., by the Rev. A. B. GROSART, D.D. Three Vols., crown 8vo, cloth boards, 18s.

Sims (George R.), Works by.
Post 8vo, illustrated boards, 2s. each; cloth limp, 2s. 6d. each.

Rogues and Vagabonds.
The Ring o' Bells.
Mary Jane's Memoirs.
Mary Jane Married.
Tinkletop's Crime.
Zeph: A Circus Story, &c.

Tales of To-day.
Dramas of Life. With 60 Illustrations.
Memoirs of a Landlady.
My Two Wives.
Scenes from the Show.
The Ten Commandments: Stories. [Shortly.

Crown 8vo, picture cover, 1s. each; cloth, 1s. 6d. each.
How the Poor Live; and Horrible London.
The Dagonet Reciter and Reader: Being Readings and Recitations in Prose and Verse, selected from his own Works by GEORGE R. SIMS.
The Case of George Candlemas. | Dagonet Ditties. (From The Referee.)

Dagonet Abroad. Crown 8vo, cloth, 3s. 6d.

Signboards : Their History, including Anecdotes of Famous Taverns and Remarkable Characters. By JACOB LARWOOD and JOHN CAMDEN HOTTEN. With Coloured Frontispiece and 94 Illustrations. Crown 8vo, cloth extra, 6d.

Sister Dora : A Biography. By MARGARET LONSDALE. With Four Illustrations. Demy 8vo, picture cover, 4d. ; cloth, 6d.

Sketchley (Arthur).—A Match in the Dark. Post 8vo, boards, 2s.

Slang Dictionary (The) : Etymological, Historical, and Anecdotal. Crown 8vo, cloth extra, 6s. 6d.

Smart (Hawley).—Without Love or Licence : A Novel. Crown 8vo, cloth extra, 3s. 6d. ; post 8vo, illustrated boards, 2s.

Smith (J. Moyr), Works by.
The Prince of Argolis. With 130 Illustrations. Post 8vo, cloth extra, 3s. 6d.
The Wooing of the Water Witch. With numerous Illustrations. Post 8vo, cloth, 6s.

Society in London. Crown 8vo, 1s. ; cloth, 1s. 6d.

Society in Paris: The Upper Ten Thousand. A Series of Letters from Count PAUL VASILI to a Young French Diplomat. Crown 8vo, cloth, 6s.

Somerset (Lord Henry).—Songs of Adieu. Small 4to, Jap. vel., 6s.

Spalding (T. A., LL.B.).— Elizabethan Demonology: An Essay on the Belief in the Existence of Devils. Crown 8vo, cloth extra, 5s.

Speight (T. W.), Novels by.
Post 8vo, illustrated boards, 2s. each.
The Mysteries of Heron Dyke. | Back to Life.
By Devious Ways, &c. | The Loudwater Tragedy.
Hoodwinked ; & Sandycroft Mystery. | Burgo's Romance.
The Golden Hoop. | Quittance in Full.

Post 8vo, cloth limp, 1s. 6d. each.
A Barren Title. | Wife or No Wife?

Crown 8vo, cloth extra, 3s. 6d. each.
A Secret of the Sea. | The Grey Monk.

The Sandycroft Mystery. Crown 8vo, picture cover, 1s.
The Master of Trenance. Three Vols., crown 8vo, 15s. net.
A Husband from the Sea. Post 8vo, illustrated boards, 2s.

Spenser for Children. By M. H. TOWRY. With Coloured Illustrations by WALTER J. MORGAN. Crown 4to, cloth extra, 3s. 6d.

Stafford (John).—Doris and I, &c. Crown 8vo, cloth, 3s. 6d. [Shortly.

Starry Heavens (The) : A POETICAL BIRTHDAY BOOK. Royal 16mo, cloth extra, 2s. 6d.

Stedman (E. C.), Works by. Crown 8vo, cloth extra, 9s. each.
Victorian Poets. | The Poets of America.

Stephens (Riccardo, M.B.).—The Cruciform Mark: The Strange Story of RICHARD TREGENNA, Bachelor of Medicine (Univ. Edinb.) Crown 8vo, cloth, 6s.

Sterndale (R. Armitage).—The Afghan Knife: A Novel. Crown 8vo, cloth extra, 3s. 6d. ; post 8vo, illustrated boards, 2s.

Stevenson (R. Louis), Works by. Post 8vo, cloth limp, 2s. 6d. ea.
Travels with a Donkey. With a Frontispiece by WALTER CRANE.
An Inland Voyage. With a Frontispiece by WALTER CRANE.

Crown 8vo, buckram, gilt top, 6s. each.
Familiar Studies of Men and Books.
The Silverado Squatters. With Frontispiece by J. D. STRONG.
The Merry Men. | Underwoods: Poems.
Memories and Portraits.
Virginibus Puerisque, and other Papers. | Ballads. | Prince Otto.
Across the Plains, with other Memories and Essays.

New Arabian Nights. Crown 8vo, buckram, gilt top, 6s. ; post 8vo, illustrated boards, 2s.
The Suicide Club ; and The Rajah's Diamond. (From NEW ARABIAN NIGHTS.) With Eight Illustrations by W. J. HENNESSY. Crown 8vo, cloth, 3s.
The Edinburgh Edition of the Works of Robert Louis Stevenson. Twenty-seven Vols., demy 8vo. This Edition (which is limited to 1,000 copies) is sold only in Sets, the price of which may be learned from the Booksellers. The First Volume was published Nov., 1894.

Songs of Travel. Crown 8vo, buckram, 5s. [Shortly.
Weir of Hermiston. (R. L. STEVENSON'S LAST WORK.) Large crown 8vo, 6s. [May.

Stoddard (C. Warren).—Summer Cruising in the South Seas.
Illustrated by WALLIS MACKAY. Crown 8vo, cloth extra, 3s. 6d.

Stories from Foreign Novelists. With Notices by HELEN and
ALICE ZIMMERN. Crown 8vo, cloth extra, 3s. 6d. ; post 8vo, illustrated boards, 2s.

Strange Manuscript (A) Found in a Copper Cylinder. Crown
8vo, cloth extra, with 19 Illustrations by GILBERT GAUL, 5s. ; post 8vo, illustrated boards, 2s.

Strange Secrets. Told by PERCY FITZGERALD, CONAN DOYLE, FLOR-
ENCE MARRYAT, &c. Post 8vo, illustrated boards, 2s.

Strutt (Joseph). — The Sports and Pastimes of the People of
England ; including the Rural and Domestic Recreations, May Games, Mummeries, Shows, &c., from
the Earliest Period to the Present Time. Edited by WILLIAM HONE. With 140 Illustrations. Crown
8vo, cloth extra, 7s. 6d.

Swift's (Dean) Choice Works, in Prose and Verse. With Memoir,
Portrait, and Facsimiles of the Maps in 'Gulliver's Travels.' Crown 8vo, cloth, 7s. 6d.
Gulliver's Travels, and **A Tale of a Tub.** Post 8vo, half-bound, 2s.
Jonathan Swift: A Study. By J. CHURTON COLLINS. Crown 8vo, cloth extra, 8s.

Swinburne (Algernon C.), Works by.

Selections from the Poetical Works of
A. C. Swinburne. Fcap. 8vo, 6s.
Atalanta in Calydon. Crown 8vo, 6s.
Chastelard: A Tragedy. Crown 8vo, 7s.
Poems and Ballads. FIRST SERIES. Crown
8vo, or fcap. 8vo, 9s.
Poems and Ballads. SECOND SERIES. Crown
8vo, 9s.
Poems & Ballads. THIRD SERIES. Cr. 8vo, 7s.
Songs before Sunrise. Crown 8vo, 10s. 6d.
Bothwell: A Tragedy. Crown 8vo, 12s. 6d.
Songs of Two Nations. Crown 8vo, 6s.
George Chapman. (See Vol. II. of G. CHAP-
MAN'S Works.) Crown 8vo, 6s.
Essays and Studies. Crown 8vo, 12s.
Erechtheus: A Tragedy. Crown 8vo, 6s.

A Note on Charlotte Bronte. Cr. 8vo, 6s
A Study of Shakespeare. Crown 8vo, 8s.
Songs of the Springtides. Crown 8vo, 6s.
Studies in Song. Crown 8vo, 7s.
Mary Stuart: A Tragedy. Crown 8vo, 8s.
Tristram of Lyonesse. Crown 8vo, 9s.
A Century of Roundels. Small 4to, 8s.
A Midsummer Holiday. Crown 8vo, 7s.
Marino Faliero: A Tragedy. Crown 8vo, 6s.
A Study of Victor Hugo. Crown 8vo, 6s.
Miscellanies. Crown 8vo, 12s.
Locrine: A Tragedy. Crown 8vo, 6s.
A Study of Ben Jonson. Crown 8vo, 7s.
The Sisters: A Tragedy. Crown 8vo, 6s.
Astrophel, &c. Crown 8vo, 7s.
Studies in Prose and Poetry. Cr. 8vo, 9s.

Syntax's (Dr.) Three Tours: In Search of the Picturesque, in Search
of Consolation, and in Search of a Wife. With ROWLANDSON'S Coloured Illustrations, and Life of the
Author by J. C. HOTTEN. Crown 8vo, cloth extra, 7s. 6d.

Taine's History of English Literature. Translated by HENRY VAN
LAUN. Four Vols., small demy 8vo, cloth boards, 30s. POPULAR EDITION, Two Vols., large crown
8vo, cloth extra, 15s.

Taylor (Bayard). — Diversions of the Echo Club: Burlesques of
Modern Writers. Post 8vo, cloth limp, 2s.

Taylor (Dr. J. E., F.L.S.), Works by. Crown 8vo, cloth, 5s. each.
The Sagacity and Morality of Plants: A Sketch of the Life and Conduct of the Vegetable
Kingdom. With a Coloured Frontispiece and 100 Illustrations.
Our Common British Fossils, and Where to Find Them. With 331 Illustrations.
The Playtime Naturalist. With 366 Illustrations.

Taylor (Tom). — Historical Dramas. Containing 'Clancarty,'
'Jeanne Darc,' ''Twixt Axe and Crown,' 'The Fool's Revenge,' 'Arkwright's Wife,' 'Anne Boleyn,'
'Plot and Passion.' Crown 8vo, cloth extra, 7s. 6d.
*** The Plays may also be had separately, at 1s. each.

Tennyson (Lord): A Biographical Sketch. By H. J. JENNINGS. Post
8vo, portrait cover, 1s. ; cloth, 1s. 6d.

Thackerayana: Notes and Anecdotes. With Coloured Frontispiece and
Hundreds of Sketches by WILLIAM MAKEPEACE THACKERAY. Crown 8vo, cloth extra, 7s. 6d.

Thames, A New Pictorial History of the. By A. S. KRAUSSE.
With 340 Illustrations. Post 8vo, 1s. ; cloth, 1s. 6d.

Thiers (Adolphe). — History of the Consulate and Empire of
France under Napoleon. Translated by D. FORBES CAMPBELL and JOHN STEBBING. With 36 Steel
Plates. 12 Vols., demy 8vo, cloth extra, 12s. each.

Thomas (Bertha), Novels by. Cr. 8vo, cl., 3s. 6d. ea.; post 8vo, 2s. ea.

The Violin-Player. | Proud Maisie.

Cressida. Post 8vo, illustrated boards, 2s.

Thomson's Seasons, and The Castle of Indolence. With Introduction by ALLAN CUNNINGHAM, and 48 Illustrations. Post 8vo, half-bound, 2s.

Thornbury (Walter), Books by.
The Life and Correspondence of J. M. W. Turner. With Illustrations in Colours. Crown 8vo, cloth extra, 7s. 6d.

Post 8vo, illustrated boards, 2s. each.

Old Stories Re-told. | Tales for the Marines.

Timbs (John), Works by. Crown 8vo, cloth extra, 7s. 6d. each.
The History of Clubs and Club Life in London: Anecdotes of its Famous Coffee-houses, Hostelries, and Taverns. With 42 Illustrations.
English Eccentrics and Eccentricities: Stories of Delusions, Impostures, Sporting Scenes, Eccentric Artists, Theatrical Folk, &c. With 48 Illustrations.

Transvaal (The). By JOHN DE VILLIERS. With Map. Crown 8vo, 1s.

Trollope (Anthony), Novels by.
Crown 8vo, cloth extra, 3s. 6d. each; post 8vo, illustrated boards, 2s. each.

The Way We Live Now. | Mr. Scarborough's Family.
Frau Frohmann. | The Land-Leaguers.

Post 8vo, illustrated boards, 2s. each.

Kept in the Dark. | The American Senator.
The Golden Lion of Granpere. | John Caldigate. | Marion Fay.

Trollope (Frances E.), Novels by.
Crown 8vo, cloth extra, 3s. 6d. each; post 8vo, illustrated boards, 2s. each.
Like Ships Upon the Sea. | Mabel's Progress. | Anne Furness.

Trollope (T. A.).—Diamond Cut Diamond. Post 8vo, illust. bds., 2s.

Trowbridge (J. T.).—Farnell's Folly. Post 8vo, illust. boards, 2s.

Tytler (C. C. Fraser-).—Mistress Judith: A Novel. Crown 8vo, cloth extra, 3s. 6d.; post 8vo, illustrated boards, 2s.

Tytler (Sarah), Novels by.
Crown 8vo, cloth extra, 3s. 6d. each; post 8vo, illustrated boards, 2s. each.

Lady Bell. | Buried Diamonds. | The Blackhall Ghosts.

Post 8vo, illustrated boards, 2s. each.

What She Came Through. | The Huguenot Family.
Citoyenne Jacqueline. | Noblesse Oblige.
The Bride's Pass. | Beauty and the Beast.
Saint Mungo's City. | Disappeared.

The Macdonald Lass. With Frontispiece. Crown 8vo, cloth, 3s. 6d.

Upward (Allen), Novels by.
The Queen Against Owen. Crown 8vo, cloth, with Frontispiece, 3s. 6d.; post 8vo, boards, 2s.
The Prince of Balkistan. Crown 8vo, cloth extra, 3s. 6d.
A Crown of Straw. Crown 8vo, cloth, 6s. [Shortly.

Vashti and Esther. By the Writer of 'Belle's' Letters in *The World*. Crown 8vo, cloth extra.

Villari (Linda).—A Double Bond: A Story. Fcap. 8vo, 1s.

Vizetelly (Ernest A.).—The Scorpion: A Romance of Spain. With a Frontispiece. Crown 8vo, cloth extra, 3s. 6d.

Walton and Cotton's Complete Angler; or, The Contemplative Man's Recreation, by IZAAK WALTON, and Instructions How to Angle, for a Trout or Grayling in a clear Stream, by CHARLES COTTON. With Memoirs and Notes by Sir HARRIS NICOLAS, and 61 Illustrations. Crown 8vo, cloth antique, 7s. 6d.

Walt Whitman, Poems by. Edited, with Introduction, by WILLIAM M. ROSSETTI. With Portrait. Crown 8vo, hand-made paper and buckram, 6s.

Ward (Herbert), Books by.
Five Years with the Congo Cannibals. With 92 Illustrations. Royal 8vo, cloth, 14s.
My Life with Stanley's Rear Guard. With Map. Post 8vo, 1s.; cloth, 1s. 6d.

Walford (Edward, M.A.), Works by.
Walford's County Families of the United Kingdom (1896). Containing the Descent, Birth, Marriage, Education, &c., of 12,000 Heads of Families, their Heirs, Offices, Addresses, Clubs, &c. Royal 8vo, cloth gilt, 50s.
Walford's Shilling Peerage (1896). Containing a List of the House of Lords, Scotch and Irish Peers, &c. 32mo, cloth, 1s.
Walford's Shilling Baronetage (1896). Containing a List of the Baronets of the United Kingdom, Biographical Notices, Addresses, &c. 32mo, cloth, 1s.
Walford's Shilling Knightage (1896). Containing a List of the Knights of the United Kingdom, Biographical Notices, Addresses, &c. 32mo, cloth, 1s.
Walford's Shilling House of Commons (1896). Containing a List of all the Members of the New Parliament, their Addresses, Clubs, &c. 32mo, cloth, 1s.
Walford's Complete Peerage, Baronetage, Knightage, and House of Commons (1896). Royal 32mo, cloth, gilt edges, 5s.

Tales of our Great Families. Crown 8vo, cloth extra, 3s. 6d.

Warner (Charles Dudley).—A Roundabout Journey. Crown 8vo, cloth extra, 6s.

Warrant to Execute Charles I. A Facsimile, with the 59 Signatures and Seals. Printed on paper 22 in. by 14 in. 2s.
Warrant to Execute Mary Queen of Scots. A Facsimile, including Queen Elizabeth's Signature and the Great Seal. 2s.

Washington's (George) Rules of Civility Traced to their Sources and Restored by MONCURE D. CONWAY. Fcap. 8vo, Japanese vellum, 2s. 6d.

Wassermann (Lillias), Novels by.
The Daffodils. Crown 8vo, 1s.; cloth, 1s. 6d.

The Marquis of Carabas. By AARON WATSON and LILLIAS WASSERMANN. Post 8vo, illustrated boards, 2s.

Weather, How to Foretell the, with the Pocket Spectroscope.
By F. W. CORY. With Ten Illustrations. Crown 8vo, 1s.; cloth, 1s. 6d.

Webber (Byron).—Fun, Frolic, and Fancy. With 43 Illustrations by PHIL MAY and CHARLES MAY. Fcap. 4to, cloth, 5s.

Westall (William), Novels by.
Trust-Money. Post 8vo, illustrated boards, 2s.; cloth, 2s. 6d.
Sons of Belial. Two Vols., crown 8vo, 10s. net.

Westbury (Atha).—The Shadow of Hilton Fernbrook: A Romance of Maoriland. Crown 8vo, cloth, 3s. 6d. [Shortly.

Whist, How to Play Solo. By ABRAHAM S. WILKS and CHARLES F. PARDON. Post 8vo, cloth limp, 2s.

White (Gilbert).—The Natural History of Selborne. Post 8vo, printed on laid paper and half-bound, 2s.

Williams (W. Mattieu, F.R.A.S.), Works by.
Science in Short Chapters. Crown 8vo, cloth extra, 7s. 6d.
A Simple Treatise on Heat. With Illustrations. Crown 8vo, cloth, 2s. 6d.
The Chemistry of Cookery. Crown 8vo, cloth extra, 6s.
The Chemistry of Iron and Steel Making. Crown 8vo, cloth extra, 9s.
A Vindication of Phrenology. With Portrait and 43 Illusts. Demy 8vo, cloth extra, 12s. 6d.

Williamson (Mrs. F. H.).—A Child Widow. Post 8vo, bds., 2s.

Wills (W. H., M.D.).—An Easy-going Fellow. Crown 8vo, cloth, 6s. [Short'y.

Wilson (Dr. Andrew, F.R.S.E.), Works by.
Chapters on Evolution. With 259 Illustrations. Crown 8vo, cloth extra, 7s. 6d.
Leaves from a Naturalist's Note-Book. Post 8vo, cloth limp, 2s. 6d.
Leisure-Time Studies. With Illustrations. Crown 8vo, cloth extra, 6s.
Studies in Life and Sense. With numerous Illustrations. Crown 8vo, cloth extra, 6s.
Common Accidents: How to Treat Them. With Illustrations. Crown 8vo, 1s.; cloth, 1s. 6d.
Glimpses of Nature. With 35 Illustrations. Crown 8vo, cloth extra, 3s. 6d.

Winter (J. S.), Stories by. Post 8vo, illustrated boards, 2s. each; cloth limp, 2s. 6d. each.
Cavalry Life. | Regimental Legends.

A Soldier's Children. With 34 Illustrations by E. G. THOMSON and E. STUART HARDY. Crown 8vo, cloth extra, 3s. 6d.

Wissmann (Hermann von). — My Second Journey through Equatorial Africa. With 92 Illustrations. Demy 8vo, cloth, 16s.

Wood (H. F.), Detective Stories by. Post 8vo, boards, 2s. each.
The Passenger from Scotland Yard. | The Englishman of the Rue Cain.

Wood (Lady). Sabina: A Novel. Post 8vo, illustrated boards, 2s.

Woolley (Celia Parker).—Rachel Armstrong; or, Love and The- ology. Post 8vo, illustrated boards, 2s.; cloth, 2s. 6d.

Wright (Thomas), Works by. Crown 8vo, cloth extra, 7s. 6d. each.
The Caricature History of the Georges. With 400 Caricatures, Squibs, &c.
History of Caricature and of the Grotesque in Art, Literature, Sculpture, and Painting. Illustrated by F. W. FAIRHOLT, F.S.A.

Wynman (Margaret).—My Flirtations. With 13 Illustrations by J. BERNARD PARTRIDGE. Post 8vo, cloth, 3s. 6d.

Yates (Edmund), Novels by. Post 8vo, illustrated boards, 2s. each.
Land at Last. | The Forlorn Hope. | Castaway.

Zangwill (I.). — Ghetto Tragedies. With Three Illustrations by A. S. BOYD. Fcap. 8vo, picture cover, 1s. net.

Zola (Emile), Novels by. Crown 8vo, cloth extra, 3s. 6d. each.
The Fat and the Thin. Translated by ERNEST A. VIZETELLY.
Money. Translated by ERNEST A. VIZETELLY.
The Downfall. Translated by E. A. VIZETELLY.
The Dream. Translated by ELIZA CHASE. With Eight Illustrations by JEANNIOT.
Doctor Pascal. Translated by E. A. VIZETELLY. With Portrait of the Author.
Lourdes. Translated by ERNEST A. VIZETELLY.
Rome. Translated by ERNEST A. VIZETELLY.   [Shortly.

SOME BOOKS CLASSIFIED IN SERIES.

, For fuller cataloguing, see alphabetical arrangement, pp. 1-26.

The Mayfair Library. Post 8vo, cloth limp, 2s. 6d. per Volume.

A Journey Round My Room. By X. DE MAISTRE. Translated by Sir HENRY ATTWELL.
Quips and Quiddities. By W. D. ADAMS.
The Agony Column of 'The Times.'
Melancholy Anatomised: Abridgment of BURTON.
Poetical Ingenuities. By W. T. DOBSON.
The Cupboard Papers. By FIN-BEC.
W. S. Gilbert's Plays. Three Series.
Songs of Irish Wit and Humour.
Animals and their Masters. By Sir A. HELPS.
Social Pressure. By Sir A. HELPS.
Curiosities of Criticism. By H. J. JENNINGS.
The Autocrat of the Breakfast-Table. By OLIVER WENDELL HOLMES.
Pencil and Palette. By R. KEMPT.
Little Essays from LAMB'S LETTERS.
Forensic Anecdotes. By JACOB LARWOOD.
Theatrical Anecdotes. By JACOB LARWOOD.
Jeux d'Esprit. Edited by HENRY S. LEIGH.
Witch Stories. By E. LYNN LINTON.
Ourselves. By E. LYNN LINTON.
Pastimes and Players. By R. MACGREGOR.
New Paul and Virginia. By W. H. MALLOCK.
The New Republic. By W. H. MALLOCK.
Puck on Pegasus. By H. C. PENNELL.
Pegasus Re-saddled. By H. C. PENNELL.
Muses of Mayfair. Edited by H. C. PENNELL.
Thoreau: His Life and Aims. By H. A. PAGE.
Puniana. By Hon. HUGH ROWLEY.
More Puniana. By Hon. HUGH ROWLEY.
The Philosophy of Handwriting.
By Stream and Sea. By WILLIAM SENIOR.
Leaves from a Naturalist's Note-Book. By Dr. ANDREW WILSON.

The Golden Library. Post 8vo, cloth limp, 2s. per Volume.

Diversions of the Echo Club. BAYARD TAYLOR.
Songs for Sailors. By W. C. BENNETT.
Lives of the Necromancers. By W. GODWIN.
The Poetical Works of Alexander Pope.
Scenes of Country Life. By EDWARD JESSE.
Tale for a Chimney Corner. By LEIGH HUNT.
The Autocrat of the Breakfast Table. By OLIVER WENDELL HOLMES.
La Mort d'Arthur: Selections from MALLORY.
Provincial Letters of Blaise Pascal.
Maxims and Reflections of Rochefoucauld.

The Wanderer's Library. Crown 8vo, cloth extra, 3s. 6d. each.

Wanderings in Patagonia. By JULIUS BEER-BOHM. Illustrated.
Merrie England in the Olden Time. By G. DANIEL. Illustrated by ROBERT CRUIKSHANK.
Circus Life. By THOMAS FROST.
Lives of the Conjurers. By THOMAS FROST.
The Old Showmen and the Old London Fairs. By THOMAS FROST.
Low-Life Deeps. By JAMES GREENWOOD.
The Wilds of London. By JAMES GREENWOOD.
Tunis. By Chev. HESSE-WARTEGG. 22 Illusts.
Life and Adventure of a Cheap Jack.
World Behind the Scenes. By P. FITZGERALD.
Tavern Anecdotes and Sayings.
The Genial Showman. By E. P. HINGSTON.
Story of London Parks. By JACOB LARWOOD.
London Characters. By HENRY MAYHEW.
Seven Generations of Executioners.
Summer Cruising in the South Seas. By C. WARREN STODDARD. Illustrated.

Books in Series—*continued.*

Handy Novels. Fcap. 8vo, cloth boards, 1s. 6d. each.

The Old Maid's Sweetheart. By A. ST. AUBYN.
Modest Little Sara. By ALAN ST. AUBYN.
Seven Sleepers of Ephesus. M. E. COLERIDGE.
Taken from the Enemy. By H. NEWBOLT.

A Lost Soul. By W. L. ALDEN.
Dr. Palliser's Patient. By GRANT ALLEN.
Monte Carlo Stories. By JOAN BARRETT.
Black Spirits and White. By R. A. CRAM.

My Library. Printed on laid paper, post 8vo, half-Roxburghe, 2s. 6d. each.

Citation and Examination of William Shakspeare.
By W. S. LANDOR.
The Journal of Maurice de Guerin.

Christie Johnstone. By CHARLES READE.
Peg Woffington. By CHARLES READE.
The Dramatic Essays of Charles Lamb.

The Pocket Library. Post 8vo, printed on laid paper and hf.-bd., 2s. each.

The Essays of Elia. By CHARLES LAMB.
Robinson Crusoe. Illustrated by G. CRUIKSHANK.
Whims and Oddities. By THOMAS HOOD.
The Barber's Chair. By DOUGLAS JERROLD.
Gastronomy. By BRILLAT-SAVARIN.
The Epicurean, &c. By THOMAS MOORE.
Leigh Hunt's Essays. Edited by E. OLLIER.

White's Natural History of Selborne.
Gulliver's Travels, &c. By Dean SWIFT.
Plays by RICHARD BRINSLEY SHERIDAN.
Anecdotes of the Clergy. By JACOB LARWOOD.
Thomson's Seasons. Illustrated.
Autocrat of the Breakfast Table and The Professor
  at the Breakfast Table. By O. W. HOLMES.

THE PICCADILLY NOVELS.

LIBRARY EDITIONS OF NOVELS, many Illustrated, crown 8vo, cloth extra, 3s. 6d. each.

By F. M. ALLEN.
Green as Grass.

By GRANT ALLEN.
Philistia.
Strange Stories.
Babylon.
For Maimie's Sake.
In all Shades.
The Beckoning Hand.
The Devil's Die.
This Mortal Coil.
The Tents of Shem.

The Great Taboo.
Dumaresq's Daughter.
Duchess of Powysland.
Blood Royal.
Ivan Greet's Master-
  piece.
The Scallywag.
At Market Value.
Under Sealed Orders.

By MARY ANDERSON.
Othello's Occupation.

By EDWIN L. ARNOLD.
Phra the Phœnician.   Constable of St. Nicholas.

By ROBERT BARR.
In a Steamer Chair. | From Whose Bourne.

By FRANK BARRETT.
The Woman of the Iron Bracelets.

By 'BELLE.'
Vashti and Esther.

By Sir W. BESANT and J. RICE.
Ready-Money Mortiboy.
My Little Girl.
With Harp and Crown.
This Son of Vulcan.
The Golden Butterfly.
The Monks of Thelema.

By Celia's Arbour.
Chaplain of the Fleet.
The Seamy Side.
The Case of Mr. Lucraft.
In Trafalgar's Bay.
The Ten Years' Tenant.

By Sir WALTER BESANT.
All Sorts and Condi-
  tions of Men.
The Captains' Room.
All in a Garden Fair.
Dorothy Forster.
Uncle Jack.
The World Went Very
  Well Then.
Children of Gibeon.
Herr Paulus.
For Faith and Freedom.

To Call Her Mine.
The Bell of St. Paul's.
The Holy Rose.
Armorel of Lyonesse.
S. Katherine's by Tower
Verbena Camellia Ste-
  phanotis.
The Ivory Gate.
The Rebel Queen.
Beyond the Dreams of
  Avarice.

By PAUL BOURGET.
A Living Lie.

By ROBERT BUCHANAN.
Shadow of the Sword.
A Child of Nature.
God and the Man.
Martyrdom of Madeline
Love Me for Ever.
Annan Water.
Foxglove Manor.

The New Abelard.
Matt: Rachel Dene.
Master of the Mine.
The Heir of Linne
Woman and the Man.
Red and White Heather.

ROB. BUCHANAN & HY. MURRAY.
The Charlatan.

By J. MITCHELL CHAPPLE.
The Minor Chord.

By HALL CAINE.
The Shadow of a Crime. | The Deemster.
A Son of Hagar.

By MACLAREN COBBAN.
The Red Sultan.   The Burden of Isabel.

By MORT. & FRANCES COLLINS.
Transmigration.
Blacksmith & Scholar.
The Village Comedy.

From Midnight to Mid-
  night.
You Play me False.

By WILKIE COLLINS.
Armadale. | After Dark.
No Name.
Antonina.
Basil.
Hide and Seek.
The Dead Secret.
Queen of Hearts.
My Miscellanies.
The Woman in White.
The Moonstone.
Man and Wife.
Poor Miss Finch.
Miss or Mrs.?
The New Magdalen.

The Frozen Deep.
The Two Destinies.
The Law and the Lady.
The Haunted Hotel.
The Fallen Leaves.
Jezebel's Daughter.
The Black Robe.
Heart and Science.
'I Say No.'
Little Novels
The Evil Genius.
The Legacy of Cain.
A Rogue's Life.
Blind Love.

By DUTTON COOK.
Paul Foster's Daughter.

By E. H. COOPER.
Geoffory Hamilton.

By V. CECIL COTES.
Two Girls on a Barge.

By C. EGBERT CRADDOCK.
His Vanished Star.

By H. N. CRELLIN.
Romances of the Old Seraglio.

By MATT CRIM.
The Adventures of a Fair Rebel.

By S. R. CROCKETT and others.
Tales of Our Coast.

By B. M. CROKER.
Diana Barrington.
Proper Pride.
A Family Likeness.
Pretty Miss Neville.
A Bird of Passage.

'To Let.
Mr. Jervis.
Village Tales & Jungle
  Tragedies
The Real Lady Hilda.

By WILLIAM CYPLES.
Hearts of Gold.

By ALPHONSE DAUDET.
The Evangelist; or, Port Salvation.

By H. COLEMAN DAVIDSON.
Mr. Sadler's Daughters

By ERASMUS DAWSON.
The Fountain of Youth.

By JAMES DE MILLE.
A Castle in Spain.

The PICCADILLY (3/6) NOVELS—*continued.*

By Mrs. CAMPBELL PRAED.
Outlaw and Lawmaker. | Christina Chard.

By E. C. PRICE.
Valentina. | Mrs. Lancaster's Rival.
The Foreigners.

By RICHARD PRYCE.
Miss Maxwell's Affections.

By CHARLES READE.
It is Never Too Late to | Singleheart and Double-
Mend. | face.
The Double Marriage. | Good Stories of Men
Love Me Little, Love | and other Animals.
Me Long. | Hard Cash.
The Cloister and the | Peg Woffington.
Hearth. | Christie Johnstone.
The Course of True | Griffith Gaunt.
Love. | Foul Play.
The Autobiography of | The Wandering Heir.
a Thief. | A Woman-Hater.
Put Yourself in His | A Simpleton.
Place. | A Perilous Secret.
A Terrible Temptation. | Readiana.
The Jilt.

By Mrs. J. H. RIDDELL.
Weird Stories.

By AMELIE RIVES.
Barbara Dering.

By F. W. ROBINSON.
The Hands of Justice.

By DORA RUSSELL.
A Country Sweetheart. | The Drift of Fate.

By W. CLARK RUSSELL.
Ocean Tragedy. | Is He the Man?
My Shipmate Louise. | The Good Ship 'Mo-
Alone on Wide Wide Sea | hock.'
The Phantom Death. | The Convict Ship.

By JOHN SAUNDERS.
Guy Waterman. | The Two Dreamers.
Bound to the Wheel. | The Lion in the Path.

By KATHARINE SAUNDERS.
Margaret and Elizabeth | Heart Salvage.
Gideon's Rock. | Sebastian.
The High Mills.

By ADELINE SERGEANT.
Dr. Endicott's Experiment.

By HAWLEY SMART.
Without Love or Licence.

By T. W. SPEIGHT.
A Secret of the Sea. | The Grey Monk.

By ALAN ST. AUBYN.
A Fellow of Trinity. | In Face of the World.
The Junior Dean. | Orchard Damerel.
Master of St. Benedict's. | The Tremlett Diamonds
To his Own Master.

By JOHN STAFFORD.
Doris and I.

By R. A. STERNDALE.
The Afghan Knife.

By BERTHA THOMAS.
Proud Maisie. | The Violin-Player.

By ANTHONY TROLLOPE.
The Way we Live Now. | Scarborough's Family.
Frau Frohmann. | The Land-Leaguers.

By FRANCES E. TROLLOPE.
Like Ships upon the | Anne Furness.
Sea. | Mabel's Progress.

By IVAN TURGENIEFF, &c.
Stories from Foreign Novelists.

By MARK TWAIN.
The American Claimant. | Pudd'nhead Wilson.
The £1,000,000 Bank-note. | Tom Sawyer, Detective.
Tom Sawyer Abroad.

By C. C. FRASER-TYTLER.
Mistress Judith.

By SARAH TYTLER.
Lady Bell. | The Blackhall Ghosts.
Buried Diamonds. | The Macdonald Lass.

By ALLEN UPWARD.
The Queen against Owen.
The Prince of Balkistan.

By E. A. VIZETELLY.
The Scorpion: A Romance of Spain.

By ATHA WESTBURY.
The Shadow of Hilton Fernbrook.

By JOHN STRANGE WINTER.
A Soldier's Children.

By MARGARET WYNMAN.
My Flirtations.

By E. ZOLA.
The Downfall. | Money. | Lourdes.
The Dream. | The Fat and the Thin.
Dr. Pascal. | Rome.

CHEAP EDITIONS OF POPULAR NOVELS.
Post 8vo, illustrated boards, 2s. each.

By ARTEMUS WARD.
Artemus Ward Complete.

By EDMOND ABOUT.
The Fellah.

By HAMILTON AÏDÉ.
Carr of Carrlyon. | Confidences.

By MARY ALBERT.
Brooke Finchley's Daughter.

By Mrs. ALEXANDER.
Maid, Wife or Widow? | Valerie's Fate.

By GRANT ALLEN.
Philistia. | The Great Taboo.
Strange Stories. | Dumaresq's Daughter.
Babylon. | Duchess of Powysland.
For Maimie's Sake. | Blood Royal.
In all Shades. | Ivan Greet's Master-
The Beckoning Hand. | piece.
The Devil's Die. | The Scallywag.
The Tents of Shem. | This Mortal Coil.

By E. LESTER ARNOLD.
Phra the Phœnician.

By SHELSLEY BEAUCHAMP.
Grantley Grange.

BY FRANK BARRETT.
Fettered for Life. | A Prodigal's Progress.
Little Lady Linton. | Found Guilty.
Between Life & Death. | A Recoiling Vengeance.
The Sin of Olga Zassou- | For Love and Honour
lich. | John Ford; and His
Folly Morrison. | Helpmate.
Lieut. Barnabas. | The Woman of the Iron
Honest Davie. | Bracelets.

By Sir W. BESANT and J. RICE.
Ready-Money Mortiboy | By Celia's Arbour
My Little Girl. | Chaplain of the Fleet.
With Harp and Crown. | The Seamy Side
This Son of Vulcan. | The Case of Mr. Lucraft.
The Golden Butterfly. | In Trafalgar's Bay.
The Monks of Thelema. | The Ten Years' Tenant.

By Sir WALTER BESANT.
All Sorts and Condi- | For Faith and Freedom
tions of Men. | To Call Her Mine.
The Captains' Room. | The Bell of St. Paul's.
All in a Garden Fair. | The Holy Rose.
Dorothy Forster. | Armorel of Lyonesse.
Uncle Jack. | S. Katherine's by Tower.
The World Went Very | Verbena Camellia Ste-
Well Then. | phanotis.
Children of Gibeon. | The Ivory Gate.
Herr Paulus. | The Rebel Queen.

By AMBROSE BIERCE.
In the Midst of Life.

TWO-SHILLING NOVELS—*continued.*

By FREDERICK BOYLE.

Camp Notes. | Chronicles of No man's
Savage Life. | Land

BY BRET HARTE.

Californian Stories. | Flip. | Maruja.
Gabriel Conroy | A Phyllis of the Sierras.
The Luck of Roaring | A Waif of the Plains
Camp. | A Ward of the Golden
An Heiress of Red Dog. | Gate.

By HAROLD BRYDGES.

Uncle Sam at Home.

By ROBERT BUCHANAN.

Shadow of the Sword. | The Martyrdom of Ma-
A Child of Nature. | deline.
God and the Man. | The New Abelard.
Love Me for Ever. | Matt.
Foxglove Manor. | The Heir of Linne.
The Master of the Mine. | Woman and the Man.
Annan Water.

By HALL CAINE.

The Shadow of a Crime | The Deemster.
A Son of Hagar.

By Commander CAMERON.

The Cruise of the 'Black Prince.'

By Mrs. LOVETT CAMERON.

Deceivers Ever. | Juliet's Guardian.

By HAYDEN CARRUTH.

The Adventures of Jones.

By AUSTIN CLARE.

For the Love of a Lass.

By Mrs. ARCHER CLIVE.

Paul Ferroll.
Why Paul Ferroll Killed his Wife.

By MACLAREN COBBAN.

The Cure of Souls. | The Red Sultan.

By C. ALLSTON COLLINS.

The Bar Sinister.

By MORT. & FRANCES COLLINS.

Sweet Anne Page. | Sweet and Twenty.
Transmigration. | The Village Comedy.
From Midnight to Mid- | You Play me False.
night. | Blacksmith and Scholar
A Fight with Fortune. | Frances.

By WILKIE COLLINS.

Armadale. | After Dark. | My Miscellanies.
No Name. | The Woman in White.
Antonina. | The Moonstone.
Basil. | Man and Wife.
Hide and Seek. | Poor Miss Finch.
The Dead Secret. | The Fallen Leaves.
Queen of Hearts. | Jezebel's Daughter.
Miss or Mrs ? | The Black Robe.
The New Magdalen. | Heart and Science.
The Frozen Deep. | I Say No!'
The Law and the Lady | The Evil Genius.
The Two Destinies. | Little Novels.
The Haunted Hotel. | Legacy of Cain.
A Rogue's Life. | Blind Love.

By M. J. COLQUHOUN.

Every Inch a Soldier.

By DUTTON COOK.

Leo. | Paul Foster's Daughter.

By C. EGBERT CRADDOCK.

The Prophet of the Great Smoky Mountains.

By MATT CRIM.

The Adventures of a Fair Rebel.

By B. M. CROKER.

Pretty Miss Neville. | Proper Pride.
Diana Barrington. | A Family Likeness.
'To Let.' | Village Tales and Jungle
A Bird of Passage. | Tragedies.

By W. CYPLES.

Hearts of Gold.

By ALPHONSE DAUDET.

The Evangelist ; or, Port Salvation.

By ERASMUS DAWSON.

The Fountain of Youth.

By JAMES DE MILLE.

A Castle in Spain.

By J. LEITH DERWENT.

Our Lady of Tears. | Circe's Lovers

By CHARLES DICKENS.

Sketches by Boz. | Nicholas Nickleby.
Oliver Twist.

By DICK DONOVAN.

The Man-Hunter. | In the Grip of the Law.
Tracked and Taken. | From Information Re-
Caught at Last ! | ceived.
Wanted ! | Tracked to Doom.
Who Poisoned Hetty | Link by Link
Duncan ? | Suspicion Aroused.
Man from Manchester. | Dark Deeds.
A Detective's Triumphs | Riddles Read.

By Mrs. ANNIE EDWARDES.

A Point of Honour. | Archie Lovell.

By M. BETHAM-EDWARDS.

Felicia. | Kitty

By EDWARD EGGLESTON.

Roxy.

By G. MANVILLE FENN.

The New Mistress. | The Tiger Lily
Witness to the Deed.

By PERCY FITZGERALD.

Bella Donna. | Second Mrs. Tillotson.
Never Forgotten. | Seventy - five Brooke
Polly. | Street.
Fatal Zero. | The Lady of Brantome.

By P. FITZGERALD and others.

Strange Secrets.

By ALBANY DE FONBLANQUE.

Filthy Lucre.

By R. E. FRANCILLON.

Olympia. | King or Knave ?
One by One. | Romances of the Law.
A Real Queen. | Ropes of Sand.
Queen Cophetua. | A Dog and his Shadow.

By HAROLD FREDERIC.

Seth's Brother's Wife. | The Lawton Girl.

Prefaced by Sir BARTLE FRERE.

Pandurang Hari.

By HAIN FRISWELL.

One of Two.

By EDWARD GARRETT.

The Capel Girls.

By GILBERT GAUL.

A Strange Manuscript.

By CHARLES GIBBON.

Robin Gray. | In Honour Bound.
Fancy Free. | Flower of the Forest.
For Lack of Gold. | The Braes of Yarrow.
What will World Say ? | The Golden Shaft.
In Love and War. | Of High Degree.
For the King. | By Mead and Stream.
In Pastures Green. | Loving a Dream.
Queen of the Meadow. | A Hard Knot.
A Heart's Problem. | Heart's Delight.
The Dead Heart. | Blood Money.

By WILLIAM GILBERT.

Dr. Austin's Guests. | The Wizard of the
James Duke. | Mountain.

By ERNEST GLANVILLE.

The Lost Heiress. | The Fossicker.
A Fair Colonist.

By Rev. S. BARING GOULD.

Red Spider. | Eve

By HENRY GREVILLE.

A Noble Woman. | Nikanor.

By CECIL GRIFFITH.

Corinthia Marazion.

By SYDNEY GRUNDY.

The Days of his Vanity.

By JOHN HABBERTON.

Brueton's Bayou. | Country Luck

By ANDREW HALLIDAY.

Every-day Papers.

By Lady DUFFUS HARDY.

Paul Wynter's Sacrifice.

Two-Shilling Novels—*continued.*

By THOMAS HARDY.
Under the Greenwood Tree.

By J. BERWICK HARWOOD.
The Tenth Earl.

By JULIAN HAWTHORNE.

Garth.	Beatrix Randolph.
Ellice Quentin.	Love—or a Name.
Fortune's Fool.	David Poindexter's Dis-
Miss Cadogna.	appearance.
Sebastian Strome.	The Spectre of the
Dust.	Camera.

By Sir ARTHUR HELPS.
Ivan de Biron.

By G. A. HENTY.
Rujub the Juggler.

By HENRY HERMAN.
A Leading Lady.

By HEADON HILL.
Zambra the Detective.

By JOHN HILL.
Treason Felony.

By Mrs. CASHEL HOEY.
The Lover's Creed.

By Mrs. GEORGE HOOPER.
The House of Raby.

By TIGHE HOPKINS.
Twixt Love and Duty.

By Mrs. HUNGERFORD.

A Maiden all Forlorn.	A Modern Circe.
In Durance Vile.	Lady Verner's Flight.
Marvel.	The Red House Mystery
A Mental Struggle.	

By Mrs. ALFRED HUNT.

Thornicroft's Model.	Self Condemned.
That Other Person.	The Leaden Casket.

By JEAN INGELOW.
Fated to be Free.

By WM. JAMESON.
My Dead Self.

By HARRIETT JAY.
The Dark Colleen. | Queen of Connaught.

By MARK KERSHAW.
Colonial Facts and Fictions.

By R. ASHE KING.

A Drawn Game.	Passion's Slave.
'The Wearing of the	Bell Barry.
Green.'	

By JOHN LEYS.
The Lindsays.

By E. LYNN LINTON.

Patricia Kemball.	The Atonement of Leam
The World Well Lost.	Dundas.
Under which Lord?	With a Silken Thread.
Paston Carew.	Rebel of the Family.
'My Love!'	Sowing the Wind.
Ione.	The One Too Many.

By HENRY W. LUCY.
Gideon Fleyce.

By JUSTIN McCARTHY.

Dear Lady Disdain.	Camiola.
Waterdale Neighbours.	Donna Quixote.
My Enemy's Daughter.	Maid of Athens.
A Fair Saxon.	The Comet of a Season.
Linley Rochford.	The Dictator.
Miss Misanthrope.	Red Diamonds.

By HUGH MACCOLL.
Mr. Stranger's Sealed Packet.

By GEORGE MACDONALD.
Heather and Snow.

By AGNES MACDONELL.
Quaker Cousins.

By KATHARINE S. MACQUOID.
The Evil Eye. | Lost Rose.

By W. H. MALLOCK.

A Romance of the Nine-	The New Republic.
teenth Century.	

By FLORENCE MARRYAT.

Open! Sesame!	A Harvest of Wild Oats
Fighting the Air.	Written in Fire.

By J. MASTERMAN.
Half a dozen Daughters.

By BRANDER MATTHEWS.
A Secret of the Sea.

By L. T. MEADE.
A Soldier of Fortune.

By LEONARD MERRICK.
The Man who was Good.

By JEAN MIDDLEMASS.
Touch and Go. | Mr. Dorillion.

By Mrs. MOLESWORTH.
Hathercourt Rectory.

By J. E. MUDDOCK.

Stories Weird and Won-	From the Bosom of the
derful.	Deep.
The Dead Man's Secret.	

By D. CHRISTIE MURRAY.

A Model Father.	A Life's Atonement.
Joseph's Coat.	By the Gate of the Sea.
Coals of Fire.	A Bit of Human Nature.
Val Strange.	First Person Singular.
Old Blazer's Hero.	Bob Martin's Little Girl
Hearts.	Time's Revenges.
The Way of the World.	A Wasted Crime.
Cynic Fortune.	In Direst Peril.

By MURRAY and HERMAN.

One Traveller Returns.	The Bishops' Bible.
Paul Jones's Alias.	

By HENRY MURRAY.
A Game of Bluff. | A Song of Sixpence.

By HUME NISBET.
'Bail Up!' | Dr. Bernard St Vincent.

By ALICE O'HANLON.
The Unforeseen. | Chance? or Fate?

By GEORGES OHNET.

Dr. Rameau.	A Weird Gift.
A Last Love.	

By Mrs. OLIPHANT.

Whiteladies.	The Greatest Heiress in
The Primrose Path.	England

By Mrs. ROBERT O'REILLY.
Phœbe's Fortunes.

By OUIDA.

Held in Bondage.	Two Lit. Wooden Shoes.
Strathmore.	Moths.
Chandos.	Bimbi.
Idalia.	Pipistrello.
Under Two Flags.	A Village Commune.
Cecil Castlemaine's Gage	Wanda.
Tricotrin.	Othmar.
Puck.	Frescoes.
Folle Farine.	In Maremma.
A Dog of Flanders.	Guilderoy.
Pascarel.	Ruffino.
Signa.	Syrlin.
Princess Napraxine.	Santa Barbara.
In a Winter City.	Two Offenders.
Ariadne.	Ouida's Wisdom, Wit,
Friendship.	and Pathos

By MARGARET AGNES PAUL
Gentle and Simple.

By C. L. PIRKIS.
Lady Lovelace.

By EDGAR A. POE.
The Mystery of Marie Roget.

By Mrs. CAMPBELL PRAED.
The Romance of a Station.
The Soul of Countess Adrian.
Outlaw and Lawmaker.
Christina Chard

By E. C. PRICE.

Valentina	Mrs Lancaster's Rival
The Foreigners	Gerald

By RICHARD PRYCE.
Miss Maxwell's Affections.

Two-Shilling Novels—*continued*.

By JAMES PAYN.

Bentinck's Tutor.
Murphy's Master.
A County Family.
At Her Mercy.
Cecil's Tryst.
The Clyffards of Clyffe.
The Foster Brothers.
Found Dead.
The Best of Husbands.
Walter's Word.
Halves.
Fallen Fortunes.
Humorous Stories.
£200 Reward.
A Marine Residence.
Mirk Abbey.
By Proxy.
Under One Roof.
High Spirits.
Carlyon's Year.
From Exile.
For Cash Only.
Kit.
The Canon's Ward.

The Talk of the Town.
Holiday Tasks.
A Perfect Treasure.
What He Cost Her.
A Confidential Agent.
Glow-worm Tales.
The Burnt Million.
Sunny Stories.
Lost Sir Massingberd.
A Woman's Vengeance.
The Family Scapegrace.
Gwendoline's Harvest.
Like Father, Like Son.
Married Beneath Him.
Not Wooed, but Won.
Less Black than We're
Painted.
Some Private Views.
A Grape from a Thorn.
The Mystery of Mir-
bridge.
The Word and the Will.
A Prince of the Blood.
A Trying Patient.

By CHARLES READE.

It is Never Too Late to
Mend.
Christie Johnstone.
The Double Marriage.
Put Yourself in His
Place.
Love Me Little, Love
Me Long.
The Cloister and the
Hearth.
The Course of True
Love.
The Jilt.
The Autobiography of
a Thief.

A Terrible Temptation.
Foul Play.
The Wandering Heir.
Hard Cash.
Singleheart and Double-
face.
Good Stories of Men and
other Animals.
Peg Woffington.
Griffith Gaunt.
A Perilous Secret.
A Simpleton.
Readiana.
A Woman-Hater.

By Mrs. J. H. RIDDELL.

Weird Stories.
Fairy Water.
Her Mother's Darling.
The Prince of Wales's
Garden Party.

The Uninhabited House.
The Mystery in Palace
Gardens.
The Nun's Curse.
Idle Tales.

By AMELIE RIVES.

Barbara Dering.

By F. W. ROBINSON.

Women are Strange. | The Hands of Justice.

By JAMES RUNCIMAN.

Skippers and Shellbacks. | Schools and Scholars.
Grace Balmaign's Sweetheart.

By W. CLARK RUSSELL.

Round the Galley Fire.
On the Fok'sle Head.
In the Middle Watch.
A Voyage to the Cape.
A Book for the Ham-
mock.
The Mystery of the
'Ocean Star.'

The Romance of Jenny
Harlowe.
An Ocean Tragedy.
My Shipmate Louise.
Alone on a Wide Wide
Sea.

By GEORGE AUGUSTUS SALA.

Gaslight and Daylight.

By JOHN SAUNDERS.

Guy Waterman.
The Two Dreamers.

The Lion in the Path.

By KATHARINE SAUNDERS.

Joan Merryweather.
The High Mills.
Heart Salvage.

Sebastian.
Margaret and Eliza-
beth.

By GEORGE R. SIMS.

Rogues and Vagabonds.
The Ring o' Bells.
Mary Jane's Memoirs.
Mary Jane Married.
Tales of To-day.
Dramas of Life.

Tinkletop's Crime.
Zeph.
My Two Wives.
Memoirs of a Landlady.
Scenes from the Show.
The 10 Commandments.

By ARTHUR SKETCHLEY.

Match in the Dark.

By HAWLEY SMART.

Without Love or Licence.

By T. W. SPEIGHT.

The Mysteries of Heron
Dyke.
The Golden Hoop.
Hoodwinked.
By Devious Ways.

Back to Life.
The Loudwater Tragedy.
Burgo's Romance.
Quittance in Full.
A Husband from the Sea.

By ALAN ST. AUBYN.

A Fellow of Trinity.
The Junior Dean.
Master of St. Benedict's.

To His Own Master.
Orchard Damerel.

By R. A. STERNDALE.

The Afghan Knife.

By R. LOUIS STEVENSON.

New Arabian Nights. | Prince Otto.

By BERTHA THOMAS.

Cressida.
Proud Maisie.

The Violin-Player.

By WALTER THORNBURY.

Tales for the Marines. | Old Stories Retold.

By T. ADOLPHUS TROLLOPE.

Diamond Cut Diamond.

By F. ELEANOR TROLLOPE.

Like Ships upon the
Sea.

Anne Furness.
Mabel's Progress.

By ANTHONY TROLLOPE.

Frau Frohmann.
Marion Fay.
Kept in the Dark.
John Caldigate.
The Way We Live Now.

The Land-Leaguers.
The American Senator.
Mr. Scarborough's
Family.
Golden Lion of Granpere.

By J. T. TROWBRIDGE.

Farnell's Folly.

By IVAN TURGENIEFF, &c.

Stories from Foreign Novelists.

By MARK TWAIN.

A Pleasure Trip on the
Continent.
The Gilded Age.
Huckleberry Finn.
Mark Twain's Sketches.
Tom Sawyer.
A Tramp Abroad.
Stolen White Elephant.

Life on the Mississippi.
The Prince and the
Pauper.
A Yankee at the Court
of King Arthur.
The £1,000,000 Bank-
Note.

By C. C. FRASER-TYTLER.

Mistress Judith.

By SARAH TYTLER.

The Bride's Pass.
Buried Diamonds.
St. Mungo's City.
Lady Bell.
Noblesse Oblige.
Disappeared.

The Huguenot Family.
The Blackhall Ghosts.
What She Came Through.
Beauty and the Beast.
Citoyenne Jaqueline.

By ALLEN UPWARD.

The Queen against Owen.

By AARON WATSON and LILLIAS WASSERMANN.

The Marquis of Carabas.

By WILLIAM WESTALL.

Trust-Money.

By Mrs. F. H. WILLIAMSON.

A Child Widow.

By J. S. WINTER.

Cavalry Life. | Regimental Legends.

By H. F. WOOD.

The Passenger from Scotland Yard.
The Englishman of the Rue Cain.

By Lady WOOD.

Sabina.

By CELIA PARKER WOOLLEY.

Rachel Armstrong; or, Love and Theology.

By EDMUND YATES.

The Forlorn Hope.
Land at Last.

Castaway.

OGDEN, SMALE AND CO. LIMITED, PRINTERS, GREAT SAFFRON HILL, E.C.

www.ingramcontent.com/pod-product-compliance
Lightning Source LLC
Chambersburg PA
CBHW030805020726
47499CB00006B/1776